(Hunter's Moon)

(The Garden)

(Immortal Dracula)

(Hunter's Moon the Garden)

ISBN (978-0615913377)

Printed in USA Kalorama Books (kaloramabooks.com)

Dedication

This book is dedicated to all my family and friends that I lost along the way. Your faces will always be with in my dreams. Your pictures shall forever hang on the wall of the eternal. I hope you all found peace in the next life.

Table of Contents

Foreword

A thousand sunrises
A thousand sunsets
Still I never shall witness death
The bitter sweet taste
Of this accursed fate
Gabriel comes to me in wings
Never in bones
I shall never reach home
My Home is to forever walk alone
A curse to forever walk the earth
This prison that I will never escape
I lost all that I love
Through my immortal blood

Alucard Esruc

Preface

This book was developed through an idea of a good friend. He told me I should write my story. I had no thoughts of ever sharing my story. I had no idea my life would be so interesting. Many moons and suns have rise and set throughout my lifetime.

These accounts or events that I write are my views alone. Sometimes my memories may get a little clouded. I recall things as I write. The memory of this old man is not what it used to be.

Introduction

The things you know about me are mostly true but let me tell you about my story through my eyes. This is not the story of Vlad III Dracula. His myth was written from me as I was born long beforehand. I have been here many moons before that story was told.

I read all of the many books about Dracula even though some of the accounts are truth. They made most of it up to make their or should I say, my story better. I found one of the famous ones wondering through my castle. I was going to kill him but I chose not to so I gave him a copy of my book for my story to be told instead. He rewrote my story into his own.

I was here long before Christ and his disciples, Philip, was my favorite of them all. Oh, how he made me smile. I still miss him till this day. I guess there is a reason why I had this curse placed upon me.

I have regretted that day for all of my days. Let me tell you the real story from the beginning so brace yourself as you may not be ready for this. People always fear things they do not understand. I have been described as an evil blood sucking demon. I will let you be the judge of my story, what you would do if you lived this long? Yes, I have done many wrong things in my life but who hasn't?

Chapter 1: The Garden

It all started outside the Garden of Eden. I know what you are thinking, "Oh my God! You're Adam! No, I'm not. Let me finish the story". Outside the Garden of Eden was pure joy. The only thing that could have been better was to be in there but the almighty would only let me touch the gate.

From these bars, my hopes and dreams bloomed as a young boy and only my hands and face could touch or go pass the bars. The flowers moved with my hands as I touch them, so I touched the flowers as often as I could. I was told that the animals used to talk and snake had legs and to never trust any snakes. I never stayed away from them of course as they were some of the most beautiful and mysterious animals to ever come across my eye.

We never went too far away from the garden and as a matter of fact, we slept right outside the gate. I often asked father why we never go anywhere but I knew the answer and I didn't want to leave anyway. I guess my curious attitude and always wanting to know everything is the reason why I'm in this mess in the first place. I wasn't born when humans were allowed to live in the garden and I did ask father why. He would never tell me.

All he would say is to just stay away from the snakes. With my nature being curious all the time, I asked the almighty why and he would only laugh and say "that is not my story to tell you." In case you're wondering if I have seen God, then the answer is no. I have just heard of his voice from the heavens with the sun shining.

I often stopped by at the gate asking if I could come in everyday while knowing the answer in my mind. He would always laugh and asked me if I will ever give up. I told him no every single time and then I'll laugh and walk away with a smile. In case you are wondering, all the stories about God being mean uptight, seeking revenge, is all a lie. He is kind, funny, generous and straight to the point person or whatever he really is. I talked to him every day just to understand more about it.

It's probably the reason all the last born children is differently rebellious in nature, questioning things all the time and wanting to do things their way. To the fathers and mothers reading this, I'm sorry and I am to be blamed for cursing the last born. Hell! I place tons of curses on man but we will get to them later. Why, everyone was away working hard I was at the gate, the hell with hard work. I wanted to be in the garden.

I knew humans once lived in there but we can't now. I want to know the reason and I wanted to just be there. The garden's residency was the place you now call Africa. It was home to me. I was of the same color as sand and I was told that I was made from sand but I never believed it.

I know you have been waiting for me to describe the garden and I shall do it to the best of my abilities with words to describe a place where words can describe. Bear with me as I have been on this earth for many moons. Though I have only seen through the gates of Eden, to me, enjoying delicacy eyes narrow for the smart people reading, you caught on that I broke the word down by letters and I tend to do that very often to have you see throughout my journey that I do that with things that mean something to me.

My Eden, my beautiful Eden. This garden of wonderful colors that have extinct. Yes, some colors are extinct till this day as I have not seen them again. Some of the lost colors are what we would now call light purple and the true color of the sun filled the flowers in the garden. No one has seen the true color of the sun since it's more than just yellow. There is a reason you go blind starring at the sun.

No mortal eyes is meant to have this gift because we lost it through our sins (our sins means my family). The flowers glowed at night with the color of the sun and the light purple. The bees were shining day and night. You could feel the wind as they take flight. The plants were alive but in a different way.

It's not how you see them today nor did they get up and walk. They moved with the wind and danced together like a couple with a heartbeat. The trees bear fruits as big as my head and the sun shined brightly. This was heaven. There was no castle in the sky and this was it.

The streams sparkled with gold glitters. The roses held the color black and were incrusted with jewels; they are the kings and queens of flowers. For this old man, it's hard to describe it. It was just beautiful and a wondrous place. The sun always shined even in the rain, the rain was just to cool down the life-force for the garden and everything around it.

The temperature was always mild during the day and night. It was never too hot and it never got too cold. There was a stream that flowed from the garden to the outside of the gate. You could see gold shining glitters in the stream and it made the stream looked magical. The water from the stream was pure as the almighty himself and it had a sweet taste to it.

Our land was full of livestock that we only kill once a week for food. We ate fruit and vegetables on the rest of the days even though we kill the livestock only once a week. It's hard to kill something that you have watched grow even if we did it for food. It was especially hard for my brother because he spent the most of time with them.

To ease my brother's heart, I would always offer my livestock. My mother saw what I was trying to do so she would always hug me. As for my father, well, let's just say he didn't approve of the way I did things. He wanted a simple life and I rarely ever did anything simple unless I was outside the garden doing nothing.

Now, let's get back to the story. As time goes by, I looked up and I'm a grown man but with my attitude from the younger days. I did everything I could to please the almighty but nothing seemed enough. It seemed like everyone loved my older brother more than me because of his heart.

He did everything through his heart whereas I did everything through my mind. To do everything with your mind is to think too much and that's just what I did. In the old ways, using only your heart was fine but you must now find balance. I learned to love my brother the way he was with his never questioning anything nature. You tell him to do it and it will be done without asking any questions.

Not me I questioned all I searched for answers I had to know but still everything was fine till that day that forever changed life as we know it. The story that you know is different from the truth. The almighty never asked for us to please him, we asked him what can we do to please you he told us just to give him our best gift.

So we told our father on what we were planning to do and he told us to not mess this up. Actually, he directly told me not to mess it up because he knew there would be no problems with my older brother. He said that if we do it right, the almighty would probably let us back into the garden and forgive our sins, sins of the father. The pressure he placed upon us was more than you could ever imagine.

Being the man I am, I thought of giving him my cow but no, that's not good enough. He is the almighty. Why does he need a cow when he is the king of all? Wanting to outdo my brother so bad that I remembered the jewels I have found in the cave so that's what I will give him. The day finally came when father said to me to make him proud; he said to my brother I know you will do well.

After hearing the praise he said to my brother and of what he said to me, it made me felt uneasy and envious. That didn't help me at all and I was thinking in my head that I know I am going to screw this up. So we both walked to the gate together with him and his sheep in his arms. I thought it was funny as I was with my jewels meant for a king.

So the almighty asked us to present our gifts. I told my brother to go first because all he offered was a sheep and I knew I would win this so I placed the jewels in front of the almighty. Nothing went according to plan. The almighty took his gift and left mine there.

He said to my older brother that he gave him the gift out of the kindness of his heart and told me that my gift was to make my brother look bad and he was very disappointed in me. The almighty never said that to me no matter what I did. Something came over me. I heard the almighty saying, "Calm your heart Cain", but I couldn't so I picked up a rock and hit Able with it as hard as I could.

We have seen things die before but I thought it was just the animals that could die and not us, plus I have never even had that thought in my mind. The sky turned black and the almighty sent a rumble through the skies, "Cain, what have you done my son?" I saw father running up, looking at the sky with a look of pure terror. "Cain, what have you done my son," while holding Able in his arms.

I was at a complete loss for words for the first time in my life "I, I don't know. I'm sorry." I saw my father crying. The time stopped. All was still. The almighty paused the world and we were the only thing that moved.

Then, I heard a word that I have never heard before and that would stay in me for all of my days. The almighty exclaimed, "Murderer Cain! You have killed your brother!" I said to the almighty that you can bring him back to life since you're God. The almighty answered; "My son, it does work that way but you must be held responsible for your actions for now as you have brought death upon this world" I have yet to come to understand what he meant.

The almighty said, "For your actions of being the first murderer and bringing death upon the world, you will be the only one that can never die and your father should have told you why you're not allowed in the garden. He disobeyed me and now, no human can ever step foot in the garden again". Not understanding these words, the almighty pick up the Garden of Eden and raised it into what we now call heaven. My father ran behind, chasing the garden while screaming, "No! Come back!"

He then walked up to me and told me the story. I fell to my knees and asked why he didn't tell me about it. Then, my mother came out crying after finding out what had happened to her son. Father told me to leave and never come back again and that I was no longer his son. Mother gave me a hug and whispered in my ear that she will always love me no matter what I do.

Be safe on my journey. She told me to forgive my father for his words as people always say things they don't mean when their heart is broken. Hearing those words from my father, seeing my mother weeping and seeing my dear brother dead was just too much to handle. I just ran and ran till I couldn't run anymore. I fell to my knees and called up to God but he didn't answer me. The only word that I could think of was that I felt that I was forsaken.

God didn't forsake me but instead I had forsaken him. Just like I have forsaken my whole family and I didn't deserve to hear God's voice. In case you are wondering now and you know the story of the bible, a lot of things in there are misinterpreted. Abel was the oldest and I am the youngest son of the four ever born.

Before I continue my story, I would like to say that I'm so sorry for this curse I have placed upon us. You can never understand how I feel or how it was to live without death. Wondering for days, months and years through vest jungles, woodlands and deserts the land was full of Dodo birds. I can understand why they are extinct because these were some tasty birds.

Plus, they were some easy targets and their meat is good. Their big blue bodies with small wings with yellow feet and red neck feathers help them stand out. They couldn't fly and they weren't the smartest of animals so I eat them all the time. All the wildlife I came to see that weren't in the garden filled my heart with joy.

Father once told me about the king of the beast which the almighty placed his crown upon was a very large brown noble animal with mane full and has the looks and presence of a king. He told me in the presence of other animals that they used to blow their heads at the sight of him. I will never forget the day I came across the king. I saw him resting on a rock with the rest of the females on the ground, surrounding him there just in silence as they lay around him.

Watching from a distance, I wanted to know more about this king. He ruled with an iron fist. They worshiped the ground he walked on. He did none of the hunting. The females would bring him his food. Fascinated by him, I stayed near him but never getting too close.

However, he noticed my presence and he would stare in the direction I was in and moved on. One day, some dog-like creatures with stripes attack the king this was the moment I waited for to see the king in action. He stood up proud with chest and fought them all off by himself. The way he raised his paws and cut through the air sent chills down my spine.

He was the strongest thing I ever seen, standing five feet high and fifteen feet long with brown mane and black highlights strength from head to tail. Needing to know more about him, I followed him for months. Then, I did one of the dumbest things ever. Remembering the stories of my father, I walked up to him with my head down to show him respect.

He stood up like the day he was attacked and I heard the sound of thunder coming from the heavens but this came out from his mouth. Falling down onto my knees, "Is this God?", with fear in every part of my being, I cried out forgive me almighty, I'm sorry. All I felt was claws and teeth. He moved so fast I could do nothing.

He did not try to eat me but he tried to kill me. I thought this was my time. I was going to slip into nothingness and feel my brothers pain for the sins I have committed. Blacking out, my world went dark and I could no longer feel my heartbeat. I felt pain before but that was nothing.

Hitting my foot on a rock, I fell out of many trees. I even got stung by a bee but this was different as I tasted death for my first time. Slipped into nothingness, there I see a figure so I said God and the figure said no "so you are the one my hands can never touch, my name is Gabriel I think we should become friends because I know I shall see you again." I blacked out. I'm dead.

I remember nothing after that but sunrise came, I woke up with the bright light shun upon my face. Father told me stories about other beings like us but not like us. He called them angels. God's warriors; the ones he called in for war. I have never seen an angel before but I had this feeling that I have now. Gabriel he said, friends he said.

Why would he want to be my friend if he is in God's hand? No matter what, I shall look for Gabriel my friend when I taste death and hopefully that won't be many times. This is what the almighty meant by I can never die but he never said I won't feel pain and the pain I felt took months to heal. Finally, I recovered completely but this time, I had a feeling of invincibility.

I'm the immortal one. I kept telling myself because I still needed the courage to face the lion again. If you really think I wasn't going to go back to the lion, then you have not been listening to my story. I guess that I wanted his respect because I lost my father's and God's plus he was the only one around that could take away my loneliness.

Since he was the king of beast, the almighty is the king of all and I felt the closer I get to the lion, the closer I could get to God. So once again, I went back to the lion with my head down in respect. The lion looked at me like, "Oh, it's you again." Don't you ever learn?"

He rose up again and I was thinking in my head "Not again." I heard the heavens rumble once again through his mouth and can you guess what happened? Everything went black. I saw Gabriel again; Gabriel laughed "I told you I would see you again my friend just didn't think I would be this soon." Once again, I was awaken by the sun.

I need to figure this out as my way is not working so I observed the family closely and came up with an idea. I brought him food, dropped at his feet and backwards. Doing this everyday for a month, he finally walked up to me. I was very scared but I didn't move. He sniffed and peed on me.

Standing there, shocked by what he did. He just marked me or something by doing that. After that moment, I was allowed to be around and this is what I call the Pride. Yes, I was the first to give them that name. I name them that because they were proud noble beasts the king of beasts.

I was so happy now that I have a family again. I know it is not the same but it was something. I learned so much being with Able. Yes, I named him, as humans we name everything we see. It helps us to understand what we see and are trying to learn.

It was only fitting that I named him Able because I missed my brother so much and I was so truly sorry for what I have done. After a while, he started to answer to Able. Whenever I call out his name, he would come and that brought joy to my heart. Even though he ruled, he still showed everyone love by brushing himself against them.

He made sure everyone ate but after him of course. He watched out for everyone and protected all from harm. He played with the young and that amazed me of how something so strong could be so gentle. It showed in how he played with the young and never once hurting them. Through this play, he was teaching them skills to survive and letting them know he was the king.

Understanding that I need to be better on the hunts, I sharpen the rocks and branches to join in. One day, the laughing dogs attacked the pride. I used the tools I made to help fight. Tossing rocks and striking them with the braches I made, we managed to fight them off.

By this time, I learned to copy the thunderous sound that came from his mouth. Using it after the victory, I saw Able looking at me with pride; he walked over and licked me. That was the first time he ever did that and after that day, he played with me like the rest. Never once did I ever think that he was going to hurt me.

We ran through the forest with the voices from the heavens. We could clear the forest within minutes and I looked up to him as a father. By his side till the very end, at his end he laid across me using this sound of happiness that shook through his whole body. When he died, I wept like the day I made the garden leave. Deciding to stay there to guide the youth, I was now the king of the pride and I was proud of it.

Doing everything I remembered him doing until one of the younger ones showed he would be king. His name was Leo. I was proud for Leo as he watched my every move. During hunts, Leo would join me and while I would charge from the front, he would flank them from behind. I would let Leo carry the food back to the pride.

This was a necessary act to show the pride their new king. Loving Leo like a son and a great son, he was loyal and strong, gentle and as strong as Able. I knew the pride would be alright once I started my journey forward. One day, I went on a hunt without Leo and brought the food to him in front of the whole pack and bowed to show the pride that he is now the king.

They walked up to him and lay on the ground and I heard the thunderous sound coming from his mouth. I was proud. I walk over to him, gave him a hug and a kiss and started on my journey. Needing to see the world if this place was so great, I needed to see more.

After all, I'm immortal and I had nothing but time. Traveling for months until I seen a sight for two of sorest eyes ever more humans. You cannot understand the joy that entered my heart. A tear fell from my eye. Never have I ever dream that there were more humans in the world. I thought the almighty was so mad at us that he let us die off through my father and mother.

Chapter 2: Village of Sun and Sand

Seeing this village of people, I didn't know whether to run to them or keep my distance but being the cool cat that I am, I walked over. The people all stared at me like I was a ghost. It gave me the chills and I had an eerie feeling but I pressed on. "Are these people of my brothers and sisters?

Did mother and father bear more seeds?" One of the oldest persons in the group exclaimed "Halt! Who goes there?" I could tell from the beginning he was the old lion. This was about the year one thousand AH; can you guess what AH means? If you can, you're sharp.

It means After Human. In case you're wondering, the earth is over a million years old as the almighty created it a long time ago. Father once told me the earth was full of giant snake-like creatures that roamed the land. They were wild as nature himself and as tall as the sky with teeth sharper than the king of beast with flying ones and ones that owned the sea.

He told me the almighty showed him the bones of the creatures and that I taught him the almighty is not to be played with. He told me the almighty was disappointed in his creations so he encased them in ice forever. He said the almighty wanted creatures closer to himself so he created humans. Now back to the story, upon approaching the humans, my heart was beating fast with excitement.

It was a joy to me as the world has more of the human population. As I approached the village, I see people running to a tent and out popped the elder of the tribe, the chief. As I walked through the village, I saw wonderful things. Children running around playing, collecting sticks to play.

I saw women planting and harvesting the garden. I saw the men practicing fighting and throwing branch spears at made-up targets. That brought a smile to my face. I guess I wasn't the only one who thought of that. Also, I wondered why they had to make them.

The elder approached me with the king's mane draped over his body, encrusted with the jewels that I have tried to give to the almighty. Was he the king of men? That thought ran through my head. All of the other villagers stood behind him as he approached.

Welcome my son. My name is Jacob. I have never seen another human besides the ones that live in the villages. Where are you from? My name is Cain and I come from Eden. I saw a strange look on his face as his eyes became narrow. Jacob said welcome to the village of Sun.

"You are welcome to stay here. Just obey the laws of our village." I said thank you to him with the biggest smile ever and all of my teeth was showing. "Jacob, come my son, let me show you around." We walked around the village. He showed me the garden and told me that if I help out in the garden, I can eat the produce.

I told him I had no problem with that. He showed me the open field where the children would play. The sight of children playing brought back times of me and Able running outside the garden. The children ran up to me smiling. I guess they were happy to see a new face.

He took me to the training zone where the man were practicing throwing the spears made of branches. I wanted to ask why there was a need for that but I remained silent. He took me to the living quarters and this place was full of tents made by the skin of some strange creature. He walked up to one that was encrusted with jewels.

This one is yours. I thanked him and asked why I was given one with wondrous beauty. He smiled and said because it's the only one empty.

It felt a little odd that a stranger was given this beautiful sleeping tent but I was happy I had it.

Jacob said I will leave you now and feel free to join in whenever you like. One thought ran through my mind and I began to rub my fingers on my tent. The texture was smooth. It was light brown with big dark brown spots. It made me wonder what animal this lovely skin came from.

Wondering around the village, the people smiled at me and introduced themselves. This was the first time I heard people used the same last name. Everyone's last name was Sun and I thought to myself that it was clever to use the name of the village. Being very interested in the training camp, that's where I went first.

Seeing them tossing the spears in the air and doing something new made me very interested. Seeing two people training together one on each side with the spear in hand swinging it at each other was a joy. Thinking they were trying to kill each other, they began to twirl the spears around with one hand never dropping it. Swinging it at each other with such grace, it had the look as if two people were dancing.

They each dodged or blocked every strike and it was like magic. They stopped and asked me if I would like to try. I said "Yes, I'd love to," and so he tossed me the spear. I caught it and he said "Very good. Now let's see what you've got."

Holding the spear between my hands and began to swing, he dodged it without hesitation. He swung and hit me in the arm. I jumped back all of a sudden as something came over me. My animal instincts or my king of beast instinct kicked in. Leo and Able reminded me on what I was taught.

No man shall ever be able to defeat me. Remembering who I was, what I was, what I learned and remembering that I was once a proud noble king, the look in my eyes changed as they became narrow when I see my target. I began to twirl the spear like how I saw them did. I stood up like Able and my opponent looks have changed and the fear in them started to show.

Abraham, the one who gave me the spear had a surprised look on his face. Everything went in slow motion, I grabbed the spear with both hands and struck like lightning, I broke my opponent spear in half. The impact sent him flying to the ground. Abraham then came running in with a big smile on his face and asked "How did you do that? Can you teach me?"

Beginning to calm down, I told him yes and tossed him the spear. I told him to grab the spear with two hands, raise it over his heard and strike. He did just what I told him to do and cut through the wind. He began to cheer asking me how I learned that and I told him it was from my family.

"Abraham, you must have had a strong family." I smiled and said yes. I did walk back to my tent and went to sleep as I was tired from my long journey. The next day, I woke up with the sun shun upon my face.

I remember that sunshine like it was my first. The light parted the dark. It drowned the dark like a washing wave. The yellow met the red pure fire for the earth and I had forgotten for a moment that I was cursed. Raising my hands in the air, yawned and smiled, this will be a lovely new day.

I proceeded to the garden after I got up. I was the first one up in the village. I found a nice grassy spot and dug it up. Picking up some seeds, loosen the ground and planted the seeds. Placing the soil back on top while gently bowing my head and blessed the seeds.

Being taught by my father to bless almost everything and that everything is a blessing. Father told me that the almighty placed everything in the world for humans. He told me we are the kings of this world and that we should treat it like a queen. I picked some flowers and I placed them around my seeds.

I have always love flowers and always will. It gave my place in the garden since the days of Eden. Bowing my head one last time and I returned to the training grounds. I started to carve out fresh spears for more training. I stood up strong and placed the spear in my hand and began to twirl it.

Wanting to practice twirling until I got it down packed, I could now twirl it in both directions. Raising the spear over my head and use what I called the king's thrust, I repeated until my shoulders hurt. I began to rotate my shoulders with the spear in hand and then some kind of natural instinct kicked in a twirled it while I rotated my shoulders. This will be called the wind cutter and I practiced for hours until the villagers started to awake from the tents.

The children popped out, running straight towards the playgrounds. I started to run around playing with the kids while remembering Able. I taught them lessons as we played, telling them to always keep their eyes open as you never know what's around the corner. Keep your heads up high and shoulders square and be proud that you're villagers of the Sun.

The rest of the villagers watched us play and it brought smiles on their faces. All I could do was to picture myself being here and calling it home. Jacob walked up to me and said let’s take a walk so we started to walk around the village. There are branches stuck in the ground by the edge of the village.

Asking him why was the branches in the ground, he told me it's there to mark the edges of the village so the people won’t stray out too far. He told me its safety in numbers and I said that's a great idea. He asked me where I am from and what my name is. I told him my name is Cain and I come from Eden.

Jacob said Cain Eden is a nice name. Cain you're welcome to live here as long as you like. I see you will fit in here just nice. I told him thank you I would really like that.

I told him that it's nice to finally see other human beings on my long journey as I haven't seen any other human in over 100 years. "Jacob, you must have traveled far." "Yes, I have. It has been for many moons and suns." Sleeping under the stars and I've made many wishes upon them.

Jacob wished on a star. That's new but what is the reason for this? I don't know, I really can't tell you by just looking at them. It gave me hope especially the ones that move and they made me wished on them more. Jacob asked, "What was your wish Cain?"

"My wish is to see another human, Jacob." I guess it worked. I will try that for now on. Jacob smiled and his smile made me smile while we share a few laughs along the way. Asking him if this was the only village with people, he told me no and that the village of the sea is south of us and that he would take me there tomorrow.

I was pleased at the thought of more people. He bid me goodbye and walked away. Just before he left my sight, he turned and told me we will have to change your name because the villages tend to be afraid of outsiders. I said ok and asked what my name should be.

He asked what would you like to be and I told him to call me Leo, Leo Sun. He smiled and he said that he likes that name. What does it mean? I told him King Jacob that he should change his name to Almighty Sun.

I told him that I will see him later, bowed and walked away. That made me laugh and like having a new friend. The sky started to dim. I have been working all day long and it's time for some sleep.

Shutting my eyes and drifting to sleep, there was Gabriel. He said, "Hello Cain." "Hello Gabriel." "Cain, I see you're getting stronger and you can now hold some words with me." "Remember Cain, this is a dream.

We don't have to be in the dark and you can shape this world." So I started to concentrate on Gabriel. "How did I know you would take us here, come on let's go inside the gate." I told him no, even in my dreams I'm not worthy.

Gabriel said, "Cain, what you say to me and do will just be between us. After all, we are friends." "That's fine Gabriel but I just rather sit outside the gate so we both just sat there smiling."Woken by the sun, had a big smile on my face with my two friends.

I guess my life isn't too bad. As soon as I hopped out the tent, Jacob was right there. I laughed and told him not to scare me like that. He said, "Sorry. Let's be on our way to the village of the Sea.

We won't be back here for a couple of days. Grab a spear and take one of the shacks and let us hurry up. I'd like to get there before sundown." So off we went. On our way out, we were met by the young ones and they told us to be safe on our trip and gave us some fine rocks and asked us to trade them for sea rocks.

We told them sure, we would love to. I placed the rocks in the shack and the children said thank you. Off we went with spears in our hand on our day long journey. On our journey, I saw what my skin was made from. It was the tallest animal I have ever seen.

I asked Jacob a question that I already knew. "Did my tent skin come from that?" I was told yes. I then asked him how he killed a beast like that. They are not too smart; they only eat leaves and are a nice calm creature.

We only kill them when needed. We never kill them for fun because they are beautiful so we want to keep them around. I told him that's good. I love nature and the creatures of this world are a gift to us. Jacob a gift you say never even thought about it like that.

After all, they give us food and shelter and we should not take it for granted. Jacob agreed that it's time for us to eat. Let's go catch a dodo bird. I said, "Jacob, I love those. They are so tasty and easy to catch. Jacob there is a nest of them down the hill. Let us go get two of those."

We went down the hill and caught us two and cooked them up real nice. We separated the meat from bone, placed the meat in the sack and continued on our journey. Jacob asked me if I was tired. I smiled and told him that I've walked many miles just to get to where I am now and this is nothing to me.

I said to him "Are you tired old man?" he smiled and said don't let this old face fool you. I still got a lot of life left. About halfway on our journey, I saw something I've never saw before. A big creature with blue and grey elongated nose. It hangs all the way to the floor with bones sticking out of their faces.

There were a lot of them together. With a big smile, as you can see I liked to smile and nature brings me joy. "Jacob, what are those? I've never saw those before." He told me they are called trunks and they are very dangerous. We must keep clear of them.

So we kept our distance but I didn't take my eyes of them because they were so beautiful and strong. I watch the way they interacted with each other. They moved in a line and when they stopped, the biggest ones stood in the back and front. Finally, we arrived at the village of the sea.

It was by a sea that was so vast no land was in sight for miles and miles it almost made my heart stop. The villagers of the sea greeted Jacob with open arms. I saw the village elder came out his tent with the king's mane draped over him just like Jacob. They hugged and Jacob called out my name.

This is Leo Sun, a new member of our tribe. Leo, this is Michael the village elder. Welcome to our village Leo. You are welcome to stay for as long as you wish. Oh, there is just one free tent. The other has to rest under the stars with blankets.

With a smile on my face, I told him I'm used to sleeping under the stars as they bring me hope. It was nice to hear the same words from two different people "you can stay here as long as you like." Hearing people say this to a person they didn't know was a great thing. Michael hope you say that's different, then Jacob interrupted and said I will tell you all about it. Come, my old friend.

We have a lot of catching up to do and turned to me and told me to look around. I went to the sea as my first spot and placed my feet on the sand for the first time in my life. Jumping around on my feet, I had to do that to get use the heat. It was rough and grainy it took in the warmth from the sun and held it in each grain. I've heard many stories of the sea but it didn't compare to being here.

Sitting there till the sun started to set; the sea showed the same sight what the almighty created was a masterpiece. I bowed my head and walked back to the village. I walked up to the tent area as everyone was already inside. I saw my blankets already spread out with those beautiful spots again.

I shall not have any problems sleeping tonight. Laying my head down, I closed my eyes I still remember this dream me and Leo laid on the sand making, the heaven's thunder comes from our mouth. Sensing someone was there, it could only be Gabriel. I bet he was in the background watching us with a smile.

The sunrise woke me with tears in my eyes "Oh, how I missed my other family." That dream brought joy in my heart as those were happy tears. I wiped my eyes while smiling and stretched. As I arose, I was greeted by Jacob. "Good morning old man." "Jacob, how did you sleep? I guess it was well?" I told him yes, he told me to come with him.

We walked up to Michael's tent. Michael popped out, "Good morning Leo. Jacob told me all about the stars," he smiled and said I shall now wish upon the stars. We walked up to another tent. Michael said my daughter will show you around the village. Out popped a short hair woman with skin golden as the sun.

"This is my daughter Eve, Eve Leo, Leo, Eve" she said nice to meet you. I didn't even say anything. I was at a loss of words for the second time in my life. Jacob elbowed me and smiled. Finally, I said hello and she was laughing all the way and I could not help it but to smile.

It’s funny the first two women in my life I loved had the same name. Michael said come on Jacob, let's leave these two and be on our way. Just hearing her name brought my mother's face back in my mind. Those big brown loving eyes that she always gave me, "Oh, how I miss them.”

Now back to the new village. Eve with that short hair, big cheeks and that round brown eyes the most beautiful thing I have ever seen. Till this day, she is still the most beautiful thing I have ever seen. She said come on lets go, you do talk right? I smiled and told her yes. Forgive me, I have never in my life had a loss of words but this is the first time I had a reason.

She smiled of course. You can see this is the sleeping area and we are going to the sea. No need to walk you around a village, they are all the same. Let’s go to the beach and sea. I told her I’d love to so we took a walk on the beach.

All of a sudden, she ran right into the sea but before she jumped in, she tossed off all her clothes. Even though I didn't really see anything, it was the first time I saw a woman naked. She told me to join her. I was afraid and I didn't know what to do.

The sight of her brought upon new feelings in my life, it sent chills through my body. My body was turned on even with my eyes closed. Next thing I know, I am naked in the water floating around. The warm water gave me a hug and a wave washed over me. I tasted sea water for the first time. Asking her what was this taste in my mouth; she told me it was sea spice.

I put my head in the water to taste it again. She laughed and told me not to drink too much or it will dry me out. Seeing some hard spider looking creatures with claws, I asked her what are those and she told me those are sea spiders and that the sea is full of wonderful life. She grabbed my hand. I was nervous when she said come we can go further.

We moved deeper into the sea and she then said, "Let me show you something." She went under the water and began to move without walking. The feeling of being shocked and amused at what type of magic is this. I thought the almighty have removed or hid all the magic left in this world.

Then she popped back up you try I told her I have no magic in me. She laughed and told me it's not magic. I just have to hold my breath and move with the sea by using my feet to guide me while I was under water. So I held my breath, jumped in and began to move my feet.

I was doing it but I was just not as good as her. I popped back up. That was fun and I would like to learn how to do that. She said you will in due time. Just give yourself some time to learn.

She asked me if is this your first time seeing a women really naked and I said yes, besides my mother but this is not the same. She asked me where my mother is and I told her that she was dead. "I'm sorry to hear that. I bet she was a lovely woman." I told her yes and thank you. Eve said, "Let's get back to this happy moment, no need for sadness," and I agreed.

We walked back to the beach after the short swim. I was red and I tried to look away but it was hard. She told me it was ok and that it's natural to look. All of a sudden, I heard a noise and I asked her what that was.

She said it was the sound of a horn. I asked her what does it mean and she said just watch. Then all of a sudden, everyone came running out, tossing their clothes. I saw Jacob running and I laughed. I thought to myself that I just saw too much of that man.

We sat on the beach watching the others swim and play in the water. People of all ages and sizes were together in laughter, splashing water all around and all I could do was to smile. We sat there and talked for hours, talking about the things we like and the things we like to do. I told I was on a long journey and that I slept under the stars every night.

I told her I use to gaze at the stars and make wishes upon them. Eve said you wished on stars? That's the best thing I've ever heard. Tell me more. What do you wish for? I told her to just see another face and she said it worked.

I think I will make wishes on them. I didn't understand why my wishing on stars made people that happy. Did it actually give them hope? Telling her the ones that shoot across the skies were the ones I wished on the hardest.

It's rare that you ever see one but when you do, it's like magic and something has to be there. All those lonely nights I had it was the only thing that kept me going. She told me I was strong and that she would like to be that strong one day. I told her she is and she has nothing but strength.

"Now tell me why is your hair so short?" She laughed and said, "Oh, you noticed I see. It was in my way so I cut it off." "How did you cut it off?" She told me she sharpens a bone on a stone and grabbed her hair with both hands and cut it off. "Now the real question is do you like it?"

I told her it brings out her face and that you could see it clearer. What I wanted to say was nothing should be in the way of that beautiful face but she always find ways to make me loss for words. The sun started to set and the people began to leave the water and put their clothes back on. Wasting the whole day with Eve doing nothing, this was the best thing I've ever done in my life.

I walked her to her tent and wished her goodnight and that I'll see her tomorrow. I then walked up to my blankets and laid there. Is this the love my mother told me about? I don't know but there is one thing that I know. I just want to be around her.

Didn't know if I should close my eyes and dream or stay up and just remember this day. All I know was that, I wanted to see her again and that I hoped she felt the same way too. I finally closed my eyes and went to sleep. I woke up this morning by this strange light.

Eve was lying right beside me. Eve said wake up sleepy head, it's time to take a swim. Without any further thoughts, I just hopped up out my blankets and we ran towards the sea. I had no problem taking off my clothes this time. I guess seeing the others gave me the strength to do it.

She laughed and said, "I see you had no problems this time removing your clothes." Telling her no and that seeing the others do it made it less hard. She asked me if I'm ready to swim again and I told her yes, I'm ready. I was born ready in the manliest voice.

She smiled and said, "Leo, show me that man in you." I held my breath and jumped into the water. This time, I swam a little longer and she showed me a trick. She told me that if I use my arms to swim on top of the water, I would be able to swim longer. So I tried to do what she told me and it worked for a minute but I couldn't keep it up.

She told me it takes time to build the strength to do it longer. Wanting to keep trying till my arms was sore, she told me enough for now. Let's just sit here while we float around and talk. "So Leo, did you wish upon any stars last night?" I told her that I haven't made a wish in many moons.

I didn't felt the need to because my wish came true. She told I should never stop doing it so my hope will never fade. Asking her if she did wish upon a star and she said yes but she's not going to tell me what it was. "I thought that telling your wish before it happens will lose its power.

We shall see if it comes true." I said yes, we shall see. Alright, come let us walk around the boring village this time. We left the water, put our clothes back on and began to walk around the village. She took me to the garden.

This is my spot in the garden and I made you a spot next to mine. Here, plant some seeds. I started to loosen the dirt, planted my seeds right next to hers. I looked up and began to look around. She asked me what I'm looking for and I told her to wait right here.

Walking over to some wild flowers, I picked some and brought them back to our spot in the garden. Reaching out my hand, I gave her one and she smelled it and placed the rest around our spot. She told me to wait right here. I watched her walk to her tent and she came back out with something in her hand. Eve said, "This is yours. I made it from the bones of the king of beasts." All I could do is to tell her that I love it and placed it around my neck.

That was my first gift given to me by someone else other than God or my family and getting it from her was even better. We walked to the training grounds and watched two of the men in the village practice. One of the men asked me if I wanted to practice. Eve elbowed me so I said sure and he tossed the spear over to me.

I began to twirl the spear in directions and my opponents said, "You look like you've done this before." I said maybe a once or twice. He said that's good. "I don't have to go easy on you," and he struck me in the arm twice as he was fast.

So I raised the spear over my head and used the strike of the lion and broke his spear in half. Eve stood up cheering, "That was great Leo! How do you do that?" I said that it just came naturally to me and I tossed the spear in the grass and walked over to Eve.

Then I remember the children who gave me the rocks to trade. "Eve, I have a favor to ask the children if they want to trade rocks. I have them in my sack. I will go to my tent and get them." She said ok, I'll get some of our stones.

We traded rocks after that and I kept them in my sack. The day started to wine down. Jacob told me we are leaving in the morning. I wasn't ready to leave yet but it was time. I walked Eve to her tent and made my way to my blankets.

I didn't go to sleep right away. All I thought about was Eve and how I wasn't ready to go. I went to sleep eventually. The sun woke me up. Jacob was already ready. He told me to grab my things and let's get going. I grabbed my things and turned towards Eve's tent.

"Oh, how I'm going to miss her." Then Eve popped out her tent saying, "You didn't think I would let you leave without saying goodbye did you?" I hugged her and she told me to make sure I come back to see her. I told her I will and you can bet on it. As we walked away, I turned and looked at Eve and waved goodbye.

Jacob said not to worry as I will be seeing her again. I smiled and said I know. Jacob said, "I think someone is in love." I told him that he's probably right. I never had these feelings before. We made our way back to the village right before the sun went down.

The children ran up to us asking if we did get the sea rocks. I pulled them out my sack and handed it to them. They ran off happy. Making my way to my tent, all I could do was to think about Eve until I fell asleep with her in mind. I woke up the next morning to screams. I had over slept.

I popped out of my tent seeing the villagers running everywhere screaming, "Run for your lives! It's the king of beasts!" I looked around and saw two male lions large. The heaven's thunder came from their voices and it scared all the villagers.

Thinking that I must do something, I ran to grab a spear. My instinct started to kick in and I began to growl as I ran up to the lions. One by one I gather them both. The villagers stopped running and I heard them saying someone has to help Leo before he gets killed. They ran to pick up their spears and surrounded the lions but they were too scared to do anything.

I told them to hold their ground; the lions let loose the thunder of the heavens and the villagers started to shake. I swung my spear at the lions but they dodge it. I must do something fast. My memories kicked in and I let out the thunder from my voice.

Both the villagers and the lions were surprised. Now this is my moment to strike, I stuck the spear in one of the lion's chest and the other lion tried to run but I managed to stick the spear into his neck. Raising my spear in the air and let out the biggest of what I now called a roar, the villagers dropped their spears and bowed to me. As I turned and looked, I was in shock the villagers were all on their knees.

I looked and saw Jacob dying; I tossed my spear and ran to him. Jacob thanked me for saving his family. "No problem. It's the least I can do after all the kindness you have shown me." Jacob said, "I knew you would come," he told me. "Who told you what?" Jacob said, "The almighty told us of you and how you brought death upon this world.

He told us that he kept trying to make more humans but we all had failed him. It was the reason I told you to change your name. He told me even though you did what you did; you still had good values in him. He told me you would come my way and that I should treat you with kindness. The village is now yours Leo." He died right in my arms and I wept like a baby.

Chapter 3: King of the Sun

The villagers came up to me and called me king. They told me we must burry Jacob so no animals will come back to the village. I said ok and they took him off. I stayed on the ground crying. They dug the hole in the back of the village. I saw other graves there too. I never went to the back of the village before.

Everyone said a few words while they laid Jacob in the dirt but I said nothing. The villagers walked off crying while I stayed at the grave. "Gabriel, I know you're there. Why did Jacob have to die?" I got no answer and I stayed there till it got dark. I finally got up and went to the tents to check on the villagers.

They were happy that I came to check on them as they still had fear in their souls. I went to my tent and fell asleep. I was outside the garden crying. Gabriel walked over to me and said, "Cain, I heard you called out to me. I don't know why God does what he does nor do I ask."

I said this is my entire fault that I have brought death to all. Gabriel said this is true. "Cain, you are my friend so I will not lie to you but you must not dwell on the past because the future is always bright." I shall always remember those words as it made me look forward to the next day. I went through Jacob's things the next morning and found his sack with a lovely mini spear he carved from a mini branch.

I figured out that I would give all his things to Michael. I told the villagers that I will be back in a couple of days and that I was going to the village of the sea to tell them of the news. I was thinking about how I'm going to tell them of the bad news while making my way to the village. I finally made it to the village of the sea. The people walked up to greet me.

Walking up to them with my head down, they knew something was wrong.

Michael and Eve walked up smiling while the rest of the villagers moved to the side to let them pass. Michael said, "Leo, it's so good to see you. Where is Jacob?" I had my head down. I finally raised my head with tears in my eyes and told her that he didn't make it.

Michael asked what you mean by he didn't make it. Lions attacked the village and I couldn't save him. The villagers started to cry and Michael started to weep in tears. I told him I'm sorry and gave him Jacob's sack telling him that I think Jacob would have wanted him to have it.

Michael said thank you my friend. I shall cherish it forever. Eve came running up to me and gave me a hug and told me she was sorry. With tears in her eyes, she told me Jacob was like another father to her and that she will miss him dearly. That just brought more tears to my eyes.

I told her I was sorry too. Eve said, "What do you have to be sorry about? You did everything you could. You should be proud and the courage it took just to walk here to tell us the news shows me just how strong you are." I hugged her tighter with every word she spoke.

The sun started to set the villagers walked to their tents with tears. Michael walked to the sea for a moment alone. Eve told me to come with her. She took my hand and walked me to her tent she asked me if I would like to join her and I told her that I would love too. We laid there in the tent looking right at each other.

She smiled and said her wish came true. I asked her what her wish was and she told me that I would see her again. I then smiled and she kissed me. She said I wished the reason you came back was for a different reason.

We began to roll around in the tent. I guess all the emotions I was feeling came out. I got my clothes off fast. She rolled on top of me and took her clothes off. I started to feel emotions that I have never felt before. The passion to just kiss her, to hold her, to love her and to just be with her there took me over.

I rolled back on top of her and she smiled asking, "Why Leo? What has come over you?" You my love Eve said you think it's going to be that easy and rolled back on top of me. She was so strong, so beautiful, and so passionate. She asked me if I was ready and I told her I was born ready.

She put me inside of her. I found my Eden no longer was I outside the gate; the gate has finally opened for me. She was so soft and warm. She asked me how does it feel? With many thoughts running through my mind, I told her soft and warm and I have found heaven. I then asked her how it feels and she told me we felt like one person and that she could feel me inside of her.

Everything about this moment was perfect I'm not going to go into any more details. You can figure out the rest. We make love till the middle of the night for my first time and I like to think I was good. Hell, since I'm a man, I always have to think that way. I am the king after all but on a serious note, I hope I did a good job.

We finally went to sleep.

We lay in the tent naked all night. I woke up with the feeling someone was watching me as soon as I opened my eyes. Eve jumped on top of me asking, "Ready for round two?" Woman you must have read my mind. Once again we made sweet love. The days I spent there, you could see us running around, chasing each other from tent to tent at least three times a day.

I no longer wanted to be outside heaven's doors. I wanted to be outside Eve's doors. Time passed so fast and I have spent six days in the village of the sea. It was time for me to go. Telling her I shall return that and I must get back to the village.

She said no you must return to your village, it's your village now they need you. Kissing her goodbye, I made my way back to the village, hoping I will be seeing her soon. The villagers greeted me with smiles and hugs. I could tell that they were waiting for me to return.

"Welcome home Leo. We have missed you. Come, we have something to show you". We walked up to my tent. They infused my old tent with the skin of the lions I've killed. They told me that's not all and brought out a robe made of the king of beast mane. "This is your new robe. You're now the elder of the village and that we will look to you".

I took the robes and thanked them. "I'm honored and I shall wear it with pride". All I wanted to do was to go back my tent and sleep. Life from then on in the village was different. I was the one they were looking for, for answers. Being the king of the lions was much easier they just reacted to me. The villagers wanted answers, they wanted a guide, and they wanted safety.

I tried my best to provide them with all that. I trained all the men in the art of the spear. We dug spears in the ground on the borders of the village sideways so that they stick out. We often find dodo birds stuck to them. Man, those birds are dumb.

We use the fresh kills for food. For the not so fresh kills, we use them as bait to catch other animals and we use the feathers to stuff our blankets. The bones were used to make cutting tools necklaces and anything else we could think of. They used to ask me strange questions like why is the sky blue.

Or what makes the stars shine? I could only give one answer to those questions because the almighty made it that way. Weeks passed and I missed my beloved Eve. I made a wish on the stars to see her again. It was time to take my journey back to the village of the sea. The day before I set out, I've seen a figure approaching in the sunset.

I looked out and it was a human. I went to the edge of the village to greet them. To my eyes delight, it was my beloved Eve. My heart stopped. Is this a dream? She came running towards me and gave a hug and a big kiss. I touched her face and told her how much I missed her.

I told her I made a wish on many stars just to see her face that wasn't in my dreams. She told me that she made wishes too. I pictured us under the same sky, under the same moon and wishing on the same star, just to help us find our way back to each other. We both had that look in our eyes it was tent time.

We made love that day till the sun came up. Oh, how I longed to see your face. I've dreamed of us becoming one. I told her that I wanted her to stay with me in my village and she said yes and that she has even told her father that she might only come back to visit. She said he told her to follow her heart and that he was happy for us.

We are not married but she was what you now call a wife to me. The days passed by so fast as they always do when you're happy. I used to watch her play with the children thinking to myself, it would be nice to have one of our own. The years went by without luck but that never stopped us.

Remembering our conversation in the tent one day, I told her I'm sorry my love. We will keep trying. She told me she might be one of those who couldn't have children. I told her not to think like that and it will happen. Only time will tell.

She told me that she is happy as long as we are together. I told I felt the same way. We never managed to have any children but that didn't stop tent time or how we felt about each other. We just looked at the children of our village as our children of our own.

That helped dearly with the disappointment and it helped us to accept the fact that we will never have any children. We spent many happy days and nights together under the moon and stars. We never once had a fight although we might have had disagreements but we have always found out how to bring each other's heart back to life. Whenever she disagrees with me, I would wait for us to get to the tent and put my feet in her face.

The thought still makes me smile because she couldn't stand it but I would do it. All she could do was laugh and jump on me. "You make me sick you know. I don't like that but you do it all the time and the way you do it you think you're so slick." Whenever I have disagreements with her, she would jump on my back and say who the king is now and tell me to run faster.

Every time I have disagreements with her, I would wait for it but she would always jump from a different side. After a while, I would just walk away and smile because I knew she was coming. Oh, how I loved her. I used to bring her flowers almost every day. She loved roses with the thorns. I think it's because it reminded her of herself so beautiful with passion.

Whenever I see that look on her face, I take her back to the village of the sea. She loved the sand and the sea so I had to bring her back. There, we would swim together, sitting on the beach, watching the sunrise and sunset. Watching the sea reflecting back the moon and the stars, seeing the sands twinkle back at the stars was always a delight.

These memories both haunt and bring joy to my heart. Just writing it down makes my eyes tear up. We were a great pair. She was the sun and I was moon. She was the beach and I was the sea I kept coming back to her. Her love was sea deep and vast with so many new wonderful things to discover together. I just adorned her so much from those laughs we had in the tent, the walks we went on, all those small things were big things.

Her nickname was sea and my nickname was star or Wishman. That was another name that she liked to use. I used to let her trim my beard but I was always nervous every time. She would hold my face saying hold still you big baby, how many times have I done this for you and you should be used to it by now.

The years went by. She got older but I stayed the same. She would say that she wishes she had my blood and that face that never ages. She had the look of what we now call a forty five year old but I still had the look of what is now considered a thirty year old. She would say things like, I know I'm not crazy but it seems like you never age.

I would give her this if only you knew face. I forgot about my curse until the day she brought it up. It was around that time that the villagers started to notice I didn't age. They started asking my secrets. They started to eat what I ate, watching my every move and trying to copy everything I do.

Noticing Eve was slowing down a little, so I would pretend I was tired. She would smile and say Leo you don't have to pretend. I know you're not tired and you haven't aged a bit. She told me she appreciates everything that I'm doing and that she loves me. I would smile and tell her that I was tired but she never believed it.

More and more years went by; she looks like a person at the age of sixty. As you see we aged very well.

Still looking thirty, I stayed by her side loving every single minute of her. She would say that I still love her after all these years and I’m a gift from the almighty himself. Always telling her, I'm no one’s gift and that I just love her and nothing more.

Eve said I'm an old woman but you're still the same beautiful man whom I first met. You can have any girl you want. I told her I want no other love, you're the only one I want. She told me she was getting tired and that she wanted to see the sea one last time.

I told her ok and made our way to the village of the sea. She wasn't doing too great on our trip there so I put her on my back and carried her to the village. On my back she said who's the king now and that made me smile. I was about to break down from the thought of me losing my love.

"Just a little further Eve, we are almost there." We finally made it to the village. She asked to go to the sea so I took her there and we sat down looking at the sunrise. Eve said, "My love. I don't have much longer left in this world. I just wanted to tell you how much I love you."

I said you do know there is something that I have always wanted to tell you but I was too afraid. My name is not Leo. She said she had figured it out. My real name is Cain Eden, Eve said, "Cain? So you're the one we heard stories about?" "Yes, my love.

I'm the curse on the world Eve, you're not a curse you're my gift. Always remember that." "I will never judge you on one mistake you made. I will judge you for the two hundred years you spent by my side showing me nothing but love. You're not Cain to me. You're my beautiful Leo noble, strong like the king, my king and my love."

Telling her to rest, she began to rub my necklace and passed away on my shoulder. I stayed there with her on the beach asking Gabriel to please look after my beloved wife. I carried her in my arms to dig her grave next to her father. I placed some flowers in the grave with the body. I said a few words and grabbed my things and made my way back to village.

For two days, I didn't sleep walking back home. It was like a dream to me. I don't really remember walking at all. I just remember getting back to the village. The villagers saw me come back without Eve. I saw tears in their eyes. They walked up to hug me, telling they're sorry for my lost and I told them thank you and walked to my tent.

That was the longest, lonesome walk I've ever took. Just walking to our tent knowing she will no longer be there was awful. The tent smelled like her. I cried my eyes out. I felt Gabriel's hand on my shoulder. I saw a teardrop fall from nowhere. My life felt like it had just lost two hundred years of life through one day of death.

I finally understood my curse and I'm to be blamed for the death of Eve. Forgive me, I must get myself together just to finish writing this, for the person who finds this, those water spots are my tears. I cried myself to sleep. This dream had no garden or the sea was plain darkness. Gabriel walked over to me but he didn't say a word.

He just sat there beside me, allowing me to cry. Why should I get up? I didn't want to wake up to face another day and I know the future will not be bright. My Eve was enjoying valuable emotions while I enjoy every second of her.

I slept till mid-day. I didn't even leave my tent that day. I stayed in there crying, rubbing the side she used to sleep on. It took me a couple of days just to leave the tent. I had a dream in the darkness.

I saw a bright light and it was Eve "Leo, get up. You are a king. The world needs you." I woke up and took my first step outside the tent. The villagers were waiting for me and they greeted me with hugs.

They told me that they were glad to see me and that they are there for me and there is no need to suffer. Those kind words gave me hope and the dream gave me hope. Slowly, I started to get myself back to normal but I could never forget my Eve. I would often take trips back to the village of the sea to sit by her grave.

Sitting on the beach, talking to her, hoping she could hear me or that

Gabriel would give her the message. Always drawing her face on the sand so I could never forget how she looked like. Many years passed. The villagers started to be afraid of me.

Everyone else was getting old and dying but I stayed young. Hearing whispers in the village "Cain", I think they started to figure out who I was. One day, in the middle of the night, I packed my stuff and made my trip onwards. I gave the village one last look before I set off.

It was my home for over three hundred years. It was hard to just get up and leave but it was something I had to do. Wandering through the desert for so many years, I can't tell you how long it has been. I would draw Eve's face in the sand with spears.

Sometimes, I would circle the same spots and see my old drawings it made me give a half smile. Just wandering till I found myself in a great city, I saw nothing like before, a city of sand and stone. In was full of people, more than I ever dreamed of. Traveling from the southern tip to the northern tip of this land to the Northwest is where I found this city.

Chapter 4: The Land of Ra

Egypt is what they now call the place. The real name is a name I can't spell but I will try Rahahankh. If I remember the translation correctly means the sun gives life to this land from heaven. The humans here came a long way from the last time I saw one.

This place was thriving but there was something strange about this place. The people here were different. They didn't feel like the villagers I once held in my hand. These people had goals in life. Just how long was I in that desert? To them, it was about moving forward.

The people never stayed in one place too long. They didn't seem to enjoy life at all. This fast pace environment can probably help me forget my past. I told no one my real name "Cain" died once I left the village Leo is to be my name from now on. I met many new people and they all asked me where I came from.

I told them that I was from the land of the sea all the way south at the tip. Everyone I told was in pure amazement. They could not believe that I survived the desert for that long. I was told the "Gods" must be with me. Hearing the S in gods but I thought nothing of it.

I was soon to find the S had more meaning than I thought. Walking through the city I could hear people whispering that I was the one who travel a thousand years through the desert and lived. He is the one blessed by the gods. People would walk up to me asking if I could get the gods to bless them. They would bring me food and walk up to me just to touch my hand.

I never had a problem finding a place to stay. I was offered places to sleep. These houses are what they called them. It was very different from the tents I was used to. Made of rocks and stones, they were hard as the wind could not shake them, the rains could not soak them nor did the thunder shake them.

They always asked about my robes and how I got the king of beast's mane? Was I a king and if so why did you leave? I would just smile and say I am no king but just a man and that my kingdom is everywhere. Sometimes, I just need to keep my big mouth shut. They took what I said wrongly.

They called me "Leo the king of the desert" I would bow my head when they say it. I thought nothing of it. I even liked it as it made me feel special. Getting so used to the name and the treatment, I think I let it go to my head. Walking around the city like I was king, walking over to people and looking over their food knowing that I would get some for free, it was great.

I also got to sleep in one of the best houses with the finest blankets. I always kept on the king's mane just to make sure everyone knew I was king. They gave the finest robes incrusted in jewels clothing fit for a king. I did well playing this role but was I really playing? I was really a king after all.

Just like everything in life, all good things must come to an end. Playing king for about three weeks was great until one day; I left a house that I was staying in. As soon as I walked outside the house, I was greeted by some men with spears and curved blades of which I have never seen before. They asked me if I was Leo.

In my kingly voice, I said yes I am him and they raised their spears and told me to come with them. I said ok and began to walk with them. I asked them where they are taking me. They told me to keep quiet and that I am going to see the "real king". I knew I was in real trouble now.

We hopped on an animal with two humps and went on a long trip. Man, it was hot outside. The sun felt like it was leaning right on me. I asked if we can stop and they said no and told me to shut up. I asked if I can at least get a drink of water.

One of the men gave me a glass container full of water and I thanked him for that. One of the men smiled and said there is no way you're a king. You are way too nice and the others started laughing. I began to laugh with them but I really didn't get the joke.

Finally, we arrived at the gate and you know when we got there I said finally, they all looked me and shook their heads and one said I guess I was wrong, he might be a king after all and they all laughed. He hopped off the two humped beast. They told me to start moving and poked me with the spear. I said, "Ouch! What was that for?" He said to just move.

This structure was unlike anything I have ever seen. It was massive stone walls. The size of three men standing on top of each other and it was long and wide as a river. Did God himself build this? No man could have done this. It was marvelous.

We went pass the stone walls only to find what I called; the biggest house I have ever seen. It was marked with symbols and carved by the stones. I rubbed my fingers across them while we walked. The inside was full of statutes, deck out in the finest robes. We walked into this large room that had drawings of human like figures on the all walls.

I was lost in its beauty. I was told to wait right here in the center of the room. Some of the guards walked off while the rest stood there with their spears pointed at me. Asking them what was going on; they told me I was going to meet the real king.

The guards walked back in, surrounding a man with this funny looking thing on his head. It was the golden color of the sun. It even shined just like the sun. Who was this man? The thing on his head was encrusted with the shiny rocks that I've found in the caves.

It made his appearance "godly." He sat in a chair made of the golden substance which is also encrusted by the rocks. He sat down like he was the best person alive. I asked him what the meaning of this is. He screamed silent and the guards poke me with a stick.

They grabbed my shoulders and forced me on my knees and said to bow before your king. In a total disbelief, the only true king I knew was the almighty. This was all new to me. He asked me who I was and I told him I'm the king of the Village of the Sun.

Telling him that I came from a land far away, the word sun seemed to bring them shock. He asked me where this village of the sun was and I told him it is all the way south by the sea. He raised his hand and the guards dropped their spears. He told them to leave us and they walked out immediately.

He stood up and walked to a drawing of a strange man like creature. He said there is a prophecy about a man that will travel from the south sea and that he will change Egypt at its very core. Ra the God of the sun will bless him on his journey here. He asked me how long did I travel and I told him it was over a thousand years.

I crossed the desert land. He asked if I've traveled that far through the desert and did not die. I told him yes and that my journey was long and a tough road to get here. I don't know how I've made it here. I just walked till I found this strange place.

He said it's true that I must be him and that I was guided here by Ra. I was confused for I didn't know of this Ra person is and why would he guide me here. He told me to get up of my knees and follow him. He told me his name was Kadjet Narmer Menes or Pharaoh Narmer Menes. Kadjet means immortal star or one chosen by the stars.

I asked him what pharaoh was and he told me pharaoh was the king. Pharaoh was more than a king. He is the ruler of Egypt and that all were under his power. He told me that he wanted me to be his advisor, I asked him what an advisor was and he told me I'm will be the person he will look after for guidance and answers. I was telling myself that this is a job that seems to follow me.

I told him I will do it. He was delighted to hear that. He clapped his hands and the guards popped out and he told them that I will be his new advisor and told them to show me to my chamber. The guards said right this way my lord. In my head, "I was like; oh I'm their lord now."

Looking at the guard that poke me with the spear and I asked him weren't you the one who poked me? I saw fear in his eyes. He lowered his head and said yes I'm sorry my lord. I grabbed his spear and poked him back.

Do you like it when you get poked with a damn spear? He answered, "No, my lord." I told him to not do it to others then. I heard the pharaoh laugh and said that I will be a wonderful advisor. They showed me to my chamber. It was definitely a wonderful chamber to live in.

It was filled with books or should I say pictures of the man like creatures with the sun, the moon, the stars and many other thoughts of humans. My walls also were filled with these drawings. I looked on the floor. There was a giant drawing of a man reaching out to the sun.

Fascinated by the drawings, I began to open the books to learn more about them. These books I found with the words Ra written on them, was this the man that the pharaoh was talking about? These books helped me to learn that Ra was the God of the sun and that they felt he was devoured by the sky every day and was reborn every morning. I found that the Egyptians worshipped him above all other gods and that he was the God of gods.

Guessing that saying I was the king of the village of the sun made the pharaoh believe I was the man from the prophecy. Learning of Anubis the God of The dead or what the Egyptians called the underworld. I was fascinated by the underworld matters after I found a book on it. Finding out that the underworld was the place human souls get judged and this was the home of many of their gods.

The more information I found, the more I started liking Ra. Ra must fight his way through from the west to east every day for the sun to rise and set. Ra had to fight Apep everyday on his journey from the west to the east. They even had woman gods in which they called goddess.

Bastet was one of Ra's daughters. She was the goddess of protection. I also found that Isis was a one of the goddesses of protection. I just loved the sound of her name. Hathor was also a goddess of protection. It seems as if all the women were here for protection.

Is it because our mothers are seen as our protectors? Ma'at was the goddess of justice and was one of RA's daughters. I finally found some other goddess that was not here for protection. Sekhmet was the goddess of war. It was told that you could hear her battle cries when battles were fought.

Seshat was the goddess of writing and Tefnut was the goddess of the rain. The last goddess I saw was Nut, the goddess of the sky. All her drawings show her holding up the stars. All the readings helped me find more gods. Osiris was the God of resurrection and fertility.

He recycled life through our children. Atum was the God of creation and perfection. He was the first God and his name sounded so close to my father, Atum and Adam. It made me wonder if there were any connections between the two. Staying up long passed when Ra set the sun, I learned the Egyptians worshipped many gods and there was a God for almost everything.

I thought to myself. The human imagination is a grand tool or was it that the almighty had a mother, a father, a brother or a sister? I read everything I could till I got tired. I wanted to know everything about the Egyptians as much as I could. I was wondering what the change was in humans that made them stray away from the God I knew and loved.

I woke up the next morning to a knock on my chamber. I was told to get ready and that my clothes were behind a door on a rack. I went into the door and saw many clothes. Are these really all for me? The clothes were different. It was lighter than and not as heavy as the robes I wore.

All the clothing was made from silk. It had many areas for air to flow. The top was one piece by itself and the bottom was another piece by itself. I found some clothing that looked like the pictures of Ra. They were bright as the color of the sun on the top and black on the bottom.

The guards walked me to the Pharaoh's chamber. I found the Pharaoh sitting on his chair. He asked me to step forward and gave me a beautiful golden necklace that he called the "eye of the sun "and told me to wear it at all times. He said the priests had blessed it so that the wearer will always have protection.

The necklace was beautiful. I thanked him for it and he told me that I can now take off the bone necklace. I told him I will never take off the necklace because it was a gift from my queen who is now in the underworld. You will like how I just tossed that word at him that I've just learned.

He told me he understands and I told him that I will put in on over top of it. The necklace was very heavy. It weighs over two pounds as it was solid gold at about 14 inches long, 3inches in widths and 1 inch thick. All the links were connected to the middle where they would turn into the sun. I understood right there at that moment that these metals and shiny rocks was worth more than the entire world.

I had a new goal in mind which was to gather and store as many of them as I could. Pharaoh Menes told me to take a walk with him so that I can learn the Egyptian culture. He told me of the gods they worshipped. Ra "the sun" was the most important god. He told me that he believed that I was Ra, resurrected in the human form.

It is the only way I could have survived being in the desert under the sun. Also, being the king of the village of the sun and wearing the king's mane, no doubt that I'm the one. With a smile, I agreed with him. I didn't have the heart to tell him the truth or was it because I was fascinated by all of this.

I think it was the second one plus the fact that I was there as a king again was also a plus. He told me of my duties and tasks. My duties were to advise him on matters concerning the kingdom. My tasks were to maintain order in the kingdom so he doesn't have to.

He told me that he is trying to be a kind ruler but it's hard because the people always want things from him without doing any work. So most of the time, he rules with a closed fist. No one questions his words on anything he says. To the people, he is half man and half god. I am the sunrise and the sunset.

He told me my first order was to go collect taxes in the town where I was staying. Hopping on my camel and rode off into the desert sun, I hated the sun, some god of the sun I was. I walked around the town that day. The people were so nice to me and I collected taxes from everyone. Seeing me in my new clothing made them all bow their heads.

Since I was dressed up like Ra, they all called me Ra-Noor. I had no idea what Noor meant. Being the man that I was, I gave each of them a red shiny stone to show my thanks for all that they had done. I told them this will be the only time for now. I work for the pharaoh and I will be collecting taxes on the first day after every full moon.

I told them it was the pharaoh's orders. That was a lie but I figured having a schedule will make things easier for me and the people. So I collected all the food and shiny rocks that I could and made my way back. I presented Menes with the taxes. He was pleased. I told him that I will collect taxes after every full moon.

He was pleased with the idea. I told him that it will give the people time to have better gifts. He told he knew I came to him for a reason and told me that I did a job well done. I bowed my head told him thank you my lord and retired to my chamber.

I continued to read up on the underworld as I needed to know the place humans go when they die. I needed to know this for my father, my mother, my beloved wife and my poor brother. I could just picture them sitting outside the gate looking inside, wishing they could be there. This is when I found out that they had many names for the underworld such as Duat, Akert or Neter-Khertet. This place fascinated me or more like it gave me hope for my family.

Maybe all wasn't lost maybe and I didn't ruin everything. The underworld was a place under the earth. It's where every human's soul has to go. It was still full of life. Even in death, a giant flowing river gave life to plants and trees. The drawings were grand.

I could picture my wife sitting by the river with her short hair and a big smile. I could see my mother and father sitting under a tree just enjoying the breeze. I could picture my brother in the fields in his sleep. This place of souls had many wonders; it had lakes, caves walls of iron and a lake of fire.

The lake of fire had no real information I looked through almost every book in my room but there was nothing. As I looked deeper into the picture, I saw human hands reaching out of it. As I found more information, I read that we will be blessed by the spirits or Akh and this is what the Egyptians called and that we must find our way through the dangerous landscape. We must pass many tests and travel through many gates full of guards. I found that this was not the afterlife but only a journey to it.

There was a map of the underworld from the day you die. There is a starting point and an ending point. The end was freighting to say the least. "The weighing of the heart" is where Anubis used what I think, was a feather who was Ma'at in her judge form. If your heart was lighter or heavier than the feather, you will be rejected and eaten by Ammit "the one who devours souls." The souls that pass the test would be allowed to travel to the Paradise of Aaru.

It began to get late and I was tired. I will learn more of this Aaru tomorrow. I woke up the next day with two things on my mind; the lake of fire and Aaru. I left my room and went straight to the Pharaoh and asked him if we could talk. He said sure and asked what's on my mind Ra-Noor, with a smile on his face. You don't think I don't know what's going on in my kingdom? I know everything as I have ears all around. I smiled and asked him about the lake of fire. He said, "I see you have been studying our ways."

I said yes and he told me that the lake of fire is where the bad people spend the rest of their life in eternity on fire. He said that he was the first Pharaoh and Egypt had many kings before him. He was the only king to have the ruled all of Egypt. I asked him if he knows what happened, he told me his father was the king on one side and his mother was the queen of the other side. They got married and united both sides hence making him the king of both sides.

He said being the Pharaoh means that he can never see the lake of fire no matter what he does. I didn't understand these words right away. Asking him about Aaru, he said Aaru was the "Reed Fields". It is where the souls who lived life with a kind heart go. The heart is where the soul lives and this is the reason why we are judged from the heart. The feather of Ma'at was the judging point of the heart.

You must have read where your heart can't be heavier or lighter than the feather. It's much more than that. A heavy heart means that you have lived your life with much pain. That pain is from all the wrongs you lived with without trying to right your wrongs. The heart being lighter than the feather means that you had no cares in the world but only thoughts about yourself. We must have a balance within us to achieve what is called Noor.

Noor is light, bright, shining or hope. The people see you as hope. I see you as hope Leo; I hope we can make Egypt the greatest kingdom ever. I told him the same goes with me with my signature grim. We took a walk through the courtyard. It was beautifully filled with lotus trees. These trees grow flowers and from them, the big white flowers will give the courtyard a smell that could only come from Aaru.

The flowers also grew in the water it was a magical sight. I spent most of my time in the courtyard. It was just me and my garden complex. Still dreaming and hoping that I could be inside the garden, using my wondering eyes. To me, Egypt was about enjoying greatness years of perfect treasures. I loved that place. It was one of the few places I thought of as home. The years went by and life was just beautiful but I had this empty feeling inside. I asked Menes for a favor and I told him that I will be back soon and made my way off.

While making my way south on my journey this time, I saw countless numbers of people roaming the desert lands. I gave them water when I passed by them. I wanted them to live as the desert can be a cruel place. I finally reached my destination, my home. The village of the sun and I was very happy about it.

Looking back at the place that brought so many happy years enlightened my heart. I looked around the village but no one was there. Everyone was gone. After seeing my old tent, I rubbed my fingers across it. That familiar feeling widen my eyes. I went inside the tent and my memories started to come back to me. It still had her scent. No one has slept in here ever since I was gone?

While I lay inside the tent, I rubbed on the spot she used to lay on. Oh how many years has it been? I feel asleep after that. I had dreams of us two together again but this time it was different. She asked me how my life was going. I had to ask her what she meant and she gave me that big smile.

I woke up immediately after that. Was this a dream? Was that really her? I just knew that I didn't want to wake up. I grabbed our blanket and made my way further south. As I approached the sea, that familiar smell came up to me. Oh what a joy to be back here. The sea was in sight. My Eve, how are you doing my love?

The village of the sea was also empty and not a single person in sight. I made my way to the sea with one thought in mind. I must watch the sunset. Sitting there on the beach just waiting to see that familiar sight when the sea shows the sun being devoured made my happy.

I smiled the whole time and it never once left my face. It’s time to do what I came to do. The years weren't kind to the village of the sea. The village was falling apart or should I say, it was apart. It looked as if a storm came through it. I wanted to pick up the pieces but there was no point so I left it alone. I made my way to the place I came to see and the sight of it brought tears to my eyes.

My beloved, here is where you rest. I stood over it. The roses I planted still grew there. Bending over to take a smell and for some reason, they smelled sweeter. I thought that it might be my mind playing tricks on me.

Standing over her talking, I asked my love how long has it been? I hope you're happy and at peace. I hope you found Aaru and maybe the almighty will let you in the garden. Look at me; I'm a king again with my head up high. The mighty Ra-Noor let the thunder flow from my mouth. I'm doing fine my love.

I miss you every single day of my life over a thousand years and I still love you like it was just yesterday. I kissed the ground and placed some seashells on her grave. I then hopped on my camel and rode off in the night.

Looking up at the stars, making wishes upon the stars. It never shined so bright in the desert and off the sand before. It was just magic. Making my way back to my new home upon arrival, I took my last breath of my past. It is time to see the brighter day of tomorrow. The years went by. Menes had a son in which he named him Nor-Aha. He was named after Horus, the god of the sky.

Chapter 5: New Bonds

He loved Nor-Aha very much. Menes was a great father. His wife Anta was beautiful with a long flowing silky hair. She was a walking goddess and he worships the ground she walked on. I also treated Nor-Aha like a son. We play in the courtyard very often and Anta will always be there watching us. I learned the art of sword. Menes would often say why does my advisor need to know the art of the sword? I would give him my grin and tell him that it would be for the times when I need to protect the ones in which I have come to love.

Menes taught his son how to be a king while I taught him how to be a person. I took him on my runs in the city to teach him how to deal with the people. Wanting to show him that a little kindness can go along the way. By teaching him how to use a sword in the courtyard, you could hear two pieces of wood crashing together and that is a sign of me and the young prince in training.

Menes would often joke and asked if I am trying to take his son away from him. "All he does is talk about you," said Menes. I would tell him, "No my lord. I just want him to be a strong man." After that, Menes would send woman into my chamber around this time. I haven't been with a woman since my wife. I would turn them away initially but I'm only human with passion. I tried to hide; it was only a matter of time before it came out. The years have been very kind to me. I was strong. My muscles were as hard as a rock. I wasn't the biggest man but I was 180 pounds of pure muscle.

Menes sent a woman in who looked like his wife and I could no longer hide it. I jumped on her like a lion. She loved it. She smiled and said to give her more. I answered her request and with all my strength, I picked her up and walked her to the bed.

There was no wasting of time. She was ready so I placed myself inside of her. The beautiful feeling of it being so warm, so soft and so wet was just too much. I was done in like three minutes but she told me it was ok. I told her I know because it's not over yet and got back on top of her. We made love for hours and she told me that she will be back often. I don't know what happened to me but I awoke the sleeping lion and you could hear moans throughout the castle coming from my chamber.

I was alive again, living and loving life maybe a little too much. I started having more than one woman at a time. I was starting to be known as Ra-Leon, the king of the bedroom. I love to hear women calling my name when we made love.

Women were lining up to go to my chamber and I never had a problem being alone in my bed. My bed was always filled with naked women. My bed was large enough for four people so I made sure I had four naked women in there. I never really had the same woman in my bed because I loved the first timers. No two women ever felt the same. Some were softer than the others. Some were warmer than others and some were much wetter than others.

I made love to hundreds of women so keep your daughters locked away and keep your wives inside because I was on the hunt for them. I had countless wives in my chamber all telling me their husbands don't make love to them anymore. I didn't let this interfere with my day job. I was a night time lover. Yes, I wanted it during the day but my duties were first.

During this time, our priests saw an opportunity with Nor-Aha and since they could not convince Menes to give them absolute power they looked towards him. One of the priests named Amen, who was basically the leader of the priests wanted to be in power under the throne. Amen was an evil man. He took taxes behind the king's back from the people and he told them it was to please the gods. Amen told the people he could talk to the gods by giving him money and he would personally deliver their message to the gods. I knew Menes knew about it. After all, he knows about everything but I could never understand why he let him get away with it.

Amen would gather all his so called god taxes to build wealth and power to his priests. He walked around like he was the Pharaoh wearing his golden masks and silk robes. As he walked through the city, he would pretend to bless the people and instead of saying thank you, the people would say amen. His power grew as the pharaoh become sick. I would find him around Nor-Aha whispering things into his ear, trying to get in his favor because he knew he would be the next pharaoh soon. I tried to keep him away from Nor-Aha but it was hard from tending to my duties and checking on the king.

His wife Anta stayed by his bedside with a sad look on her face. He would touch her face softly and tell her not to worry and she should go and do the things she loves. She would always tell him no and just stayed by his bedside unless I was there. When it was just me and him, still calling me Ra-Noor, he told me to look after his son and make sure he that grows up to be a strong pharaoh. He told me that Anta will stay queen until Nor-Aha is ready to be king.

He told me that Amen was plotting to kill me so I have to be careful. He told me Amen sees me as a threat to his plans. I told him not to worry about me as it’s not easy to kill me. He said he knows with a smile "he who walks through the desert for a thousand years." After our conversation, I had my eyes out for Amen's plot to kill me. I thought he would send a woman into my chamber so I didn't let any women stay in my bed after I was done. They were all hurt, thinking they did something wrong but I gave them all the same answer of "no my dearest, the pharaoh is sick and I need to be ready by his bedside," and they all believed it.

One day after collecting the taxes in between the city and the castle, I was met by three men. It was Amen's guards. I asked them what was this all about. They then jumped off their camels and said that it's time for me to die. These men had no clue who they were dealing with. I was more than Ra-Noor and I was Leo, king of the beasts. I was Leo, king of the village of the sun and first and foremost I was Cain, the oldest living human and the first murderer.

I gave them a chance and I told them to put down their swords but they all laughed. I must believe that I am really Ra with my signature grin. I said you totally have no idea and I jumped off my camel with my sword drawn. They all came at me at once. I blocked the first attack but the second attack landed, cutting my arm with the third attack barely missed my neck.

I reached for my arm in pain with the blood gushing out. They regrouped on the other side and they told me it's over. I said never and charged in like a lion. I rotated my sword and swung it at all three of their heads at the same time. They jumped back in terror. I let out my roar and the guards eyes got large.

In soft voices, they said Ra-Noor but it was too late for them. I struck my sword in one of their chests. I grabbed his sword and charged the next guard. He swung his sword but I blocked it and slit his throat clean. The last guard dropped his sword and told me to spare him almighty Ra-Noor. Without mercy, I swung both swords, one to the right and the other the left and took his head off. I grabbed his shirt to wrap my arm and made my way to the palace.

I was thinking in my mind that if they tried to kill me, he might try to kill the Pharaoh so I raced off. Upon reaching the palace gates, the guards asked me what's wrong. After seeing the blood coming from my arm, they called for assistance but I didn't take it and I went straight to the Pharaoh because that was my only concern at that time. The staff tried to help me but I refused so they followed me around on my walk. The noise stirred up the palace.

I saw Nor-Aha came running out shouting "Ra-Noor what has happened?!" I smiled at him and told him that I was alright. I reached the pharaoh's chamber. Anta opened the door as she must have heard the noise. She looked at my arm and asked what had happened to me and if I'm alright.

I told her that I'm fine. I saw the fear in her eyes as she was afraid for me. I asked her if Pharaoh was alright and she said yes. I calmed down after hearing that and entered his room. He asked me what's going on. I told him all is fine. He saw my arm and said that it's not alright and sent in his staff.

The staff had bowls of oils and clothes. They stood beside me to clean the wound and sewn it with a thread. I could feel the needle piercing through my skin. I could feel my skin forming together with every pull of thread.

This was very new to me as I have never seen anything like this before.

Once they finished, I could see my flesh closing up together and they told me to make sure that I don't move the arm too much until it heals. I thanked them and they left the room. Menes said it was Amen was it not and I said yes it was. Should I send for him? I said no because we have no proof but do not worry he will get his judgment when the time comes.

I told him to rest and that I will be fine and left his bedside. I closed his doors. Anta was waiting outside. She rubbed my arm and asked me if I was alright and I told her that I am. She said that she can't lose me and her husband so I will have to be careful because she needs me around.

She hugged me, allowing me to feel her soft skin on mine. It gave me an old familiar feeling. She smelled of oil and her hair smelled like roses. I kissed her on her forehead and told her that everything will be alright and not to worry. I walked away while she stayed there watching me as I walked away.

Menes began to grow really ill. I barely got a chance to get to know him. He died at a young age and the kingdom mourned his lost. It was said that Amen poisoned him and that was the reason he died. It didn't matter.

His wife and son had just lost a great man. His funeral was grand. The people came far and wide to show respect to the first Pharaoh but Amen had other plans. Before Pharaoh died, he had a tomb built for him and his wife. You see, the Egyptians had this belief that the tombs would glide their souls to the underworld to make their passage swift to Aaru.

During his funeral, Amen sacrificed some people who did not follow him and by the time the queen, his son and I arrived, it was too late. Hundreds of people lay in a trench beside Menes’s tomb. It was the most haunting thing I have ever seen. Anta and Nor-Aha couldn't even look. They grabbed me and put their heads under my arms. I held each one in a different arm with eyes of fire. I stared at Amen and that he must die for this crime.

I kissed Anta on her head and hugged Nor-Aha and told them that it will be alright. I told them to go back to the palace and wait for my return. They didn't want to leave me alone but I told them to go and I will be alright. I just need to know that they're safe.

They rode off, looking back at me the whole time. It was time to kill Amen once they got out of my sight. Amen knew I had come to kill him. The look in my eyes was clear. He said from a distance, "So Ra-Noor, you came here to die.

Thanks for saving me the trouble." He sent his guards to attack me but I was thrilled. One by one, I slay them down. The sound of swords crashing filled the air. I was brutal on them. I dismembered off their heads, arms and legs. You could hear them screaming as I passed. They moved in slow motion as I was hastened by my rage. I killed at least thirty men with about ten of them who got away. Amen asked them where they were going. "Do not run you cowards! It's only one man!"

I have finally made my way up to him. He draws his sword and swung into my direction. I let him stab me in my stomach as I fell to the ground. Amen celebrated as he raised his sword in the air saying victory was his. The mighty Ra-Noor has fallen to him and he is a true god. I had my head down like I was dying while he said the kingdom was his. I pulled my head up and looked straight at him. He asked me what I'm going to do now. I gave him a grin and he asked what's so funny that I'm about to die. I stood up and told him that I can never die by your hand or the hand of any man.

He asked me how am I still alive. Die already. I gripped my sword tight and slice off the hand that held the sword. He fell to the ground. I could see the fear in his eyes. He asked me who I was and I told him that my name is Cain and I was the third human ever born. I'm over five thousand years old and I will now send you to your "real maker." Yes, I was there when the world started. Tell the almighty that Cain said hi. He said this cannot be. No, don't kill me. I struck him in the leg, broke the other one and tossed him in the trench.

I looked over the top of him and told him that he will die slowly and that he must stuffer for his crimes and walked off. I hopped on my camel and rode off to the palace. I saw the guards with their spears drawn in the middle of them as I reached the palace. I saw Anta and Nor-Aha and gave them a big smile. They had the look on their faces of relief. I must have lost a lot of blood because I collapse the next thing I knew. I hit the sand with my eyes wide open. I saw them running towards me. I couldn't move, I couldn't speak nor could I hear. Once again, everything went black and I found myself outside the garden with Gabriel.

Gabriel said, "Hello my friend. It's been a while. Sorry, I haven't visited you but I have been real busy collecting souls. The humans are starting to die faster now." Those words didn't make me feel better but I told him I have been fine but just in a little pain right now while smiling.

Gabriel said, "Yes, I see that. I heard your little death speech and it was touching. I asked him if he liked it and he said it was a little too much but I got my point across. I smiled and told him I will do better the next time and I shall work on it. We stayed outside the garden, feeling the breeze while catching up on old times. I asked him if he got Amen yet. He told me no but coming real soon. He told me he appeared to him after I kick him in trench.

This was the first time I ever gave more life to a soul because I wanted him to die slow. Like you have said before, he needs to suffer for what he has done. I thank him for that. We don't have that much time. They are calling for you. Can you hear them? I started to listen hard and I heard Anta and Nor-Aha calling out for my name. I told him yes and I shook his hand and told him that I will see him around soon and closed my eyes. I was back in reality when I opened my eyes to see Anta and Nor-Aha at my bedside.

With tears in their eyes, they said thank the gods that I'm alive. I smiled and told them I barely survived but I will live. They said the helpers told them that I could still die but I told them not to worry and that it will take more than this to kill me. They asked me about Amen.

I told him that he is lying in the trench with the people he murdered. I told them they no longer have to worry and I told them they can leave and that I will be alright. They both said no. I reached out my hand and put it on Nor-Aha head and told him to go and rest for I shall be here in the morning. He said alright and made his way to his chamber. I looked at Anta and told her that she can go too. She told me no. I already lost one man I love and I'm not about to lose another.

I thought nothing of the words she said because she said it as a friend. I turned my body away and went to sleep as I needed more rest to heal from the wound. I woke up the next day to find Anta and Nor-Aha by my side sleeping. I said good morning and they woke up with smiles on their faces. They said I seem to be doing better. I told them yes and that my body has a little more life in it now. I also asked them if I could get some water. They didn't call for the staff. Instead, they got up and returned with water and grapes.

In Egypt, grapes were only fed to the Pharaoh, his queen and his son. So from seeing them bringing me grapes had brought me joy. I never had grapes before. It was juicy and sweet. Anta fed the grapes to me as if I was the king. I think she did that to show her respect for me.

I pretty much rested that whole day and once in a while, I would wake up to see them still by my bedside. I would touch both of their heads and go back to sleep, making them smile. I stayed in bed for about a week and they were there the whole time. I finally regained my strength. I woke up in the middle of the night and saw them sleeping by my bed. I then covered them with blankets to keep them warm from the chilly night.

I quietly walked outside as I didn't want to wake them up. I walked outside to the courtyard and watched the stars. The sweet smell of lotus flowers set up the mood for the night. I heard footsteps getting closer to me. I wasn't afraid and I turned around slowly to see who it was. It was Anta with my blanket around her. Anta asked when I got up. I told her not too long ago and she said she didn't hear any noise from me getting up. I told her I didn't want to wake them up.

She sat beside me and asked what I was doing. I told I was looking at the stars. She looked up and said, "Beautiful! I love the stars. Nothing like them at all." She asked me why I was looking at them and I told her not to laugh if I'd tell her about it.

I said I look at them and make wishes. She looked at me and asked, "Wishes? What do you mean?" I told her the stars gave me hope. I have been in many hopeless situations. She said my husband told me you wondered the desert for over a thousand years but I didn't believe him. I thought he was just talking nonsense. Is it true? I told her yes and she said no one can live that long. I smiled at her and said that I wish it was true. She rested her head on my shoulder and we just watched the stars in silence.

We return to the room. Nor-Aha woke up and said, "Ra-Noor, you're moving about. This is wonderful." I told them to go to their rooms and meet me outside in the morning. They asked what for and I told them it was a surprise. Just be there and they agreed. The morning came and I was outside waiting. I saw them coming through the door and I smiled. I asked them if they are ready to go. The guards then gathered but I told them that we do not need the guards.

They said ok and we went off. They kept asking me where I was bringing them the entire journey and all I told them was they will find out when we get there. We finally made it to the place. We all stopped and they began to cry.

I told them they never got a chance to mourn or say goodbye so here is your chance. They thanked me but I was hoping the sandstorms would have covered the bodies because they didn't need to see them. I was right. The bodies were covered. They walked into the tomb. I waited for them outside. They came out with smiles and tears. They hugged me and said thank you. We rode back to the palace and I could sense the burden lifted from their shoulders.

I often checked up on the queen to see how she was doing. She would tell me that I didn’t have to do that. I would bow my head and say yes I do need to because you're my queen. She would say that I have no king or queen because I am the king. As soon as I recovered, I went back to my passionate ways with a different woman every night. One night, I heard a knock on the door.

I was shocked because I told the guards to not let anyone pass because I needed a break. I opened the door and to my surprise, it was Anta. I asked her if there was something wrong. She said no and asked if she could come in. I opened the door and let her in. I asked her what was troubling her. She paused and told me that her heart is troubling her. "Your heart," I asked. She said, "Yes, my heart. I love my husband and I always will." I moved in closer to her and she turned around to kiss me. Without hesitation, I kissed her in return.

We stopped and she said is this wrong. I told her I don't know. She told me she always has thoughts about us but she has always loved her husband so I kept them to myself. She said she must have been lonely. I moved in closer to her and hugged her. I could feel that soft skin, the smell of oil and the scent of rose from her hair was just too much for this me.

I tossed her on my bed and jumped on her. I looked her right in the eyes and kissed her. I started to kiss her neck. She moaned. You have to remember that she has not been touched for years. Every kiss and every touch made her moan. I started to make my way down to her breast with my lips.

Her breasts were round as a melon, about the size of a large apple. She had the body of an hourglass, a goddess in my bed. I made love to her for hours and she moaned the whole time. She called me Ra-Leon as I moved in and out of her. We both enjoyed this moment of passion. She stayed there in my bed naked, lying on my arm.

The thought of her being there turned me on again and so I jumped on her and we continued making love. She said twice in a night. I must be a God and she asked me to make love to her like no one has ever done it before. Of course, I did it for another hour. My passion was flowing through my body. I haven't felt this way ever since my beloved Eve passed away.

I gave her my all. I could feel her soul connecting to mine. We became one, one body, one mind, one soul, one breath and one heartbeat. I gave her all my love that I have held inside. She could feel it as I had her heart in my hand. She lay in my bed all night.

I held her as she slept soundly, kissing her neck while she sleeps. From that moment onwards, we were secret lovers. We are not just two people making love but two people in love. No other woman could come into my chamber from then on. I had all the guards to stop them at the gate. I heard women yelling "Ra-Leon, make love to me!" outside my window for over thirty days. I had a balcony built at my window that faced the courtyard so we could be alone and watch the stars together. We made love under the stars with the cool breeze and the lovely lotus scent over many nights.

I made love to her almost every night. She would ask if I am trying to get her to bear my child. Knowing that I couldn't have any children, I would tell her that is only a dream come true. I never told her that. I just let her believe it so she would be happy. Every chance that we got to be away from the guards, we would use it to chase each other around the palace. We would stop and get ourselves together when there were guards around.

One day, while in the courtyard training, Nor-Aha he told me he had followed his mother one night to see where she was sneaking off too. He said he was surprise that it was my room but he should have known because she always looked at me differently. I told him that I'm sorry he had to find it out that way. He told me that I have no reasons to be sorry for.

My mother is happy again. He told me that he has always thought of me as a father and so he will address me as father privately. My heart skipped a beat from the sound of those words. I reached out my hand to shake his but he smacked my hand down and hugged me instead. He said thanks for everything that I have done for his family and whispered the word "father" into my ears. I hugged him tighter when he called me that and I even shed a tear.

Nor-Aha was about twenty at that time and he was growing up to be a great man. It was time for him to become Pharaoh so Anta and I made plans for his ceremony. We held nothing back with trays after trays of food from faraway lands. His table was filled with delicious grapes. We had music playing and beautiful women dancing around but still I couldn't keep my eyes off Anta. She was the most beautiful women in the room. The white crown with a long golden silk dress, she shined like a star as if she was my star to wish upon.

It was time to crown Nor-Aha, the Pharaoh. He sat in his father's chair while we stood in lines on the left and right. The queen walked down the middle with his father's crown on a pillow. I was the closest one to Nor-Aha. Anta smiled as she walked by me beautiful. She finally made it up to Nor-Aha and held the crown in the air, over his head and said a prayer before placing it on his head. Anta said to him, "May you be a great Pharaoh, my son." She then bowed to him and took her place in the line next to me.

The priests walked over to bless the crown and the new pharaoh. Did you think the priests died with Amen? You should know by now that nothing is more powerful or more evil than religion.

The new Pharaoh stood up and walked to the balcony where the people waited outside the palace gates. They cheered loudly when he stepped on the balcony.

He raised his hands and the people cheered even more. The people outside were having their own party with drinks, music and food. They were just there, dancing around being happy. It was a joyful day in the kingdom and all was happy. The pharaoh walked down the line, shaking everyone's hands and kissing the ladies hands. He walked up to me and Anta and gave us both a hug and said thank you mother, thank you father. Those words always brought me joy. They could put out the lake of fire.

The party went on far pass the moon. Anta and I sneaked out to my room for an hour. We ran around the palace like children while all the guards were at the ceremony. I chased her to my room, pulling up her dress to get a peek at my prize. She would laugh and twirl, making the dress go up higher then pulling it down, saying catch me if u can.

We often stopped at a wall by door to kiss and touch each other. She loved to rub my stomach. My six packs of muscle turned her on. The day of the ceremony was the most fun time we ever had. The freedom to be ourselves and to not hide our love was joyful. Don't get me wrong. We loved to sneak around with the thoughts of having no one else knowing about this, kissing and touching each other with people around the corner was fun. It was just this time that it was different. Freedom is bliss.

The ceremony was finally over. People started to leave. I returned to my room, waiting for that knock. Nothing could have sounded more beautiful than that. My knock came and this time, I hid behind the door while she walked right in. She looked around for me but it was too late.

I already jumped on her. She laughed all the way to the floor. She said, "Still playing games I see." I said, "Yes." I looked at her in the eyes and told her that I love her for the first time ever. I always showed her that I love her but I never told her. Her eyes got big. She smiled and said she has been waiting to hear those for a long time. She said she loves me too and asked me to kiss her and bring her to Aaru tonight.

I told her I will answer her request and she said that I better do so. We made love till Ra reached the east and brought out the sun. I opened my shutters to let some of the light in. Dust particles were moving through the light, shining on Anta like it was magic.

She asked if I was going to just stand there and suggested that we sleep through the day. This was the longest time she ever stayed in my room. We were there sleeping for hours. We spent the rest of the day together and the rest of the night by each other's side. We ate and drank in bed. It was a lazy, beautiful day.

A couple of years went by and I noticed that Nor-Aha was getting lonely. So I told him that it's time to get him a wife. He smiled and stood up, joyfully saying, "Bring it on! I need a queen." So I sent the word out to the kingdom that the king was looking for a queen.

I hopped on to my camel and rode into the city, looking for the most beautiful women that I could find. People stopped me in the streets, telling me they have a sister, mother, or daughter that was beautiful and I told them to go get her. I walked through the city, inviting all the beautiful women I saw to palace on the night of the full moon.

It was only a few days away from the night. He was nervous yet excited to have that many beautiful women in one room just for him alone. In case you are wondering, the pharaoh was no virgin. After all, living with Ra-Leon for all those years had some effects on him. Yet, he was still nervous.

I guess the thought of finding the one you love and spending every night of your life with someone can get to you. The night of the gathering finally came. I walked up to Nor-Aha and grabbed him and asked if you are ready my son. He said yes with a big smile on his face. I told him that's my boy and ran outside to greet all the women. I had to make sure that only beautiful women entered the palace.

Hundreds of women showed up to have a chance to be queen but I only allowed fifty women in the palace because I didn't want Nor-Aha to be overwhelmed. It was just like his pharaoh’s ceremony but this time, it was all women. He walked around the room, kissing all the women on the hand. He started to dance with some of the women. I saw this as a chance to have fun. I walked over to Anta and whispered some naughty things in her ears. She smiled with the same thoughts in her mind.

We both turned to Nor-Aha while he was dancing. He smiled and shook his head. He waved his hand telling us to go. We ran out playing the whole way to the room. There is no need to tell you what happened next as you can get the rough idea. An hour passed, we jumped out of the bed.

We must get back to the ceremony. We didn't want to miss it for the world. We ran through the palace playing around before stopping at the door to get ourselves together. We saw disappointment in the pharaoh as he was sitting in his chair with his hand on his hand. We walked over to him. Anta hugged him, gave him a kiss and told him that it's going to be alright. I put my hand on his shoulder and told him that you will find her and nothing to worry about.

I dismissed the women. They were all disappointed. I told them that I'm sorry but the party is over. I thanked all the women for coming and the prince returned to his room. Anta and I lay in bed, talking about Nor-Aha. "What are we going to do?"

I told her not to worry and that he will find his true love. We cannot force this. It has to happen on its own. She said I'm right and we can't force love; love cannot be forced no matter how bad we want him to be happy. We lay in bed that night. There was no love making, just there in each other's company. I guess we felt sad for Nor-Aha so we just talked and slept off.

I often find beautiful women and introduce them to the pharaoh but nothing ever came from it. I never gave up and I kept trying. He would say, "Father, you don't have to keep trying." I would bow my head and tell him that yes I do need to and it is my duty. It’s hard to see your son sad I will do whatever I can to change that.

Out of the blue, I notice his mood started to change he was happier. I thought nothing of it and I was just happy that he has happy. One day on the balcony, Anta and I were just looking out. We heard some laughter and one of the voices sounded familiar. It was Nor-Aha with the crown and all running around with a woman.

We could not see her face. The sight of Nor-Aha happy made us happy. I grabbed Anta’s hand and told her to let them be alone. She said no and she wants to see them both laughing so I pulled her harder and tossed her on the bed. With a smile on her face, she asked what is it that is so important to keep her away from seeing her son being happy. I told her to hush and kissed her and made love to her.

Anta came into my room every night since the first day and we would hear Nor-Aha running around with this unknown woman. Never underestimate a mother's nose for it shall find what it's after. She snuck around the palace, following Nor-Aha till she found out who it was. To our surprise, it was the newest member of our staff, Ma’at she was named after the goddess. She was a beautiful young woman. Nor-Aha had chosen wisely and his mother was happy. In case you wanted to know, Anta was forty but didn't look a day older than thirty. She married Menes at thirteen because back in those days, you were able to have children if you were a woman.

A couple of years went by and Nor-Aha decided to marry Ma'at. The kingdom was then at peace. The ceremony was grand. It was a wedding and the crowning of a new queen. Of course, you know that we snuck off again. We loved it more than anything. Ceremonies were just pure joy in our hearts. The years went by. The pharaoh and the queen had a child who they named Djer. I know that this was not the children of my blood but in my heart, they were my children and they knew it.

My grandson, my son, my new daughter in-law and my beloved Anta was such a beautiful thought. They are my first family and I have finally found peace in my soul. Anta never believed that I wondered the desert for over a thousand years until she noticed that I wasn't growing older. She never really said anything about it because I think she was afraid of the truth. No matter what the circumstances are, she still loved me and I still loved her.

The nights in the palace were the best. Nothing has brought me more joy than being with Anta in a long time. At fifty, she looked forty and still had a great body with scent of oils and roses in her hair. At this time, my grandson was seven; the future Pharaoh Djer. Anta and I (I want to say me and the other person's name, I know it's their name and I but that is how we spoke at that time so you might see me slip up for time to time) loved having Djer around. Children give life and light to all places. He called me father Ra-Leo. There was no such thing as grandfather or grandson at the time. Grandson was son of the son in shorts I called him next son.

He was a very handsome young man. I trained him in the art of the sword while his father taught him to be pharaoh and the cycle continues. These were some of the happiest times of my life. Anta died at the age of sixty five but she managed to see her grandson grow up, big and strong. The kingdom mourned for her lost. I did more than mourning on her lost. I lost a little more of my soul when she died.

She was buried with the Pharaoh Menes in their tomb. I visited the tomb almost every day, talking to Gabriel, asking him to keep her safe. I felt his presence almost every time when I visit the tomb. I would say I know you're there but never got a word in return. To the one who finds this, I will tell you that I didn't get a chance to say goodbye. She died when I was away and it is not always a fairy tale ending. If you have someone you love, tell them and show them that you really do. You will never know when they are going to go.

Chapter 6: The Hidden Sands

My role with pharaohs started to diminish. They started to be afraid of my never ending life and youthful face. So I put on a Ra mask to hide my face from all and join the ones I hated the most, the priests. I joined the priests for one reason and one reason alone; to be next to pharaohs. I tried to guide them right but the other priests just wanted to get rich. I started to see the downfall of the kingdom of Egypt. All it did was harden my heart.

Egypt was my home, the place I truly loved. It is saddening to watch pharaoh after pharaoh take Egypt's riches. The hearts of men began to change. Greed controlled almost every pharaoh. From pharaoh to pharaoh, Egypt faded away from its roots. From pharaoh Meneith, to pharaoh Anedjib, they began to lose the peace loving Egypt and the downfall of Egypt begun when pharaoh Semerkhet came.

He was a greedy man who wants everything to himself. He taxed the people once a week and they was glad when he died. They cheered at his tomb and threw parties in his name or should

I say his death. He was the one who started off enslaving the Hebrews. In case you're wondering they were Egyptians just the lower class who also believed in different gods.

The second pharaoh of the second dynasty, Raneb, tried to bring Egypt back to its former glory by dividing Egypt into two states, an upper and a lower. He gave both of his sons a kingdom each but they didn't want to be king. They wanted to be pharaoh instead. So they fought each other's state Egypt vs. Egypt. It was a war of its own people. I buried many people in those years and my heart withers away slowly. I tried to help the people as much as I could through prayers and lies. I told them all was going to be alright when I knew it wasn't.

An all-out war between Egypt, many innocent people died. I buried mothers, sons and daughters. The heart of man turned cold. The war finally stopped when Nynutjer won the war and became pharaoh but the people still suffered. God must have gotten mad with us when Nynutjer, son of Senedj become pharaoh. It rained for seven days straight and flooded the Nile.

The flooding of the Nile changed the life in Egypt and it is what you see today. The flooding of the Nile changed the landscape of Egypt. It washed away the plants and trees that gave Egypt life. With no plants or trees, Egypt became a true desert. Our lands began to drought and our once fertile land become cracked and hot. The pharaoh tried to please the gods with sacrifices of people but that didn't work and he died very young.

The first pharaoh of the third dynasty, Djoser, brought what I called "the living dead". At first, he gave the people a decent wage but he got greedy and started reducing them. He was the first to build a pyramid from the people's love, the idea that they were a part of building something to please the gods but his greed made them hate this stairway to the gods. The pharaoh believes the gods would love the pyramids and they also thought this would guarantee them a place in Aaru so Djoser passed this teaching down to every pharaoh.

Every pharaoh who came next would do the same but Sneferu had a different idea. He was the first pharaoh of the fourth dynasty, the builder of the first true pyramid. He was the most evil of all the pharaohs before him. See, Egypt had already conquered many surrounding lands long before he was born.

Sneferu had an idea. Rather than paying workers to build the pyramids, he used slaves instead. He paid the overseers a wage but he beat the slaves as their wages. He brought slaves in from Libya, Jordan and Israel so that the pyramids would be completed much sooner.

These were all Egyptian lands they moved the majority of the Hebrews there and left the pretty and strong in Egypt. They tortured the slaves; steadily whipping them. They used both the old and young ones. He never used woman because he felt they weren't strong enough to help out.

I tried to oversee the pyramid building so the guards wouldn't beat the slaves. The guards didn't even care that I was there and I understood why because the other priests were there telling them that the slaves need to work harder. They would say that this is a stairway to the gods. We need to please the Gods so work harder. With this in mind, the guards beat them even more and since they were Hebrews, no one even cared.

I tried to control the beatings but no success will come out of one against the kingdom. Yes, I said the kingdom because even the so called Egyptians didn't care. They didn't want to do that work and through the teachings of the priests, they told them they were inferior to us. They were taught all non-believers are going to the lake of fire so you need not worry about them. Not all Egyptians felt this way. Some would bring them food at night at the slave's quarters. The slaves would always say that it's a blessing to them for the food they had received. No one would bring them food during the day. The risk of being out casted was more than they could bear.

I often went to the quarters to feed them and give them medicine for their wounds. The Hebrews fascinated me more than the other slaves. They stayed strong no matter how many times they got whipped. They sang and danced in the slave quarters almost every night.

They prayed all the time but I didn't know who they were praying too.

I would hear them speak of the almighty but just what almighty do they mean? It took a while before they trusted me because they had a good reason too. The other priests would walk through the slave’s quarters and find the ones who prayed to their false god. They would make them give up their faith for their life. Most choose to give up their faith but some wouldn't even if it cost their lives. Some would be killed on the spot to instill fear into the others. The others were taken to the streets where the Egyptians would stone them to death.

The stoning was such a painful death and they made sure the Hebrew people see the way they are being stoned to death. Walking from the quarters to the pyramids, they stoned them right along that path. Seeing their fathers and sons dead brings tears and fears to their people. Even though their woman didn't work on the pyramids, they were slaves too. Just the women had different tasks. They were to serve the pharaoh by cooking and cleaning.

Their women were beautiful but you dare not say it out loud it could be your death. So all the Egyptian men stayed away from the women and the one who passed the rule gets to keep them in his chamber every night. They stayed in the slave quarters with the men. It was always joyful when they returned to their families. After a while, they began to trust me as I wanted to know more about their god.

They called him the almighty. They said he created all life but he created humans for a special purpose. I asked what this purpose might be. They told me the purpose was for us to follow his ways. I still didn't get why he created us to just follow his ways. It wasn't until I met Joseph that I really understood. Joseph was around fifty, still stronger than most twenty five year olds. I had many conversations with him. He told me he didn't believe God created us to follow his word and he thought it had to be more than that.

He told me that he thinks the almighty created us just to fill the void in this empty world. That everything else came after we didn't do what he wanted. He said look at this.

We are no different than the Egyptians but yet they make us their slaves, beat us and even kill us. We both have tanned brown skin, thick full hair, brown eyes, two hands, two feet and one heart and yet our hearts are so far apart. My people just want to love and be happy with their families but your people want everything. I don't know whose God is the real God but what I do know is that none of this is right and no God would do this to anyone.

It was the first time I heard a man speak this way. He said one day, he will be released from this prison and enter Gan Eden. A familiar name heard from the past, I asked him what was Gan Eden. He told me the Garden of Eden and for the first time in thousands of years, I heard a person saying that name. The name alone brought me back to the past. I pictured myself outside once again. I asked him to tell me more and he told me it was the almighty’s house.

I just couldn't believe my ears. My dream, my beautiful dream was being told through someone else's mouth. He told me that is where all the good people will go after life. He said it was only a matter of time before he goes there. The look in his eyes showed no lies. He made me remember again on my past that I have lost long ago.

I asked him about Cain to see if he knew and his eyes had the fear of god in them. He stood up in his cell and while grabbing the bars, he asked me where I got the name from. I told him it came from a man a long time ago. He sat back down and said that Cain is the evil son. He murdered the first human and tried to burn down Gan Eden. My heart stopped. How could I have fallen so far from grace and how could they speak of such things they didn't know about.

I'm truly the world's curse. Just look at how I'm viewed in the eyes of the world. I am the origin of evil. I didn't bring Cain up to Jacob no more. I couldn't bear to hear those words. Jacob became my friend, a man who I talked to every night. I gave him water and bread while I passed out food and water to the others too. After all, I could not just show up with food for Jacob with the many hungry people around us. The Hebrew people called me Leo and there was no Ra to them.

I returned to the quarters one night and Jacob was not there. The others had sad looks on their faces. I asked them where Jacob went and they told me a guard killed him because he was trying to save a young man from being beaten. In my head, I said a prayer may you finally see Gan Eden. For the one that read this, I had a thought earlier about love and showing it and this is another reason how people in our lives don't stay long. Try to put your emotions aside and be a good a friend.

After Jacob had passed away, I told myself I would never get close to anyone again. The pain is too much to bear. I would rather be alone than to feel the pain of losing someone I care about. My heart got colder. I never took my mask off in front of people. I kept my mask on even when making love to women. They would always ask if they could see my real face. I would always tell them it's not necessary. Just sit back and enjoy. I hid my eyes because they showed pain plus I understood the eyes are the connections between two humans. I wanted no more connections with anyone.

The second pharaoh of the fourth dynasty, Khufu, started what I called, the plague of death. He started the pyramids at Giza, the largest and most grand structure no man has ever seen or dreamed of. The slaves never worked so hard before that they died in great numbers. He had them shipped in great numbers after a while and he just kept more slaves ready. He knew tons of them were going to die and he didn't even care. I didn't get involved with the matter of the slaves no more. I was done. All the death turned me heartless as the oldest human alive. I understood one thing and one thing only, and being rich is all that mattered.

As a member of the priests, life was always good and being Ra-Noor was even better. I slowly started to build my wealth when Menes was pharaoh. By now, I was the riches person in Egypt. Not even the pharaoh had more riches than me. I had my own palace, the palace of Ra-Noor and I was a pharaoh in my own right. People came far and wide just to be around the palace of Ra-Noor. I walked outside every day and people waited outside my gates just to ask for a prayer or blessing.

I would give them food, water and stones at times. I had my own staff with guards, servants and women that I made love to. Since I never took off the mask, myths and stories grow. Some said I was the same Ra-Noor that lived with pharaoh, Menes. The others said I was the son of son of Ra-Noor and that my spirit entered the body of each son. The pharaoh couldn't even touch me and as a matter of fact, they were all afraid of me.

The teaching passed from pharaoh to pharaoh that the priest Ra-Noor was immortal. He brought the flood and brought to the lands because he was displeased by pharaoh Senedj. I was untouchable. I let it get to my head for a minute and I actually thought I was a god. Let me be the one who tell you things you already know. Power corrupts all and absolute power consumes the soul. I talk about things people already know of because of one thing. Things get hidden in the past and past tells all the stories of the future.

I wrote rules down like I was pharaoh; I passed laws like I was pharaoh. One law that I passed long ago gave the priests absolute power "the law of the priest." The law of the priest still goes on to this day, the men of God cannot be questioned by any man nor shall he follow the rules of man. Not one man whom cannot speak to god can tell a man who could speak to god just about anything. This law gave all religions the power over man. I'm sorry for what I have done. No words can be said to forgive me. I do not ask for your forgiveness because I should not be forgiven for this.

One of my priests, Anubis, he was the most evil priest that I have come across so far. He figured out how to use the people more to get our brotherhood richer. He asked what the one thing that people fear the most is and I told him they fear the pharaoh the most. He smiled and said "No, it's the gods." That fact never even crossed my mind but I should have thought of all the people outside my gates. He told me to come to the balcony. He said look at all those people outside just to get blessings from us. Let's use that, let us fuel it for no one is dumber than a man who follows a God.

So from then on, we used their beliefs to enslave them even more. We placed posts around Egypt such as "in order for you to get blessings, you must make an offering to the gods." Just like cattle, we led them to our grass. The easiest people to prey on are the ones with hope or the ones looking for hope. One by one, they came giving us things they shouldn't have parted with. Some even offered their daughters if they were pretty and I took that offering right away. As you can see, I didn't care. I have already lost my way. I lost everything that I held dearest to my heart so nothing else mattered to me but myself.

I had dreams of ghosts in my bed. The memories of the two I once loved and still loved. I would wake up in tears. I moved to another room in my palace but the visions of their sad faces still haunted me. There is no escaping this so all I could do was to turn my back and face the wall. The only escape was to have women in my bed so I had one stay every night.

The offerings of daughters became my relief. Years went by and the nineteenth dynasty came. Ramses the first was the new pharaoh. He kept the priests by his side as he was afraid of death. Nothing scared him more than dying. He heard that I was the immortal one.

Chapter 7: The Never Ending Title

He made me an advisor again and I almost never left his side. He had a son Ramses II and his full name was Usermatre Setpenre Ramses II. He was around four when this strange event happened. There was another son around six months old who magically appeared. By magically, I mean his mother wasn't bearing a child so where did this mystery child come from?

The sight of him gave me chills so I kept a watchful eye on him. They named him Moses Ramses. I heard the queen found him drifting up a stream. The reasons I wanted to keep an eye on him was not because of the stories but because I saw what happened before when the kingdom had two sons. The flashes of war, the people dying and the never ending fires that consumed Egypt is a memory I shall not forget. No matter what, he became the price and the queen loved him like a true son. I figured out later on that he was just a son of one of their sisters or brothers.

They grew up like all the brothers and sons of the pharaoh I seen before.

It was competitive as the brothers were trying to outdo each other and trying to be the best at everything they do. Watching them gave me joy and sadness at the same time. I saw history repeating itself once again. I trained them both in the art of the sword. User loved it but not so much for Moses. Moses would rather be reading but like all brothers, he still tried to beat them. He lost every single time but he never gave up.

But there was something different about Moses. He held no anger towards User for winning. He would get up every time and tell User that he had done a good job with a big smile on his face. The boys were told that one of them is going to be the pharaoh one day. Pharaoh usually goes to the elder sibling but the father can choose whoever he wants. Moses never knew that he wasn't their real son and how would he his parents raise him and loved him like their own.

One day, the pharaoh asked me to bring the boys in to demonstrate what I have taught them. I think he did this as a test, not for their sword skills but for something else. I brought the boys to the throne chamber while the pharaoh together with his queen watched from their chairs. The boys were going to try even harder because of the presence of the pharaoh and the queen. Try hard wasn't the word. They fought like men but User fought like he was trying to kill Moses and of course, he won. Then something wonderful happened that none of us was ready for.

Moses stood up with a big smile, shook his brother's hand and said that he had done a good job and you're going to be a great pharaoh. It came as a surprise to all of us. User understood Moses would not have fought him to be the next pharaoh. In everyone else's eyes, Moses was pharaoh. The pharaoh told me the story of Moses after that which surprised me. In his eyes, he said that he saw Moses as a king and he wants Moses to be the next pharaoh. Since Moses was not a child from the blood, it was easier for him to choose User. After that fight, User began to change. He no longer fought his brother for everything and he learned to share. Moses was happy just to be a prince. It was something that I never seen before coming from a prince.

The kingdom was at peace but not its people. It was still full of slaves. I could see that it bothered Moses but he kept it to himself. They grew up so fast that we were having two men in the palace before I even knew it. The princes of Nile are what I called them, the Nile was the life of Egypt and so were the two princes. User was becoming pharaoh right before our eyes and Moses has the wind of the desert. They were the perfect pair of brothers from two opposite forces, one for the day and one for the night. It is understood that you can't have a day without the light and darkness.

The pharaoh passed away later on and both of the brothers mourned his lost. They never forgot the things he taught them. User become pharaoh while Moses stayed a prince even though Moses has being a prince ever since. User always looked to Moses for answers.

Moses was very wise for his age plus all the book reading fueled the desert wind he was born with. He stayed talking about Babylon, China and Japan. He said that he was going to visit these lands some day later. Babylon was a place of anything and everything. It was basically a lawless place. China and Japan, who Egypt has been trading with for thousands of years, was full of mountains, green fields and men of lighter skin.

I never visited the places but I read about them through books and drawings. Moses was the prince of the sun and by the sun; I meant that he would just lay there with a book to read all day. I guess it was a good life of not being the pharaoh. User would always tell Moses to take things more seriously but he never did. I think User was a little jealous of Moses' easy life. User being User was born to be pharaoh so he would shake off these feelings and press on as the pharaoh that he was born to be.

One day, Moses had the idea to get more serious about being prince so he went with me on my advisor duties. So off we went into the city collecting taxes, checking the water supply and crops. We stop by a store front to grab a bite to eat. All of a sudden, a girl walked up to us and said "Moses! You're alive!" and hugged him. He looked shocked and asked who she was and what the meaning of this is. She said her name is Miriam and she’s his sister. He told her that he has no sister and to stop playing games before he gets her arrested.

She said it’s true that they didn't tell him the truth. Moses yelled silence and pushed her down and put his sword to her neck. I grabbed Moses’ arm and stopped him. Miriam was on her knees crying. She said, "Moses, you're my brother. I'm just so happy that you're alive and mother will be happy too." He told her to get up and run and to leave his sight. So Miriam ran off saying "Moses, you're my brother." Moses had a strange look on his face. I touched him on the shoulder and told him that everything is going to be alright.

Moses looked at me and asked if any of this is true. All I could do was to look at him and stay silent. I guess my silence did not rest his soul so he raced off to the palace. I followed closely behind him. He went straight to the queen’s room while I stayed outside but I could hear everything. As Moses entered the room, the queen asked him what was wrong. He said some women came up to him, telling him that she was his sister and then he laughed. The queen stayed silent for a bit and that was the last thing Moses wanted to know.

Moses asked, "Mother, what's going on? Why are you so quiet?"She said, "I'm sorry." Moses replied, "Why the apologies?" "She tells only lies." She said, "I was hoping that you would never have to find out but that doesn't change anything. You're still my son." He said, "I know mother. I love you too but I need to be alone."

And so he walked to the courtyard with his head down and started crying. About thirty minutes later, User came running to the courtyard. "Moses, I'm so sorry." Moses asked User if he knew but User told him that he didn't. He told Moses that this doesn't change a thing. He's still his brother with tears in his eyes and hugged him.

Moses said, "Thank you. You're my brother too but I still need to know the truth." User said, "I understand. Go find out the truth but the truth will always be that you're my brother, the prince of Egypt." Moses said, "Thank you. I shall return."

There have been many stories of how Moses found out about how he found the blanket and the basket he was found in. He found out from his mother's undying love because she could no longer lie to her beloved son. Moses asked me to come with him and I said yes. Off we went searching for Miriam. We couldn't find her right away. It took us a couple of days staying in the city with the people.

We finally found her. Moses walked up to Miriam. She asked if we had come to kill her. Moses hugged her crying and said, "I'm sorry very sorry." She smiled and hugged him in return. This was a very touching moment. I almost cried myself. She said, "Come, mother will be so happy to see you." Moses' head rose from her arms.

He asked if mother was still alive with hopes all over his face. Miriam said yes with a big smile on her face and asked if he would like to meet her. Moses said yes. We walked on the outer parts of the city. There was a tent near the pyramids. She stopped and asked if we are ready. Moses answered yes with tears in his eyes. So we walked in the tent. Miriam said,

"Mother, Moses is home. She asked, "Moses, my Moses?" Miriam said, "Yes, mother. He is here."

Miriam grabbed her mother's hand. She was blind and that didn't help the situation. It made Moses even sadder. His mother said, "Moses, let me see your face." She placed her hands on Moses' face and started to feel. Moses moved with every feel and he leaned in with every touch. She said, "My son has finally returned," and hugged him. I left the tent as it was time for them to talk.

I looked out at the pyramids. Moses stood beside and thanked me. Miriam walked up to us and asked Moses to look at our people and our sufferings. "Moses, those are your people who are slaves." She said there is a reason you're still alive and you're the prince of Egypt. Moses looked at Miriam and asked, "So what do you want me to do?"

Moses said to her, "I'm not going to defy my mother or brother." Miriam said to Moses, "We are your real family." Moses said maybe in blood but the only family I know is the ones who raised me and loved me. Miriam said no matter what it is, those slaves are your people and returned to the tent. Moses looked at me and asked me what he should do. I told I don't know and he must follow his own heart and desires. Moses went back into the tent to tell them he will return and that he needs to clear his mind. As we walked away, Miriam came up to us and told Moses not to forget who he had hugged earlier and walked away.

On our way back to the palace, Moses was just talking about his new found truth. He said, "I can't believe I have a sister and one who so annoying. Why does she keep insisting on telling me who I am and that those are my people? So what if they are my people? Why does it matter?" I said nothing and I just let him speak as he needed to let it out. We returned to the palace. User was waiting for his return and as soon as we walked in, User was there to greet us. User said to Moses my brother has returned. Moses then hugged User and said, "Brother."

User asked Moses if he had found his family and Moses said yes. User asked him how did it go and what was she like. Moses said it was alright and they were very poor. User told him not to worry and that we will fix this issue. Moses then thanked User. Moses walked away and right before he left our sight, he turned with a smile and said that it's good to be home. User turned and asked me how he was doing. I told User that he is fine. He just need some time to get it all in. The next day, Moses and I went into the city. For some odd reasons, Moses wanted to go to the pyramids.

At the pyramids, Moses just watched the slaves get worked to the bone. One of the slaves dropped some stones. The overseer told him to get up but the slave couldn't. The overseer started whipping him and to my surprise, Moses ran over and told the overseer to stop.

The overseer turned to Moses and said it's nothing but a slave and whipped him again. Moses said stop with a louder voice. The overseer then said, "My lord, why do you care?" and tried to hit him again and this time, Moses struck his sword in his neck. Moses then ran off while everyone watched him. I know he was in pain deep in my heart.

So I walked very slowly right behind him. I finally met up with Moses. The looks in his eyes were different. He told me the god of the Hebrews just spoke to him. I asked who spoke to him and he said the god of the Hebrews spoke to him in that bush. He pointed at the bush. He said it was on fire but it didn't burn. I walked over to the bush. Although I didn’t see any fire, I could feel the heat coming from it. I turned to Moses and told him to calm down and it's the desert that is playing with his mind.

He told me that was no desert. I know what I saw. The looks in his eyes were real. I still didn't believe him but the heat from the bush was no illusion. I told him it’s alright. Let's go back home and we will talk about it. Moses said no and that he can't return. He must know what's going on. I stood there for hours, trying to talk him into coming back home but he would not. I returned to the palace. User was outside waiting for us. He asked me where Moses was and I told him that he didn't return with me.

User asked me if it was because he killed the overseer. He is the prince of Egypt and killing a lonely overseer is nothing. User told me that he is going to go get him. I told him I had no idea where Moses went. That was a lie because I knew the one spot that he would usually go.

User told me that if I see him on duties in the city, tell him to come home. All is forgiven. I told him that I will. I went to my palace thinking if Moses really did see God. I went into the city the next day to find Moses. We were there in the tent, exactly where I figured he would be. I told him what his brother said but he said he's still not coming home. Moses told me the god of the Hebrews spoke to him again and he needs to figure out what's going on. I told him to take his time. I left him and his family some food and went back to the palace.

User asked me if I saw him. I told him no but I will keep Moses on the lookout. He thanked me and told me that he misses his brother. I kept going back to Moses, trying to talk to him but nothing changed. His appearance has changed. He was no longer in clean cut or in silk robes but in a slaves outfit. I told him that his mother misses him and he would tell me that he misses them as well.

The years went by and the queen became ill. She was still waiting for her beloved son Moses to return but he never did. I told Moses the news of the queen's death and he cried like a baby and thought of his brother. I told User I saw Moses. He asked if I had told him news of the queen. I told him yes and that he cried like a baby and told me to tell you that he misses you and mother but he couldn't return just yet. User asked me to get him to come home whenever I see him again and that he needs his brother.

I told Moses what User said. He looked at me and said not to worry. I will see my brother soon. I was so delighted to hear that from Moses that I went straight to the palace to tell User of the news. User was happy. He said his brother will finally return home. True to his words, Moses returned to the palace. The guards came running in to tell us that the prince has returned. User looked at the guard, feeling all excited and asked, "Moses has returned?" and the guard said, "Yes, my lord."

User looked at me and said, "Finally, thank the gods". Moses walked in with a stick looking old with a beard. He walked up to User, hugged him and said brother, I'm so sorry to hear about mother. User said, "She asked about you until she died. Never mind that. I'm just glad you're home." User stepped back, smiled and looked at Moses. He grabbed his robes and said, "Brother, what is this?" Moses said, "In order to understand my people, I had to live as one of them."

User said, "Your people. I'm your people and you're my brother." Moses said, "This is not a reunion brother. I didn't come here to come back home." User asked, "Moses, what is the reason you came here then?" Moses said, "This is hard brother. But I came here to ask you to let my people go." User laughed and asked Moses if this was a joke. Moses told him that this is no joke and that the god of the Hebrew people told him to free the people.

User asked, "The god of the Hebrews? Who is this man?" Moses said,

"For he is no man. He is the god of all, even you." User told Moses the only god he knows is Ra and Ra has no god above thee. Moses said, "Rest assured brother, I stand before you speaking the truth." User told Moses that he will not let his so called people go. Moses told User that if he doesn't let them go, the god of the Hebrews shall lay waste to Egypt. User told Moses to leave his sight before he sends him to jail and that no man or God is going to take down Egypt. Moses walked away and said, "I'm sorry brother."

User turned to me and said go talk some sense into him. I ran behind Moses calling his name. Moses turned with a voice that was not his and said in a loud voice, "Cain, stay out of this" and walked away. I stood there in shock. Did he just say Cain? And how did he know my name? That voice I remember all too well. It was the almighty. I was shocked. My body was trembling in fear. I felt the fear that I have lost so long ago. I fell to my knees and prayed to the God that I had forsaken.

I went straight back to my palace. I didn't even go back to talk to User. I just stayed in my room in my palace. I told everyone that I wanted to be alone. I stayed there until I fell asleep. Gabriel appeared to me and I just looked at him. I was thinking why Gabriel is here. Gabriel asked me if I am alright. I asked Gabriel if the almighty had sent him here. He smiled and said no. With the same smile on his face, he said he had instilled the fear of himself into me. I said yes, he did and I have no idea what to do. Gabriel told me he couldn't stay long. I shook his hand and thanked him.

Gabriel said no need to thank him. I told him it is not for this but for being there when Anta died. He said no problem. That is what friends are for. Gabriel disappeared shortly after. I stayed there thinking to myself. I woke up the next day and went to the palace. Moses was there with User. He dropped his staff and it turned into a snake. User and I were shocked. We couldn't believe our eyes. Moses picked the snake up by his tail and snake stood straight up showing its hood. It was a cobra.

User told Moses that that was nothing and told the priest to do the same thing. They brought out a snake grabbed it by the tail and it also stood straight up and opened his hood. User said, "See Moses. Our gods allow us to do the same thing." Both of them then placed the snakes on the floor. Moses' snake devoured the other two and returned it to Moses' hand. Moses moved his hand up the snake from its tail to its head and it returned to a staff. I was thinking in my head that those priests didn't turn the staff into snake or make the snake a staff.

User being pharaoh and believing he is half man half god didn't fear what Moses had shown him. He told Moses I still will not let your people go. Moses said, "I'm sorry brother but you did this to yourself. I shall turn all the water in Egypt to blood." User said, "Your god doesn't have the power." A couple of days later, I heard screams in my palace. I ran out to check and my fountain was pouring out blood. I raced to the Nile the river and it was also flowing with blood. I fell to my knees in complete shock. I must tell the pharaoh.

I made my way to the city. The people there were all shaken up. The water ways from the Nile was blood. Since I was a priest, the people looked to me for answers. They asked me what they had done to anger the gods. I told them this happened because we enslaved the Hebrew people. The people then begged me to let the slaves go. I told them it was not my call. They said we must convince the pharaoh. I rode off to the pharaoh where hundreds of people were already gathering outside the palace gates.

The people were there trying to convince the pharaoh to let the slaves go. User told the people not to be afraid for the gods of Egypt are stronger than the god of Hebrews. He made his priest turn some water into blood. They tossed some powered into the water it turn red and poured out like blood. User told the people the god of the Hebrews is not the only one that can turn water into blood. The crowd calmed down, believing what the pharaoh just told them and walked away.

I walked up to User and told him the whole Nile was full of blood. User said, "Yes, I know. I saw it." It is a grand feet but he will still not let the people go. User said Egypt is strong and we will endure this. He was so wrong that many people died during these few months. Egypt suffered a massive drought and land would not take in the blood. Moses returned to User, still calling each other brother. User asked Moses to stop the blood. Moses then asked User if he is going to let his people go.

User told Moses that he will not let his people go. Moses then told User that he will bring the second plague to Egypt. Moses didn't wait any longer this time. He walked outside and raised his staff in the air. The sky turned black and frogs rose from the ground. Millions of them hopped around Egypt. Days went by and the frogs were still there. If you kill one, it turns into two. You couldn't go nowhere without seeing a damn frog. In our beds, in our little remaining supply of water, damn frogs.

The people gathered outside the palace again asking the pharaoh to free the Hebrew people. User called me to the palace and asked me to go the Moses to tell him that he will be letting his people go. I went to Moses and told him that User said if you would stop the frogs, he will let his people go. Moses held his staff to the sky and the frogs disappeared in the sand. Moses turned to me and said, "Cain, let's go."

Fear entered my body. I looked Moses right in eye and asked him how he knew who I was. Moses said, "Yes, Cain. It is the god of the Hebrews". Your god has told me all about you. You're the first murderer where you killed your own brother.

The god of the Hebrews said that he is very disappointed in you no matter what your curse is and you still forgot about me." I stayed silent the whole journey to the palace. The Egyptian people parted a way for Moses they stood silent some even bowing their heads. Moses walked up to User and said, "The frogs are gone now, so let my people go." User said, "No, I changed my mind. I gave User an angry look."

Moses said, "Oh brother, you never seem to learn." Moses walked outside and struck the ground. The ground turned into lice. The lice outnumbered the frogs by thousands of times. The people outside ran away screaming, trying to get away from the lice. There was no escape. There were just too many of them. User called his priests in. Everyone was scratching the itch away. Hethen asked his priests to do the same. They brought out some sand and tossed some power on it but nothing happened.

User asked them what was wrong and why nothing happening. The priest told him that they cannot do this and the god of the Hebrews may be more powerful than the Egyptian's gods. User said, "That is not possible. You better figure out how to do it." The lice lasted for four weeks and it was the worst four weeks ever. They stayed on even in boiling hot water. Egypt did not sleep for weeks.

User still refused to let the Hebrew people go so the god of the Hebrews released his next plague. This time, Moses didn't come to the palace. The sky sounded of rain. I reached my hands out but there was no water. I then noticed what the noise was. Millions and millions of flies everywhere. You just couldn't take a bite of food without tasting a fly. Till this day, if I see a fly, I will make a face like I had just tasted something bad.

User called me to the palace once again to tell Moses that he would let his people go. I went to Moses to tell him the news and he told me that he will call off the flies even though User would not let his people go. He held his staff in the air and the flies flew off with the sunset. We rode back to the palace. It was like a dream. The people parted and allow Moses to pass. The same thing happened again and User said he had changed his mind. Moses said, "Brother, you never learn. I shall place the fifth plague on Egypt and that will kill your livestock.

One by one, all our livestock died. The months went by with no meat available to the people of Egypt. I have never eaten so many vegetables in my life. You never know how much you miss something until it is gone. I craved meat like a lion and as a matter of fact, the whole Egypt did. User still refused to let the people go so the sixth plague began. The sixth plague for some reasons did not touch me or the pharaoh. Everyone else was covered with boils and sores. Even the rest of the animals that were still alive but User still did not let the people go.

So began the seventh plague, the hail fire. The sky was lit with fire. It was a beautiful sight to behold. Until we could clearly see what was coming, the hail was the size of small apples coming down from the sky. The pain from getting hit by them was akin to being hit by a rock. I guess that's what we get for casting the first stone. The hail was not alone. Once the hail hits, it sets whatever it touches on fire. It might have been dark outside but Egypt has never looked so bright before. Seeing the people outside on fire, running and screaming around made me stay in the palace. I know I am immortal but I could still feel pain.

The hail finally stopped. Over a year of deadly plagues, Egypt lost thousands of people; mothers, fathers, sons and daughters. Everyone has had enough. The people threatened to kill the pharaoh and User never left the palace. The palace was on all day watch. User told the guards to kill anyone who tried to get inside. The plague of User was the eighth plague. In my eyes, he killed hundreds alone.

The eighth plague by the god of the Hebrews and ninth plague to hit Egypt was the worst so far. The sky became black and the sun was swallowed by the largest cloud I ever seen. A swarm of locusts covered Egypt and we had very little food left to eat. The locusts made sure we would run out of food supplies. They devoured all the plants. Every part of life in Egypt had locusts on it. It was a frightening sight and if you left one on you for too long, it would bite on your flesh.

So being able to sleep was only a dream. They could even manage to bite you through the sheets. Trying to sleep with a sheet over your body did nothing. User once again asked me to tell Moses that he will let the people go if he called of the plague. On my way to Moses' tent, the locusts held on to me and the camel. The camel eventually kicked me off and ran for cover. I had to walk most of the way there. It took me hours with the locusts still holding on to me and I was bitten so many times throughout the trip.

I finally came to Moses. His tent was the only place without locusts. The locusts flew away from me as I got inside his tent. What a sweet relief. I then told Moses what User said but Moses said User is lying again but he will go to see him. This time, there were no people to part the way for Moses. Moses called off the locusts and User once again changed his mind. Moses walked outside and told us to behold the ninth plague. Moses slammed his staff to the ground, behold the total darkness. The moon vanished right in front of our eyes.

The only light that could be seen was the light from Moses' staff. User ran outside the palace running into everything in his path. User screamed out to Moses, "I will never let your people go!" Moses turned to User with a big smile and said, "Yes, you will. The tenth and final plague by god will change your mind." Seeing the last of the light walk away with Moses was like a fairytale from a book. I could not believe what I saw. If you were there that day, you would not have believed it either. I could not even think of this with my wildest imagination.

Egypt was in total darkness for three days and then out of the blue, the sun rose. It was beautiful. The sun never looked so beautiful. I thought I heard an angel sing as it rose. The people once again gathered outside the palace to demand User to let the people of Israel go. User gave no attention to them until we heard silence. It was Moses walking up. Moses entered the palace this time and User met him at the door. User said, "What brings you here?" Moses told him the tenth and final plague. Moses said, "Please brother, stop this now before it happens."

User said you have stopped being my brother a long time ago. Moses said, "I have never stopped being your brother," and bowed his head to User. User asked him what the next plague is. Moses face hardened. "Remember what father did to the people of Israel?" User said, "Father did a lot." Moses said, "That's right. You were too young to remember but you still know it all too well. I shall bring death to all the Egyptians' first born sons, eye for an eye. User said, "No, not my son. You will not take my son."

Hearing those words shocked my ears. I did not remember the pharaoh killing the first born sons. Thinking to myself where was I? I must have been in bed with some women that day. Ramses must have done that in secret.

Moses said, "I'm sorry but this is not my fault. It will happen in a week from now." During the week, Moses sent the word out to some of the people in Egypt to have Lamb's blood on the doors to save their sons. Days went by and the people started placing Lamb's blood on their doors. Of course, the word got out to all the people and everyone had Lamb's blood on their doors, even the pharaoh. I didn't place Lamb's blood on my door.

I just watched the people. Then the day came Egypt was shaken with fear. The loss of a son is a great thought to bear. The night finally came the wind whipped through Egypt like no wind before. I felt a familiar presence. Gabriel is that you? I fell to my knees for the day has begun. The blood on the doors did not trick

Gabriel. He come passed riding the wind. You couldn't see him but you felt his hand it was cold and rusty.

He touched every man in Egypt to feel if their blood was the first. All you could hear throughout Egypt was cries of no not my son. It was a sad day throughout Egypt. Seeing the mothers and fathers carrying their sons to the palace was heart breaking. Some people even killed themselves. The pain of losing a child is more than some people could bear. Egypt was half the city it used to be, half the people and half the beauty. The ten plagues turn the once beautiful city into a cursed land.

I made it to the palace to find User at the gate holding his son crying. He turned to me and said release the people; my heart cannot take any more pain. He fell to his knees holding his son. I could only think of why did it have to come to this? I went to the slave's quarters and had them released on User's orders. As each and every gate opened, they cheered saying they were finally free and Moses had done it. I told them to gather at Moses' tent and not all the slaves left.

Some of the women servants didn't go and the men who were brought by the nobles stayed. They didn't mind their lives. The people gathered at Moses' tent and Moses told them to follow. The people sang all the way to the river, where the pharaoh was waiting. The people got scared seeing the pharaoh. They thought he had changed his mind again. They asked Moses what is he going to do and Moses said nothing for he will not attack. Just like what Moses have said, User just sat there, watching.

Moses stopped at the sea. User asked Moses how he is going to get across the sea with no boat. User said, "You wanted to be free so badly. Now what are you going to do?" Hearing the pharaoh's words, the people started to question why Moses led them to the sea. Moses told the people not to worry and it will all be alright. The unthinkable, the unimaginable, the unbelievable and the impossible happened. Moses struck his staff on the ground and the Red Sea parted.

It parted from the floor up with two walls of water, one to the left and one to the right. It was a beautiful and fearful sight to behold. User had feared and wonder in his eyes. His guards dropped all their weapons and fell to their knees. Moses told the people to come. They hesitated at first and why wouldn't they? It was nothing like anyone has ever seen before. Moses stepped into the ground that was once a sea and turned and said, "It's safe, let's go."

The people stepped in with fear, looking at the walls of water. I looked at User with sad eyes because I had to go I followed the people. Half way through the sea, we noticed the pharaoh's guards charging with weapons in hand. Moses told the people not to worry just keep pressing on. So the people started to move faster and we made it to the other side. The sea closed up. It had teeth and it looked like a mouth.

It swallowed the pharaoh's guards up. They disappeared right before our eyes and the people cheered. User stared from the other side in disbelief. I bowed my head to him and begun the journey into the desert. The happiness turned to sorrow, walking in the desert with nothing in sight. The people started to lose faith and I couldn't believe that. After everything Moses and the god of the Hebrews had just done for them, how could they lose their faith?

The hearts of man is weak and fragile but also the strongest thing that beats. I have learned a lot about myself and the people. We can never seem to stand together and only the strong survive. The weak ones died off not because of the desert but it was because they just gave up. Others got tired of walking so they returned to Egypt. They would rather be slaves than to be in the desert.

Every time the people asked for something, Moses will provide it through the god of the Hebrews. Regardless of it being water or even food that he gave to us. He made it cloudy to shade the people but they were still not happy. Moses told the people that we are going to Mount Sinai so he can meet with God. We made it to Mount Sinai. Moses told the people to wait and that he will be right back.

Moses climbed the mountain like he was a young man and he left our sight very quickly. The people began to question Moses to why they're still in the desert and where is this so called promise land.

Out of the blue, the ground began to shake and fire came down from the sky. Smoke spiraled down from the sky to the mountain. It made the people kept quiet and fall to their knees. They started to pray. The fear of God grabbed hold of them. Moses spent three days up there while we waited for his return. Moses came down with two large stone tablets with words on them.

Moses asked for silence for now, he shall give us the ten commandments of God. Rule one; thou shalt put no other god before me. I thought to myself of being guilty for I have done that. Rule two; thou shalt not make unto thee any image or idol of heaven. This one was a little tricky. I didn't make myself unto an idol of heaven but I did turn myself unto an idol. I guess I am guilty of this one too. Rule three; thou shalt not take the lord's name in vain.

Finally, one I didn't do. Rule four; remember the Sabbath day and to keep it holy. This was a rule to keep us on the right path and to remember that it took God six days to reshape the earth. On the seventh day, he rested and it is the day we give thanks. Rule five; honor thy mother and father. This one was also tricky. I have never treated them bad personally. I still wronged them by killing my brother and forgetting who I was so I felt guilty again.

Rule six; the one that shook my bones. Thou shalt not kill. No need to tell you how I felt when I heard those words. Rule seven; thou shalt not take another man's wife. Guilty, guilty, guilty, I did that almost every night. Rule eight; thou shalt not steal. Nice, another one it seems that I didn't do. Rule nine; thou shalt not bear false witness against thy neighbor. One more commandment that I didn't do and the tenth and final rule; thou shalt not covert thy neighbor's house, another one that I didn't do. Who would want thy neighbor's house when I had a palace?

These stone tablets with these rules were hard to take it. He went up with no tools but came down with words on giant stones. Also, seeing this man carry them down the mountain with one in each arm is still unbelievable till this day. Moses made the people choose either God or themselves. He didn't kill the people like in the stories.

I mean, use your damn brains. He just passed a law to not kill so why would he kill? We wondered in the damn desert for a year and we spent the other year persevering. It was very trying on the soul. Of course, some of the people were going to give up and go back. I spent a lot of time with Moses after he became my friend.

Moses told me that he spoke to God face to face when was the Hebrews first king? Hearing Moses saying that he spoke to God face to face gave me chills. I wanted to ask him what he looked like but I was too afraid. The only people I knew who have ever seen God was my parents but they never talked about life in the garden.

Moses asked me about my past at the garden. I told him there was nothing like it in the world. I just wished for moments that I could have been inside. He asked me why I killed my own brother. It was hard to talk about it so I tried to hide it in my past.

I told him I regretted it till this day and not a day goes by that I don't miss him. I wish I could turn back the sands of time and I would have used my mind then. He never told the people who I was and he never judged me. He called me brother even though the others didn't like me and Moses' relationship. They tried to come between us. They told Moses lies such as I was just there to spy.

They told him I could not be trusted and that I was Ra-Noor, the priest of the pharaoh. Moses never changed how he felt about me. I spent years with people before but these two years by each other's side had made us close. I would joke with Moses at times: Didn't we see that bush before? I asked Moses if I had hit him, would God strike me down. He would laugh and say that I need not worry about God because he wouldn't be the one that would strike me down. We shared many laughter and bad times together.

The true measure of a friend is not by the good times but how we treat each other when times are hard. Moses began to grow old. I had to use my shoulder to help him walk. Moses thanked me for being here for him and my never ending love and care towards him ever since he was a child till a full grown man now.

I told him I was there for him from the beginning and will be here to the end. I raised you and I knew you would be a great man. He would grab my face and say beautiful. You never age and the beauty of youth is always showing on your face. So this is the mark that God said he had given you. I yes and told him whatever he said was true.

I would then touch his face and tell him beautiful for that old face of yours will grant you passage to the garden. Moses would smile. He always knows the right things to say. He said a hundred twenty years of kind words, you truly are a king. I told him I'm no king. The only king I see is the one on my shoulder. Moses died a couple of months later. I was there by his side. He asked me to tell him stories of the garden.

I told him the gate is pure gold. The colors of the flowers no longer live in this world. It is the most beautiful place you will ever see and may the almighty hold you in his hand. The man who had seen God face to face, even I didn't see that. Moses gave me his staff and told me to destroy it. I told him that I will and he died shortly after. We dug his grave on the bottom of the mountain in silence. His wife and his children mourned his loss.

With Moses gone, my faith left but still I fought on. Many people tried to get the staff from me. I had to hold it like I was sleeping with a woman. Some of the Hebrew people got tired of all the fighting and decided to hop on a boat and sail to somewhere else better. I have decided that I was going to join them. I didn't care where we would end up but it has to be better than this. The others who stayed saw us off and said a prayer for our safe trip.

With the staff in hand, we sailed off to another home. Saying goodbye was hard. I stared at Egypt till it left my sight. Once we got to a deep point of the sea, I tossed the staff. It has now found its home in the bottom of the Red Sea. The others screamed no looking overboard watching the staff sinks. They asked me why I tossed the holy staff of our king. I told them no man can be trusted with that power, not even myself.

After I tossed the staff, the people on board started to hate me. I saw murder in their eyes. I know someone was going to try to kill me. I had no more friends aboard the ship when I come to think about it. I never had any friends they didn't like the way Moses treated me anyway. I watched my back all the time on the ship. The looks that they gave me haunted my little sleep.

I let my guard down one time and I immediately found a knife in my back. I gripped the side of the boat, it broke off and they tossed me into the water. I could hear them cheer. I placed my body on the piece of wood to float I blacked out. For months, I drifted in sea. I had dreams of Gabriel's hand pulling me in directions, trying to keep me afloat. I know I'm immortal but the stab wound with the lack of water and the salt water in my wound took a great toll on my body.

Chapter 8: The Fire In My Soul

I finally washed up ashore. I saw some strange light colored men. I couldn't keep my eyes open. I kept blacking out. I would open my eyes to find these strange men carrying me on some type of wooden structure. I opened my eyes fully for the first time shortly after. I couldn't move or speak. I lay in the bed helpless the strange men force feed me food and water. I heard them speak but I could not understand because I wasn't really there.

I have finally regained my strength back. I tried to get out of the bed but the strange men kept pushing me to lie down. One of them spoke but I didn't understand a word they said. I tried to speak back to them but my words didn't reach. We didn't understand the same words. We spoke of a different language. At the moment, I felt hopeless as I lay in bed with tears running down my face. I wished I would have just died. Finally, I got the strength to get out of bed and I started wondering around this strange place.

The strange men all gathered in one large room, standing still, not making a sound. I walked passed them and opened the door to the outside. This cold wind of which I have never felt before sent chills to my bones. I got myself together, looked out and saw that I was surrounded by mountains. It was beautiful. The mountains had white powder on the top down to the middle. It was like I had found heaven on earth.

I had no idea where I was or who were these strange men. I was in some type of weird palace filled of long steps. I was still weak from my wounds and my trip on the sea. I tried to walk down the steps but I fell all I could remember was my body crashing on the steps. I finally stopped and I tried to get up but it was no use. The strange men came running down the steps to help me.

Being in the state I was in, I tried to fight them. Needless to say, it was very easy to capture me. After all I just went through, I trusted no one. I thought they were going to hurt me. Yes, I know that was stupid. After all, they took me in, gave me food and shelter but I wasn't in the right state of mind. I was full of anger.

Once again, they nursed me back to health. I had constant nightmare of the day they stabbed me on the ship. I would wake up screaming and once in a while, I would start to cry. The person by my bedside would always leave when I started to cry. Finally, as I regained my health again, I walked into the large room where they gathered once again and they were still. I began to talk.

All of the strange men opened their eyes at the same time, all but one person. He sat still facing the wall. There was a giant hole it front of him. I felt this power coming from him. Seeing all the men looking at me at once was a creepy sight. It was like they were all in one soul.

They stood up and one of the men walked up to me. I backed up a little. He started talking but I didn't understand a single word he said. Remember, people fear the unknown and this was something new to me so I panicked and swung. That was a big mistake. He grabbed my hand so fast and moved it to the side. He hit me in the stomach with the same hand and uses the other to toss me down. It happened so fast. I have never seen anything like it before.

I didn't like the idea that I just got tossed like that so I got up and charged at him again. This time he didn't swing right away he side stepped every punch. He used this weird hand moment to move all my punches to the side. I never laid a finger on him. All of a sudden, during one of my punches, he just dropped out of thin air and swung his leg around on the ground like a graceful dancer. I left my feet so fast I was in the air; I landed on my back so hard.

He stood over top of me smiling then reached out his hand and picked me up. I was holding my back. He bowed to me with his eyes on me and walked away and sat down in silence. In my mind, I was just trying to figure out what just happened. I sat in the corner, watching them. At this time, I realized that they meant no harm. I got up and walked outside. The cold air made me go back into the strange palace.

I often heard stories of Babylon. It was on how the people there defied God by trying to build a tower to heaven. They said God struck down the tower and set Babylon on fire. He sent lighting crashing down on all the people but no one died. Instead, the lightning burned their brains and caused them to not understand each other.

It is where the saying babbling came from. I only saw Babylon after they rebuild it. I guess this was the truth and because of that, humans were not being able to understand everyone. This strange palace held about a hundred men I think. I tried to talk to fifty of them but there were no communication.

All this did was making me angry and clouded my sharp mind. I eventually gave up trying. One day, I walked into the large room where they had gathered in silence. Every time I went it this room, I saw the same man in the same spot. It was like he didn't move. I decided to sit down and join them. I closed my eyes and sat there. I felt someone watching me. One of the men was looking straight at me and then he spoke.

He asked me what I was doing. In my head, I was like what in the underworld. I said you can understand me. I got up angry and he told me to calm down. I said all this time I tried to talk to you with no answer but you understood me. He told me yes, I understood you but you were not ready to be spoken too. What do you mean I wasn't ready to be spoken too? He told me there is too much anger in my heart. I asked him what that has to do with anything.

With a smile on his face, he said nothing and this is a peaceful place and that I have no peace. I told him there is no such thing as peace. It died with the first human. He told me I had a lot to learn and told me to sit back down and close my eyes. I sat down and closed my eyes. He asked what do I see and I told that him I see nothing but darkness. He told me to do it longer but after sitting there for five minutes, I gave up.

I told him this was pointless. He told me if this was pointless, then why these men would be sitting here. I said because you are all crazy. He laughed and said crazy to us? You're the crazy one. I calmed I never thought about how I look in their eyes so I sat back down and closed my eyes. I took a peek and I saw him smiling. I did the same thing every day. I sat there with them silently, trying to figure out what they were trying to do.

I discovered the courtyard later on. On the steps to the courtyard, there was a statue of a man sitting there in prayer. He didn't look like any of the men here. In the courtyard, the men practiced the weird hand and leg movements that they used on me. It was like one big dance. They all did it together as one at the same time. I sat there every day on the steps when the sun set over top of us, the same time every single day.

One day, I decided to join them. I walked over and stood at the end and did the moves I saw them doing. They all stopped and turned to menthe one man that I spoke to approached me. He told me to stop. I asked him why and he told me that they do this for peace. You have no peace so you cannot learn because I will use it for war. He finally introduced himself to me. He said since you're going to be in our home, I should know your name.

I thought about what name I should tell him because I have so many but the words Cain came out my mouth. He told me his name was Qiao and bowed his head and said welcome to the Shaolin Temple. I sat back on the steps thinking what did he meant by "they fight for peace." I have never heard of such a thing. Fighting is to conquer land, people and to kill.

The Shaolin Temple was beautiful. It was full of statues of the man sitting. The walls had carvings of strange letters on them. They also had statues and wall paintings of tigers fighting a strange snake like creature with arms and legs. The tiger was in attack mode while the strange snake like creature was in defense. The strange men also had this image inked on their skin.

That image must have meant a lot to these people because it was everywhere. They wore strange robes that covered their legs with a rope tied around the waist. I was still in my Egyptian attire because they never gave me new clothes. Every day, I would gather in the large room in silence trying to find this peace. I saw the same man there in the same spot in my head. I thought, man, he loves that spot. Every day, I would stay there longer than the day before. I practiced the moves I saw them doing in the courtyard in secret.

I wanted to learn more. My nature of wanting to learn will forever get the best of me. One day, I stood there in silence for over an hour. I felt the present of a man staring at me but I never looked. I finally open my eyes and I found some stillness. It was Qiao. He was smiling. He always smiles and he told me to come. We took a walk to my chamber. He opened my door and pointed.

On my bed laid the clothing of the Shaolin people. He said those are your new clothes. Maybe one day, I could wear them with pride. I told him thank you and that I would wear them with pride. Qiao smiled at me and asked what I have to be proud about. I asked him what did he mean. Qiao said these words to me that I still follow till this day.

In order for you to be proud or have pride in something, you have to achieve something to be proud of. Pride is not what you're born with. It is something that you will develop as you do great deeds that are associated with your pride. I told him that is deep and that had never crossed my mind. All my life, I was proud just being born into something. I never did anything to make me feel proud of doing.

I walked in the room, placed my new attire on for a minute and I felt proud of it. I just remembered our talk. I did nothing to feel proud of. I placed the Shaolin robes on for the first time. I never wore anything on my legs. I felt the warmth and comfort that these clothes provided me with from the cold winds. I was happy to wear this, bowing to all that passed with a big smile.

I sat on the steps at the courtyard to watch my favorite dance. Qiao looked at me and said, Cain of the Shaolin temple, come join us. I got up as fast as I could. I was eager like a child waiting for his turn. When my turn finally comes, I was happy my soul was calm for the first time in hundreds of years. Qiao told me to follow his moves. I raised my hands in the air and began to move them from side to side. I have studied these moves for months. Qiao smiled and said looks like you have been practicing.

Qiao began to teach me the way of the Buddha. He told me about the tiger vs. the dragon. I asked him what a dragon is. He told the dragons are noble creatures that once roamed the land. They were the creatures that protected the water, the sky and the land. The tiger vs. the dragon represents the two styles. The dragon is of defense and the tiger is of attack. They are Yin and Yang to opposite forces who live as one in the Chinese culture. Yin and Yang means darkness and light.

In the context of darkness and light, the dragon and the tiger represent life and there is no one side to life. It's like a truth and a lie and there are no in between. It is either one or the other. Make no mistakes through because an evil act can turn out to do well. This is the reason why we must fine balance in our lives and you can't be just one sided.

That is time I found out that I was in China. The place I only read about in books, one of the places I wanted to see. It was like a dream that I needed to see. I think Gabriel guided me here for a reason. Now that I look back on it, now that the world is mapped out I still wonder how I have made it here. Through the red sea passing through Indonesia and Malaysia, Philippines and Cambodia and making my way to China, Gabriel had brought me here for a reason.

I began to learn what Qiao called martial arts; the way of the fist. He told me to never use this for offense and that the monks of the Shaolin temple use it for peace and only when needed. Qiao told me the monks are both loved and feared that many people will try to stop us from teaching. I asked him why someone would try to stop something so good and peaceful. Then he told me about something that I already knew.

Qiao told me people fear the unknown and things they cannot control. Qiao said the king of their land wants to control the Shaolin temple for his own needs. He wants to use the power and knowledge we have to enslave the people. There, I am in another world than the one I know with different people and with different religion. I still find war, I still find slavery and I still find greed. Is there any hope left for humans?

I started to search for the inner peace and the balance that Qiao spoke of. He calling the art of silence meditation, it was a calm of the soul. I meditated every day. The deep breathes helped my troubled soul and the silence brought clear thoughts in my mind. For the first time in years, I found some but this time, I didn't forget my God. I meditated with my God in mind with the teachings of Buddha.

I started to figure out that all religions, no matter who was the God, are all tied together. All religions had a base, a god; the god wanted all the people to do right by him. Each god wanted the people to be good and not evil. Even though I knew the truth about who is the real god, I never pushed my beliefs on anyone.

One day in meditation, I heard a bell ring. All the monks jumped up and ran outside. Qiao told me to go in my room and stay there. I went to my room but I didn't stay. I felt the air and something was not right. I ran outside to find the monks fighting some men in silk robes. The men in silk robes had swords in their hands but the monks had no weapons. I ran to join in the fight by using all the martial arts moves that I learned I used.

The monks tore through the men like a wave on dry land. It was amazing to see men with no weapons win against men with swords. There was one of the men with a sword in hand was slicing the monks one by one. In him, I saw the tiger on the wall live and well in this man. He was of the offense type. He struck with force, one slice by one slice and then moved on to the next monk. I knew I didn't have a chance against him so I fought the other men.

Qiao jumped in front of the tiger and he became the dragon. This was the poetry in motion. I could tell these two had fought before. They seem to know each other's move where they both went from the tiger to the dragon with offensive and defensive strikes. I finally understood the tiger vs. the dragon. It was like one soul with two sides fighting to claim the power of the body.

The man with sword got a slice on Qiao face. Qiao dropped down and swing with both his fist to his ribs. The man flew back like he was hit by a large rock. I never saw anything like it before. The man got up, holding his ribs and ran off. The other men seeing their leader ran started to run along behind him. The victory goes to the Shaolin monks.

Not a single monk died and neither did the other men but everyone was cut or bruised. Qiao looked at me with blood running down his face, still smiling with fist to palm and he bowed. All the monks patted me on my shoulder as they walked in the temple. At that moment, I looked cool with my long hair blowing in the wind.

The blood running down my arm dressed in a monk's attire on the steps of the Shaolin temple. If mother and father could see me now, I think they would be proud of me. I looked around to see if the man with the hole was there fighting but he was not around. I walked into the temple and he stayed there in his spot. Just who is that man and why doesn't he move? I walked over towards him. The smell of must surrounded him. At that moment, my nose understood that this man didn't move at all.

He stayed facing the hole in the wall. I could feel this force coming from this man. Chills went through my body as I got near him. As I got closer to him, Qiao came to me and told me we must not disturbed the enlighten one.

He pulled me away as I stared at him the whole time. I asked Qiao who that man was and he told me his name is Buddha. I asked Buddha as in Buddhism? He said yes and he is the starter of the religion. Qiao told me he has been facing the wall for over three years. I was in shock hearing this news. No way had he stood there that long, I told Qiao there is no way he has been in that spots for over three years.

Qiao told that it was no lie. He told me he made that hole in the wall with his force. I asked Qiao why he has been sitting there for years and he told me that his is searching for peace and answers. I asked Qiao what answers and what peace and he said that he is searching for peace of mind and he is searching in what I think is the afterlife. Does this man really have the power to search in heaven? But judging from the size of the hole in the wall, I guess he does.

A week after we sewed up the wounds, the monks gathered outside my room. Qiao knocked on my door. I opened it and I was shocked that everyone was gathered in the hall. Qiao asked me to follow him. All the monks stay on the side I thought I did something wrong. We walked into the large room where we meditated. There were two chairs there. I saw Buddha there in the same spot.

In all my days here, I have never once seen a chair in this room. Qiao with a big smile as always, told me to sit. Qiao said to me, when I first came to the temple, I was a stranger but I'm now one of us. Qiao bowed his head and said thank you my friend. He picked up a jar of ink and a needle from the floor. Qiao told me that it's time to make me one of them and he began to ink my arm.

The feeling of getting poked with the needle was new to me. It was like chills with pain. Every ten pokes made the blood came flowing out. He wiped it off with a cloth.

The whole process took four hours. He told me to look into the mirror. I saw the dragon vs. the tiger on my arm. Qiao asked me how I felt. I told him that I was proud and he grabbed my shoulder and said yes, I should be proud. Qiao asked me how my arm felt I told him that it felt great.

Qiao said ok and the normal smiling man had a straight face. Qiao said what I'm about to teach you can never be used for the offensive. This is the true fist of peace. Every time it is used, it brings peace. He told me to only strike at the ribs because any place higher will kill the target. I said to him. Qiao said we need to meditate. You must fine your middle way. I asked him what a middle way was and he told me the middle way my liberation.

With a puzzled look, I asked what liberation was and Qiao said that we are children of life and death and in death life has meaning. Since we are not here to stay, we must liberate ourselves from the earth. The more wants you have, the more you will be connected to a place you cannot stay. For the only home for humans is our soul. I never heard such a meaningful way to describe life.

I told him alright knowing I may never find that liberation. Since I cannot die, I thought that there is no way for me to be liberated from this earth and earth is my home and not my soul. I sat there in thought for days. I cannot get my mind of being immortal. A week went by and I was still there but nothing happened. I was about to give up. I heard Qiao's voice. Free your mind Cain and find your place that brings you joy.

Then I heard a voice that I have never heard before. Hello Cain, I opened my eyes to find Buddha standing over the top of me with a smile. He said hello Cain. I knew you would come. I have waited over three years for you. Yisu told me you would come. In my head, I was like who is Yisu. I have never seen him around before. Buddha then said don't worry. He is not here but he is everywhere. It seems like you are ready for me to talk to you and by the way, welcome to the temple. My name is Buddha.

Hearing this shocked me and seeing him not in the corner shocked me even more. Also, who is this Yisu? Is Yisu Buddha's God? I didn't know what to say. He told me to focus. Buddha told me to find my place of joy. I closed my eyes that could only be one place; the garden.

I picture myself there as a child again, all happy and joyful. I felt myself getting free but the garden brings back memories of mother and father and my poor brother. I'm sorry. I heard Qiao voice say no Cain, you're losing it. I opened my eyes. I was done. I stood up but Qiao said no and pushed me back down. Don't give you almost had it.

I closed my eyes and listened to his voice. I heard Buddha's voice in mind. "What is going on?" "Am I imagining this?" I heard his voice in my ears. Happy place, happy place the garden filled with happy times of me with my wife, Eve; my beautiful Eve.

I pictured us together in the garden and then something started to happen inside of me. I felt this power. I saw Buddha there with us in the garden glowing. Qiao told me to open my eyes and stand up. So I stood up with a tear drop running down my face. Qiao told me to use that power and channel it through my fists. Qiao told me to swing both my hands now.

As I swung, Qiao placed a thick piece of wood in my way. I felt the life from my soul go through my hands. Both of my fists struck the wood and it broke up into small pieces. Qiao smiled at me saying, "My friend, you have found the middle way," and then bowed to me. Buddha said with a big smile on his face, "You have just learnt the Almighty push. Also, another reason we don't use it too often is because channeling the power of your soul will shorten your life with every use. It is called the Almighty push for a reason.

You're pushing out the power that was given by the Almighty God." That tear that I shed was not from sadness but joy. If you have ever cried from joy, you will then find true happiness. There, Buddha told me his work was done and went back to his place to meditate.

Qiao was in shock. He told me he couldn't believe that Buddha got up to speak. Qiao started to really teach me the ways of the Buddha. He taught me about the enlighten path, it means to release one's self of earthly objects. Qiao told me the ones who try to be perfect will never be enlightened. No matter what we have and what humans do, we will never be perfect. What we fail to realize is that we are perfect our perfect imperfections make us strive for more. It makes us seek peace search for answer that a perfect being will never find.

If one thinks that he is perfect, he will fail to see things right in front of him. If he thinks that he is perfect, he will feel that he don't need answer because of the fact he is perfect and no knowledge will be found. Qiao was the smartest man I have ever met until this point of my life. He told me the only perfect man is the one knows he's not perfect. I heard Buddha's voice again; he told me you can only gain perfection in death. There is no way I'm imaging this.

Qiao taught me the three marks of existence. Anicca; Nothing in this world will cease to exist. No matter if you believe in God or not, everything will live forever. I asked Qiao what he meant by this. He asked me to see this leaf for it will fall off this tree and touch the ground. Not being attached to the tree will cause the leaf to wither. Wither away it shall but it will not give life to the grass. We walked up to the tree in the courtyard; it was an old majestic tree. Qiao said, "You see this tree. It is my ancestor. Many of my family were buried here."

Dukkha; nothing in this world can bring lasting deep satisfaction. We can find someone to love and be happy with but if the people you love are attached to the world, you will find suffering. We are creatures not of this world and you can never find happiness by having attachment to the world. No gold, no silver and no jewels can keep you happy forever.

Anatta; self does not exist. The words I and mine mean nothing. Nothing in this world is ours. Our possessions will be someone else’s when we die. The only thing you own is the thoughts in your head and the love in your heart. For the body will be given to the earth and the soul given to god. Thus, nothing can be yours for there is no self. I heard Buddha’s voice again. This world is not of God’s so don’t be a part of the world. Is Buddha trying to guide me?

Qiao taught me the four immeasurables; loving-kindness towards all and everything. I don't hate the enemies that I fight on the battlefield but instead, I wish them peace even at the moment of strike. Always hope that a person will be well. We must do this without any exception whether the person is evil or your enemy.

Compassion and hoping that a person's suffering will diminish. I pray for my enemies and evil ones hoping that they will find peace. I wish no suffering on no one. I think that all people have goodness in them so they will be able to change.

Empathetic joy; joy in the accomplishments of a person. It can be in oneself or in another. You should be proud of yourself or a friend when they have done something to be proud of. It's good to rejoice in the happiness and virtues of a person. By sharing a little joy with a person that has lost their hope can help them find their way.

Equanimity; we must learn to accept loss and gain. This one is not easy. The fact that we are not perfect can sometimes make us feel that we don't deserve to be happy. Also, it makes it hard to accept the lost when we weren't going to win in the first place. We must accept praise and blame, success and failure. This is not to be distinguished between friends but by all beings. We are all created equally and we must not be overpowered by delusions, mental dullness or agitation.

The last thing Qiao taught me was the noble eightfold path. Number one was the right view, the right perspective, the right outlook or the right understanding is the right way of looking at life. Seeing things the way they really are. The right view is just plain wisdom. Without wisdom, you can't have the right view of life. If you don't have wisdom, you don't have the knowledge to understand what you see.

Number two; the right intentions, the right thought, the right resolve, the right conception or the right aspirations is something we all need. This will inspire you to rid yourself of bad qualities. There are things inside us all that are wrong and immoral. Qiao said sometimes, he lets his emotions get the best of him. He said living life through emotions can cause emotional outbreak, emotional outbreaks causes you to not use your mind.

Number three; the right speech and learn to say the right things. We must learn to speak the truth at all times. In speaking the truth, we can learn to use the right words to say. Just because you're right doesn't mean you can use words that would hurt others. Learning to speak the truth with the right words can bring peace.

Number four; the right actions or the right conduct learning to do what's right. One should train oneself to be morally upright. Do not act in ways that will corrupt someone or oneself. Do not bring harm with your actions and to only use force for defense.

Number five; the right likelihood and live the right way. Feed your mind and body with good things. Live life like it's the only one you got. Even though we die and become something else, remember you only live this life once.

Number six; the right effort, the right endeavor or the right diligence is to abandon all wrong. Abandon wrong and harmful thoughts, words and deeds. You should persist in giving rise to what is good and useful in yourself and others through good words, thoughts and deeds.

Number seven; the right mindfulness, the right awareness or the right attention feed your mind good memories. You must keep your mind alert at all times to encourage a phenomenal effect on the mind. Do not speak or act due to forgetfulness or misunderstanding. The body is your temple but the mind is what makes the temple breathe.

Number eight; the last of the noble eightfold path the right concentration. Without this, the other noble sevenfold path will be hard to achieve. You must find yourself within yourself the truth that lies inside. No matter what you do, you can't lie to yourself but you can only trick your mind. We must remove the layers that we use to trick ourselves and find the real us. I went to sleep that day with a peaceful mind hearing the words of Qiao who brought more understanding and meaning.

I remembered my dream till this day; I was outside the garden just as I always am. I saw a light walking towards me. As it got closer, I finally made out a figure. It was Buddha with the big smile of his. He said hello Cain, the one who can never die. I had this shocked look on my face. He said yes, I know who you are.

I will be here to guide you on your path for a person that cannot die, who can shape the destiny of life as we know it. You have nothing but time on your hands. Remember the noble eightfold path and you will do fine. He vanished after that. I had a nice feeling in my heart knowing this man is by my side.

Years went by and I have finally found peace but just like everything else, nothing seems to last. When the world is full of men, we will never find peace. The Shaolin temple was peaceful but the world around us was caving in. One day, while on a trip to a city to the east, we encountered an army of men who looked familiar to me but they were not Egyptian.

The army was burning down the city some and Qiao stepped in to help the people. Qiao said that this is not a time to be the dragon. We must be tigers or these people will all die. We rushed in on the attack. The first soldiers got their arms broken while the next ones got their legs broken. We kicked them on the side of the knee to snap their legs.

The other soldiers saw us going through their men like water. They started to attack us. Make no mistakes that two men cannot take on an entire army. However, you can definitely take on an entire army when they have swords and already thought they won. The soldiers fought with emotions while we fought with our minds. Qiao and I took down around twenty soldiers while the rest managed to run away.

We helped put out the fires in the city. Many women and children lay dead on the streets. We let our guard down but there was still one soldier left. He charged Qiao from the inside of a building. Qiao flinched back and swung, hitting the soldier in the neck. The soldier died instantly. I could see the sadness in Qiao’s eyes. I told him that it was not his fault and he said he knows but it still hurts.

Qiao stood over top of the soldier and said a prayer. I bowed my head in respect for the loss of life. Some of the people ran up to us to thank us. We bowed and said you're welcome and then we asked the people what's going on. They told us that it was the Persian Empire. In my head, I remembered hearing stories about how they had one of the largest armies and that we need to watch them.

I was thinking why they are this far away with their soldiers. The people of the city said the Persian Empire rules eastern China. I couldn't believe what I have just heard. This can't be. Qiao and I continued to move east to find out the truth. The people of the city gave us horses so it made the traveling faster. Just like the people said, the Persian Empire was in every city.

We stopped many people on our way through to try to find more answers. Most of them didn't know more than the rest but we found some who knew the whole story. They told us the Persian Empire first took Egypt and later on conquered all the lands to the west. I couldn't believe my ears. Egypt has been taken over?

I didn't want to believe it but the evidence was clear. My home has been taken over. I must do something. I looked at Qiao and said that I must go. My homeland has been taken over and I must go to help. Qiao said to go and that he'll remain there to help his people. I closed my eyes and said goodbye in my mind. I could picture Buddha in the corner smiling. I set sailed from Nepal. I packed my horse and made off. Before I go to Egypt, I must go somewhere else first. I sailed all the way south to the village of the sea.

I pulled up to the shore. Those beautiful memories started to flood. "My Eve, my beautiful Eve oh how I have missed you so." The village now had people living there. As I made my way to the village, I was met by the villagers with spears in their hand. They asked me what I was doing here and I told them that I'm here to see an old friend. The villagers said they have never seen me before and who my friend is. I couldn't very well tell him the truth now because they wouldn't believe me anyway.

Since I was taught to speak the truth, I told them I tell no lies. They made me get on my knees and they called for the village elder. The elder walked up to me and circled around me, looking all over me. He asked me what I was doing here and I told him that I came to visit an old friend. He asked me who this friend is and I told him that she longer dwells in this world. He grabbed my face and made me look him straight in the eye. With tears falling, I said please, let me she her. I meant no harm.

He turned and waved his hand to signal to the villagers to remove the spears from my face. The elder said that he sees no lies in my face and I am welcomed in their village. I bowed my head and thanked him. With the horse by my side, I walked straight to the back of the village with the elder followed me closely. I saw the rose bush. It is still growing strong so I walked over to it. The elder told me to stop because that ground is sacred to the people.

I looked at him and said that it is sacred to me too. I told him this is where my friend rest. The elder had a shocked look on his face and he asked me how I knew someone was there. With no lies in my face, I told him that it was because I placed her here and planted the roses. With a shocked look on his face, he asked me how can that be. I told him it's a long story that I do not wish to speak on.

The village elder fell to his knees. I have heard stories about the undying man who planted these roses and buried his wife and that he shall return at any given time to visit her. I didn't believe it was true. I thought it was just a myth. I turned to the rose bush and started to feel the roses. I was telling myself how it was still strong and beautiful as ever. I placed my nose in the bush. They still had that sweet smell. I fell to my knees and hugged the ground in which she lay.

I burst out crying out loud. I couldn't hold back my tears that I have held inside from the moment she died. I just kept saying I miss her so much over and over again. The pain of my never ending cursed life was too much to bear. I lay on the ground for hours just crying and crying. I didn't want to leave this spot. I finally got the courage to move. The village elder gave me a hug and asked me to go with him.

I followed him to the tent area where I saw a tent made up of lion mane. Man, did that bring back memories. I had a big smile on my face. The elder told me its mine. He didn't believe that legend was true but they made a tent just in case I returned. I thanked him for that but I'm only staying for the night because I have to go free Egypt.

Those words must have touched something because the old man ran off telling me to wait right there. The villagers came running with supplies I will need for my journey. They gave me a sword, some water and some food. They packed it all into the side of my horse. They told me the Persian Empire is an evil empire and they are aiming to conquer all of the lands.

They told me to sleep. I will need my rest for the fight that is to come. The tent was in the same spot as the old. Still rubbing the side she slept on till I fell asleep. I woke up the next day, walked to my love and told her goodbye. The villagers were waiting for me around gate. They cheered and wished me luck. Off I rode into the rising sun. It was a magical moment. With my heart, body and mind at peace, I was happy.

This trip didn't take too long. It took about two months as I had a fast horse. I called him shadow because he was black as the night. His black hair blew in the wind. He was the strongest horse I ever seen. We finally made in to Egypt. The place still looked the same but the environment was different. The Persian flags and soldiers roamed the great city.

Chapter 9: The Death of Ra

The Egyptian people were their servants I guess. They now know how the Hebrew people felt. I had a different feeling when I was walking through the city. I was watched like a hawk with every step. The soldiers told me I wasn't allowed to carry a sword. I didn't want to give them my sword but it was foolish for me to fight now. So I gave them my sword first I must find out what's going on.

I started talking to the people to ask them what has happened. They told me the Persian Empire marched into Egypt with hundred thousand men and we didn't have a chance. They killed the pharaoh and the queen and took over the throne. Cambyses of Persia was now the new pharaoh. They told me all the Egyptian people are now servants to the Persian Empire. They told me about a force that was fighting to take back the kingdom.

I asked the people where this force lay and I was told of someone on the outline of the pyramids. I walked back to my horse to find some Persian soldiers admiring my horse. They asked me where I got that from and I told them it was from a friend. They asked me where I got the strange clothes from and I told them the same thing too. I told them I want no trouble and they said I will have no trouble if I give them the horse.

I wasn't about to give them shadow so I offered them jewels that the villagers give me. They took the jewels and said that they still want the horse. I had no choice but to fight. I closed my eyes and said just let me go. They said no and what am I going to do about it. I kicked them both on the side of the knee and broke their legs. They screamed in pain the other soldiers heard them. I hoped on shadow and kicked two more soldiers as I rode off.

I made my way to the outer lines of the pyramids. I saw nothing so I decided to journey onward. I came across a place filled with tents guarded by five men. They said halt who goes there and I said a friend of the people. They asked what does this friend of the people want. I said to free Egypt and their eyes got narrow and asked me how they would know whether I am a spy or not. I showed them the eye of the sun and they dropped down to their knees and said sorry my lord.

They told me to follow them and I told them to look out for my horse as he is an old dear friend. I patted shadow on the neck and made my way to the tent. There was a young man sitting in a chair with the pharaoh's crown on his head. He introduced himself. He said his name was Ramses the fourth. In my head, I was thinking if this Ramses is the second great grandson. He asked me where I got the eye of the sun. I told him it was from an old friend. He said how it could be given by an old friend when that was given to Ra-Noor, the time before any of us were born.

I told him I knew for I was there. He didn't believe the words that I have spoken. He thought I was Ra-Noor's son. He said so you're the son of the great Ra-Noor. I know I was taught not to lie but he would have not believed me anyway so I told him yes and that I'm the son of Ra-Noor. He said great, just like old times. The son of the pharaoh and the son of mighty Ra-Noor united together once again. He said just like old times, I will be his advisor. I started to think if I could ever escape that job position.

He told me that this is the force that will take back Egypt. We fought with the Persian Empire for years, losing men steadily. We could not take back Egypt because the people were too afraid of the Persians. During this time, I knew it would take years and years to free Egypt if it was even possible. I got the idea of storming into my old palace to get my mask back. I knew I would need the mask to hide my never aging face.

So I waited for the night when the moonshines the least. I rode on the outline of the city so I wouldn't be seen. I trained shadow hard during the war to reclaim Egypt. He was a horse of war. I even made him some light armor to protect my friend. I taught him how to survive with little water or should I say, he taught himself. I taught him how to lay on the ground silent to wait for me.

I was dressed in an assassin's attire, all black with my face covered with nothing but my eyes showing. With rope in hand and sword by my side, I climbed the back of the gate. I moved fast and quiet and made my way to the Persian priest's chamber. Just my luck, the door wasn't locked. I opened the door slowly so I wouldn't wake him. I saw my mask on the dresser. I knew he would have not tossed it since it was solid gold.

The one thing you could count on was human greed and a priest's greed is ten times more. I grabbed my mask and made my way back to my rope. This was too easy but I didn't complain. I got the job done. I hoped back on shadow and rode off into the night. I bet he will be pissed tomorrow when he knows the mask is gone.

Even though that Cambyses II ruled Egypt, he almost never showed his face in Egypt. He ruled from a far and it was just the motivation we needed. Without a real ruler, the soldiers there will be weak without anyone to follow. Let's say that the plan didn't turn out too great. Every time we thought we gained ground, our feet would slip. For every Persian soldier we kill, Cambyses II sent two in their place.

It was like killing bugs but just meaningless because they just kept coming. Cambyses II even treated them like bugs. He didn't care about the soldiers. All he ever wanted was Egypt's riches. Cambyses II loved the fact that he conquered the oldest kingdom made. It was clear as day in a man, I never seen but I knew his face so well. It was on everything the flags, the coins, and wall postings.

I never disliked a face more than his. It was hard to practice my Buddhist teachings in this war. I became the tiger the dragon became hidden. The dragon always showed at the wrong times. Whenever I had a soldier cornered, I will always set him free. There was this one time where I let a soldier free, he dropped his weapon and I let my guard down. The next thing I knew, he pulled a small blade from his boot and gave me a nice wound to remember him.

I killed him there on the spot as I couldn't let this snake live. Any man who fights like this doesn't deserve to live. Plus, in letting him live, he would use these tactics to kill many kind hearted men. There was another soldiers who I have let live, I found him later on raping an Egyptian woman. I released the blood from his neck. The dragon had to hide. I'm not fighting men but I'm fighting rats.

I meditated every day in order to keep my inner peace. Even though I hid the dragon, I still needed him. I know what war can do to a man that makes him cold. The more you kill, the more you smell like blood. I hated the smell of blood. It is a thick and has a strong odor. The smell of blood and death cannot be mistaken for anything else.

Without the meditation, I would have turned into an animal. Killing changes a man it can turn you cold blooded and release the demons in your mind. Once the demons are released in your mind, you would have become lost to world. You will start killing for fun or to hear them scream. War changes a man and killing someone is always hard to deal with no matter if it's for a good reason.

It is always hard living with the fact that you killed someone where only the strong survive. I prayed for every life I took. I tried to do at the moment of death but it is a hard process when the fight never ends. The Egyptian rebels would ask me why I pray for the enemy. I said it does not matter if he is an enemy or not because he is still a living creature. The Egyptians did this to the Hebrew people not too long ago and we must learn for our mistakes.

There are two sides to war where the both of them think they are right. If you were born in Persia, you would be here doing the same thing. Some understood what I was saying while the others didn't care. They just wanted to kill the Persians. Kill Persians we did but we would have accomplished nothing. In order to make the men feel like they had accomplished something, they would collect fingers and pieces of their attire.

They used these as a way to show their manhood or who was mightier than the other. I took no parts in these games. I knew what I was fighting for but seeing these actions made me question things. If we do free Egypt, they will just come an attack again but seeing the people suffering would always give me a clear view.

We didn't manage to take the kingdom from Cambyses II. Another ruler rose up and I didn't know what happened to Cambyses II but it was clear as day we had a new ruler. Darius face replaced Cambyses II face on everything. I didn't know if Cambyses II died, was this is son or did he just loss power but he was no longer there. Darius was smarter than Cambyses II by a huge margin. He conquered the whole of Middle East and half of Asia.

The Persian Empire was at a high point. No man could win against them. Knowing this is still never stopped us from trying what man wants. We fought the soldiers with no hope of winning but the thought of dying free always lit the fires of war. The stories of the Athens and the Spartans gave us hope. Hearing how Greece constantly fought off the Persian Empire and never gave up their kingdom was a soul lifter.

We would sit around the fire drinking, telling stories of the Athens and the Spartans victories. The Spartans were the greatest heroes of them all. The stories of how they trained and the way they only kept the strong ones from birth were fascinating. I study up on their history. There must be a secret way to defeating the Persians in there.

Anoxandridas II the king of Sparta was said to be a descendant of Heracles or who we now know as Hercules. Heracles was the mortal son of a God named Zeus. It was said that Anoxandridas II possessed the strength of a god and that no one could match his strength. Well, none of this helped me at all if that is his secret, it will not do me no good.

We continued to fight with no win in sight. We got word that Anoxandridas II died and his son Leonidas was the new king. Darius was no longer the king of Persia but his son, Xerxes was. I heard as soon a Leonidas became king, Xerxes sent an army to take over Sparta. Let's say it didn't happen. The Persians forced Egyptian men to fight alongside of their army.

They send the Egyptians in first to measure the strength of the army. Since they were slaves, no one cared that they died. I would talk to the Egyptians that survived against the

Spartans. All the stories were the same. They said king Leonidas was a god. He was seven feet tall with muscles even on his cheeks. They said the Spartans always won with only a hundred men.

A hundred Spartans equals to a hundred thousand men. They fought on the battlefield with one soul and they move in groups with swords and shields. They would make circles with the huge shields with no way for you to break the defense. In my mind, there was no time left for talking. I told the men that I would ride to Sparta to learn the secret to winning.

I rode off with shadow. Me and my shadow is what I called us. I took a ship from the Mediterranean Sea. Just like in today's age, money ruled all. The rebel forces of Egypt were very rich. We took jewels and coins from the battles we fought. Plus, I would sneak back into my former palace here and there to raid my hidden safe.

I made in to the shores of Greece. The air here felt different. The salty smell and the plant life were of a familiar sight. I remember when Egypt looked like this. I found some men who I paid to tell me which way Sparta was. They told me I should be careful for the roads are full of Persian soldiers and seeing an Egyptian on Spartan lands would bring me danger.

So I brought some robes and a vile to hide my face. I saw many Persian soldiers just like they said but I never got too close. I wanted to make it to Sparta in one piece. Shadow loved the change of the land as I could see it in the way he galloped. The dirt under his feet was a joy to him. No more grainy sand and the plant life made him stop to take some bites. I didn't rush him because I knew we would be back in the harsh desert.

During the ride through Greece, the roads were full of pillars and stone monuments. The stone monuments had vines growing all over them. This land was beautiful. I kind of didn't want to go back to the lifeless desert. I finally made my way to Sparta. Approaching this great city made my heart stop. The entrance to the city had two large pillars about the size of five men standing on top of each other.

On the top of the pillars was a roof-like structure that sloped.

There were some words on top that I didn't understand. As I made my way to the pillars, there were four guards standing watch. These men had pale color skin with a sunlight tan. They stood no less than six feet tall with muscles everywhere. They wore the same style of outfits as the Egyptians but with a red cape on their backs. They told me to stop right there so I stopped and said I meant you no harm.

They asked me what I was doing in the mighty Sparta and they told me that I better have a good reason or I will die. I told them I came to seek the aid of king Leonidas. They asked me just what type of aid do I want from the king. I told them I needed help to free my people. They told me that we in Sparta have our own problems to deal with.

I told them I understand but the Persian Empire must be destroyed. They put down their weapons and told me to drop my vile. I took of my vile and the soldiers said I see you're Egyptian and I nodded my head. They said they killed many Egyptians in battle and we know they were forced to fight. They said I'm sorry that your people had to suffer the terror of the Persian Empire.

As I walked through the city, the people stared me down and never taking their eyes off me. The women even had muscles. I could see that these were no ordinary women. The children even had on the army attire they were larger than any children I have ever seen. They had the muscles of grown men in Egypt. I must not do anything to cause a problem. I might be immortal but if I could die, I bet these people could be the ones to do it.

The city had the color red all over it. The flag, the robe, the women's attire, were all red. The roofs of the buildings were all red as well. It was like they were sending a warning to people. I made it to the palace. Their palace was full of pillars circling all around the building. The palace was tall, like it was built by a god. They took me to the throne room and told me to wait here. I was nervous like a child because I'm going to meet the legendary king, king Leonidas of Sparta.

I was walking in circles, trying to figure out what to say. I began to talk to myself while waiting to meet the ten foot tall man. I noticed a women walking in and I bowed my head to greet her. She said with a strong voice, so you're the Egyptian that is looking for Leonidas? I said yes and she started to circle around me, looking at me up and down. I didn't know what to do or say.

This was one of the strongest women I have seen in thousands of years of my life. For years, the world started to keep women down. Once the men of the world understood that they were stronger than women, they made sure they kept them down. They couldn't speak their mind unless they are the queen, they had to do everything the man said to do or they would be punished but not this woman. She had life, strength and fire and you could feel it.

She said you're not weak like the rest of the Egyptians. In my head, I was like, hey, that hurts but I didn't want to start anything. Plus, she knew the Egyptians had become very weak. Our vanity caused us to not work hard. We always had slaves to do work for us so we never lifted a finger. We felt we were too good to do manual labor. That is the reason the Persian Empire took Egypt so easily.

She gripped my arms and told me, I see you have muscles. She punched me in the stomach, yes, you're strong. I wanted to toss her across the room after that because she didn't hit like a girl. A large man walked in the room laughing. He said, forgive my wife. She is what you call noisy. She turned to the man and told him, I'm not noisy I just need to see what's going on and walked up to him and kissed him.

The large man said, forgive me for I haven't introduce myself. My name is Leonidas and this is my queen, Gorgo. How may I help you? Leonidas was a tall man at about six foot six with muscles everywhere. He had woolly hair and a thick beard. His voice was as strong as a lion. I bowed my head and said thank you for seeing me my lord. He said what brings an Egyptian this far into my home. I told him about the Persian

Empire and he said, yes, they wish to conquer everyone. I told him I came here to learn about the Spartan's secrets so Egypt can defeat the Persian Empire.

Leonidas laughed and said, I have no secrets but I can show you how we train. I told him I will like that very much. He told me to take the room upstairs to right. He told me to get some rest because I will need it as they start early. I thanked him and made my way to the room. The room was just like any other room. I was actually hoping for something more.

The morning came and I got a knock on the door. I was told to get dressed in my attire. He was waiting for me outside the door. I opened the door there, wearing the attire of a Spartan. I placed on the attire. The feel of wearing the Spartan's attire sent chills throughout my body. The red rope draped over my back felt like the warmth of the sun. Placing the helm over my head gave me a sense of power.

I walked down the stairs and I was met by king Leonidas. He smiled and said you look good in the Spartan uniform but just not as good as me. Come, let's get the day started. We made our way outside and we were greeted by fifty Spartan soldiers. Leonidas placed his sword in the air and said Spartans. They placed their swords in the air and said hoo-rah. Leonidas gave me a sword together with a shield and told me to try and keep up.

He had no idea who he was talking too. We ran with the heavy shields and swords for hours. I always stayed at the front of the pack right behind king Leonidas. He turned and said you're strong for an Egyptian. There was no jealousy towards me from the other soldiers. They even cheered me on. After the run, I thought the training was over. Man, was I wrong.

For another hour, we stood perfectly still with shield up in perfect defense with sword in the air. If we fail to do it, we have to do one hundred pushups and then get back up and try again. I passed that test with ease. The next workout was a little harder. There was a course with flying logs the size of grown trees. You had to make it through the course with just a shield and your brain. No matter how many times you fail, you have to try again.

This course had platforms in which you had to move without falling off. The logs didn't all come the same way. Some came high, some came low. It was hard to time them since you have to move fast. The first time I tried the log hit me right in the side and knocked me off. The impact of the log forced my wing to leave my lungs. The second time I tried, I got almost half way but I took my eyes off the log and it took my legs from beneath me.

King Leonidas laughed; I see the Egyptian is having a hard time with this one. I said with my half grimed face, yes, the Egyptian is. King Leonidas said; let me show you how it's done. He hopped on the platform with no shield. The soldiers said, my lord, get a shield. Leonidas said I do not need a shield to do this. The first log came passed Leonidas high up. He turned his body sideways with his feet in perfect formation. He jumped to the next platform while another log came high this time and he ducked it.

He jumped to the next one. This time, the log came low and he stopped at the edge and let it pass him. He jumped to the next the log that came high and he beat it to the spot and moved to the next platform. The next log came low; he grabbed the rope and jumped on the log. He waited for the perfect time to jump off to the next platform. He did something different in every platform until he came to the last one. This time, he pulled out his sword and cut the rope and the log just flew away.

He turned and looked straight at me and said now Egyptian, show me what you got. I tried to do what he did and only made it to the three platforms. Leonidas came and picked me up. He asked me if I am the king of Sparta. With a puzzled look on my face, I said no. Leonidas then asked why I tried to do it the way he did. You must find your own strength and way to win.

With these little words, I was born again. I had a new life. I grabbed a sword, hopped on to the platform and made my way. I ducked the first log and I beat the second one to the point. For the third log, I cut the rope and the fourth log; I stuck my sword in it to slow it down. As for the fifth log, I dropped my sword and channeled my soul. I struck it with both fists and by using the Almighty push, the log broke into pieces. I heard the soldiers cheer and Leonidas say go Egyptian.

For the sixth log, I jumped over it and the last log wasn't there because king Leonidas cut it down. I made it to the end. Leonidas cheered bravo, Egyptian bravo. You're strong as they come. He asked me how I did that thing with my fists. I told him it takes years of peace to achieve. He smiled and said I don't have years but I want peace. The day became dark and he told the soldiers to retire as we have had a long day.

Leonidas told me to come with him so we could talk. We took a walk through the tall fields of grain. He asked me for the first time, what is your name Egyptian? I told him Cain. He asked me what Egypt was like under the rule of the Persians. I told him that it was slavery, rape, murder and anything else that you can name. The Persians are sucking our lands dry of everything that is useful.

Leonidas said I feel better now about the choices I have made. At one point in time, I was going to let the Persians move in thinking it would help my people live. But I didn't want my people to be slaves to no one. I'd rather us die free as Spartans. So tell me Egyptian, what do you fight for? I told him I fight for the same thing as him. I also want freedom for my people.

He said I know you're not a king but you have all the qualities of a king. You're one strong bastard. Maybe you can free your people. I told him I hope so because being a slave is worse than death. He told me I am welcome to stay here for as long I like and I thanked him for that.

I spent a year in Sparta learning the tactics of this legendary army. I understood that no matter what I learn, it could not be taught to the Egyptians. These Spartans were born for war, bred to be soldiers. No one had a chance against them. During the time I spent in Sparta, the Persian Empire sent in two armies to try to conquer Sparta. In the first battle, king Leonidas told me to go inside and wait for his return.

I didn't go inside. Instead, I stayed in the city streets to make sure the people were ok. Some of the Persian soldiers managed to sneak through the Spartan's defense. The Persian soldiers must have thought it would be easy to take the city. They charged in like they already won but they had no idea what had waited for them. The women and the children armed themselves and fought the soldiers like it was man to man. I helped fight the soldiers myself. It was an easy victory as no one in Sparta died.

I saw Leonidas and the armies come charging in but by the time they got there, the Persian soldiers had already died. Leonidas saw me in the Spartans uniform with sword and shield with my hands covered in blood bowed his head to me. The other Spartans also bowed their heads. Everyone checked to make sure all was ok. I headed to my room to rest. I heard a knock on my door a while later and it appears to be king Leonidas.

Leonidas asked if he could come in. I smiled and said this is your house. He said it maybe my house but after today, it will always be your home. Thank you for what you have done today. I will never forget it. I told him you're welcome. You have shown me nothing but kindness. It is the least I can do. He walked out of the room with his back straight, head up high and shoulders squared. I slept well that night from the battle and the words the king shared with me.

I woke up the next day and made my way outside the palace. King Leonidas and Spartan soldiers were there to greet me. Leonidas said Spartans and the soldiers said hoo-rah. Leonidas looked at me and said Egyptian the Spartans will like to salute you for helping to defend our people. They raised their swords in the air and said hoo-rah five times in a row.

Leonidas grabbed a sword and a shield and walked up to me and said, you're the first non-born citizen to become a Spartan. This is your sword and shield. The shield has some Greek writing on the inside. I asked him what it means. He told me it meant the Egyptian who became a Spartan. I smiled and he said that's not all. Then one of the soldiers walked up to me with a helmet.

This helmet was the same as any other helmet but this one had hair. The hair was the color of gold. Leonidas said the color of the hair gives rank in Sparta. The black is for the king the white is for the general's, the red is for the lieutenants and this gold is now for you, you're the one and only gold Knight so wear it with pride. I bowed and said thank you, I'm honored to be a part of the Spartans and I will wear it with pride.

During the year I spent in Sparta, Leonidas and I became close friends. Besides the fact that I wanted to learn more of their secrets, Leonidas wanted to learn more about me and the Egyptians. I made love to many beautiful women of Sparta and I was back to my old lustful ways of Ra-Noor. Leonidas would often ask me how I find the Spartan woman. I would smile and say all fire.

Xerxes sent another army to try and conquer Sparta. This time I was allowed to fight and fight I did. I got to see the fine Spartan machine work with my own eyes, swords and shields. The perfect defense was grand and I being a part of it was even better. The large shield held over the stomach so that no part of the body showed but legs and head.

We marched forward side by side, never breaking the line and form circles as the enemy got closer. I understood at that moment what made the Spartans so strong. They made sure they had no weak links. We devoured the Persian forces like an ocean. Waves and waves of Spartans soldiers in perfect defense could never be beaten. I finally found what I was looking for. It was time to make my way back home.

I told Leonidas goodbye, shook his hand as a friend I gave Gorgo a hug and a kiss. The strength of that woman always gave me chills. Me and my shadow rode off into the Greek air. I think shadow knew we were going back home because he didn't run as fast as before. I never took of the Spartan uniform and I wore it the whole way home. I caught a ship at the same spot going back to Egypt.

I was eager to return home to tell the men what I had learned and what I have seen. Stepping back on my homeland made me remember the struggles my people were going through. Shadow started to kick his feet up from the feeling of the sand. He circled a few times before he ran off. I pat him on his neck to let him know that it was alright.

He let out a grunt and I laughed and told him, come on and he finally took off. I wore the shield over my back like a true Spartan. An Egyptian, a Shaolin Monk and now a Spartan even though I'm cursed, life wasn't all that bad. As I made my approach to the rebel camp, I thought it would be cool to ride up slow. So I made shadow ride slowly. He enjoyed the nice walk in the desert air and so did I.

As I approached the camp, I heard someone yell out Spartan. That brought a smile to my face. I got the reaction that I wanted to get. They told me to halt in my head and I was like why does everyone use that word when people approached. They asked me what is Spartan doing this far out. I smiled and took off my mask. I saw a familiar face and he asked, Ra-Noor, is that you? I smiled and said yes, I have returned.

He told the guards to run and send the word that the lord Ra-Noor has returned. The people all gathered by the camp fire. It was silent. They all started to touch my shield. They have never seen a shield of such size and they were shocked that it could be held. They all wanted to hear my stories. I told them of the battles I have fought and the women I made love to. The men cheered at the thought of women which such strength and fire.

I told the men the secret to the Spartan's victory and everyone became silent, so silent that the desert winds stopped to hear. I looked around at all the men side by side with each other. They all had a puzzled look in their faces. We have to trust and watch each other's back at all times. I knew I couldn't teach them the ways of the Spartans but I knew I could teach them the ways of trusting each other.

I had the man make larger shields for us. Not the size of a Spartan's shield but larger than the ones we had. Over the next couple of months, I taught the men how to hide behind the shield so they would take little damage. I taught them how to make a shield line so it would make the Persian soldiers easy to kill. It was time for us to take back our home. Dressed in the Spartan's attire, it was time to set out.

With the Egyptian rebel forces led by Amyrtaeus, we charged into battle. The Egyptian rebel forces stormed the gates using the shield line. We marched forward taking out any Persian in our way. The Egyptian people even gave a hand to aid us in the war. I guess they were tired of being slaves. Mothers, daughters, sons and fathers fought with swords, rocks and sticks. There was no way we could lose this battle.

We stormed the palace with the Egyptian people behind us. It was a magical sight. We killed every Persian in the palace and we ripped down every piece of Persian literature they had. We finally took back Egypt and we partied for days burning flags and killing all the Persian messengers that came. Amyrtaeus was crowned the new pharaoh and the people were free again. We knew it was just a matter of time before the Persian Empire came back to take Egypt. They sent a force with five thousand men but we managed to handle them so easily.

I got word that my friend king Leonidas was killed by Xerxes through a traitor in Sparta. I placed on my Spartan attire banged my sword to my shield and said hoo-rah, hoo-rah for my fallen friend. The tales of him and his 299 men defeating Xerxes armies one after and other became legend. The 300 men became hope to those who wanted to fight the Persian Empire. The tales of how they killed the army of the immortals made your fear leave when the story was told.

We knew that would not be the last of them. For over sixty years, the Persian Empire sent soldiers in to try and take Egypt. For sixty years, we fought them off with thousands of victories. Year sixty one was followed by the most massive army to step foot on Egypt. The Persian Empire sent all one million of their soldiers to retake Egypt. We didn't stand a chance against such a force this large.

They took Egypt like the locusts that once plagued our land. Once again, we were slaves to the Persians but this time no rebel force would even put a dent in the Persian Empire. We lost Egypt for good this time. In order to make sure that the Egyptians would not fight back, the Persians treated us better this time. They gave some of us power, land and gold. They understood that in order to keep Egypt, they had to divide the people.

Nothing divides people more than money and power. Giving some Egyptians power over Persian and Egyptians alike made them not care that the people were not free. We got word that the Greek Empire was growing stronger than the Persian Empire that it was led by Alexander the Great. The Greek Empire marched on Persian owned lands and conquered every single one of them. Mazaces was the new pharaoh of Egypt and he handed over Egypt to Alexander the great with no fight.

Chapter 10: The Mask of Ages

We were told that the Greek Empire made deals with the Persian leaders that if they give up their lands, they would leave them in power over the people. Most of the Persian leaders took the deal and the ones who didn't suffered death. I was granted my palace back when the Persian Empire took Egypt for good. It seemed to happen overnight where Egypt became a Greek nation. Just like all the other rulers before, their face was everywhere.

Alexander the great did something different from most of the leaders who took over Egypt. He made his presence known, he often stayed here coming or going from battles. He led the armies not like most kings who just stayed back. Alexander was always accompanied by Aristotle, one of the smartest men I have ever met. He seemed to understand everything and if he didn't, he would find the answer.

The combination of Alexander's strength and Aristotle's mind was too much for anyone to win against. Alexander and Aristotle heard word that I once lived amongst the Spartans and the Shaolin Monks. They made me their advisor of Egypt (again with this advisor stuff) I took trips with them back and forth from Greece. Aristotle wanted me around to pick my brain. Alexander wanted me around because I was strong.

Aristotle asked me many questions like how it is so that I led the battle over sixty years ago and still look like your thirties. I told him that he wouldn't believe me if I told him so I told him that one day I might tell him about it. Aristotle wrote many pages about everything such as why do the stars shine, why does the moon give light. He wanted to know why and the reason God made it that way did not stop him.

Just in case if you have ever wondered, I often visited the graves of Eve, Qiao, Leonidas, Menes, Anta and Moses. Those five people in my life touched me more than anyone did till this date. In case you are wondering why I said five and not six, I couldn't find Buddha's grave. It was like he just disappeared. On our way to Greece is when I would visit Leonidas' grave. Alexander would always go with me, asking me about how the legendary king truly was. I told him exactly that he was legendary, kind and strong as a god. I told him that no man shall ever be as strong in heart and mind as this man.

That didn't stop Alexander. He wanted to be better than Leonidas. He wanted to be remembered long after he was dead and gone. That was his sole reason he led every army on the battlefield. He wanted to be Alexander the great. I asked them both the same question on why did a country that longed to be free and be a slave to no man turn out to enslave so many?

Alexander said the reason Greece enslaved so many lands was because they had no choice. It was either Greece or someone else but someone would do it so Greece chose this path. We felt we're the lesser of the evils. Aristotle said the reason Greece enslaved so many lands was simple. The most powerful army will always have claim to the lands. Power always corrupts and absolute power corrupts absolutely.

Aristotle answers are never simple. He said only the strong survive and the weak are preys. You're an Egyptian so you should understand. Did you not enslave the Hebrew people? When people forget the history, it will always repeat itself. The day you let history fade is the day your history will soon be your present and your future.

I asked Aristotle if he believed in the gods and he would say I wonder. I know I was taught to believe in the gods since I was a child but I often wonder if I really believed in them. Everything that was once thought of as God made in that way now has a non-God answer. I have no knowledge of how the earth became to be or how us humans was given this world.

I still feel no matter how many answers we find, we are not alone. I still believe and feel that my soul can't see it. Just like the air but I know it's there. This man had a mind greater than most of the people could still manage to remain humble. I finally understood why Alexander looked up to Aristotle even though he was king. Alexander or Aristotle never owned a slave and neither had time nor wanted one.

One was trying to be the greatest man to walk the earth while the other searches for answers to everything. Alexander returned from one of his many battles alone when he came to my palace. I thought that something was wrong. This was the first time I saw him with a sword and shield in hand. I asked him what's wrong. He smiled and said nothing. He said Cain, I didn't come here as Alexander the great but I came here as Alexander.

I need a break from being great all the time. He told me not to tell anyone that he was here yet. I told him alright. You’re welcome to stay and he said thank you. He reached out to hand me his shield although he hesitated at first. I saw the look as if he could trust me. I was puzzled by his look until I gave the shield a look. It was solid gold with the face of Zeus together with his hair blowing in the wind.

I placed a finger on it and I felt a sense of vibration running through my body. I thought my mind was playing tricks on me until I touched it again. I felt swords beating up against it and I felt the impact of the shield hitting against armor. I looked at Alexander and asked him what this is. This can't be real? Alexander said this is Aegis, the shield of Zeus.

I couldn't believe my ears. The shield of Zeus, as in the legendary God, Zeus? Alexander said yes, it crashed on mount Olympus over a thousand years ago. It has been in my family ever since it is one of the reasons no army could take Greece. I told him to keep the shield with him and showed him to his room. I told him that he could stay here for as long as he liked.

I told him Aristotle likes to stay here too but he comes to read my books and talk me another ear. Alexander smiled and said yes, Aristotle does love to talk. All I could think about that shield was that I felt its power and that thing was alive. Alexander stayed in my house without telling anyone for two days. I guess the great king needed a rest after all. I told Alexander no person can be one thing all the time and that is why there is a day and a night.

Every time I say things like that, he would smile and he will say I now see why Aristotle spends so much time with a person like you. You run your mouth just like him. We would both laugh every time. One day, Aristotle came by to read in my library. I told him that you live here and that you know the way. Aristotle would always say Cain, you are a mind reader. I would always come back with a head as big as yours as it's easy to read your mind.

Aristotle was smart in brains and in mouth too. I sat there in my courtyard under my favorite locus flower tree. Aristotle made his way towards me with a book. He handed me the book with his finger on a page. He told me to look at the picture and tell me what you see. I looked at the picture and all I saw was an ancient Egyptian drawing until I looked to the right. I saw myself beside Pharaoh Menes and the funny thing is that I don't ever remembering seeing this drawing in Egypt.

Aristotle asked me who that man was beside Pharaoh Menes. I got quiet and I didn't know what to say. I told him that it says right here in the book Ra-Noor. Aristotle told me not to be cute with him and that he could have read that himself. That man in the painting looks just like you. He even has the eye of the sun around his neck. I told him that is one of my forefathers. I could tell by the look in his eye but he didn't believe me.

Then Aristotle did something that shocked me. He grabbed my robe and pulled it up. He asked me what is that mark there on my stomach. I told him that it was a wound from a battle. He started to turn pages in the book until he found what he was looking for. There was a picture of Ra-Noor being stabbed with a half circle blade that left a moon shaped scare on his stomach. The next picture showed Ra-Noor dead from the wound only to rise up again with the raising of the sun.

I gave Aristotle a look of I was lost to try and throw him off but it didn't work. He said, so you are telling me that you have a fresh wound from a sword that has not been used in thousands of years. I got up and looked at him straight in the eyes and said, I told you but you wouldn't believe me.

Aristotle said, try me. I'm all ears now. I told him let's go to the library and talk.

I told him to take a sit and asked him if he was ready. I started from the beginning and told him who I was and who I have come to be. How many years I have lived and all the things that I have seen. The most important fact I told about was why I become immortal. Aristotle got quiet and we sat there for a long time, just looking at each other. I don't know what Aristotle was thinking about. I don't know whether he believed me or not or if he was about to freak out.

Out of the blue, he said, I have always felt that my gods were a lie. I never truly believed in them but I didn't feel alone. Remember I told you that in our talk. You said to me with a smile that we are never alone and I thought your look was strange but I thought you were being your normal smart self.

I always had an idea that you were something more than you seem to be but this is so much more. It's hard to believe this even though I saw the truth with my own eyes. The funny thing about us humans is that we still find a way to trick ourselves from the truth. Things that we can't understand or are afraid of make us lie to ourselves.

Aristotle said I'm sorry to hear about your brother. I know nothing that I can say that will make it better. You did something wrong, no doubt, but you shouldn't be punished forever for it. Aristotle said what I am saying is that I'm not a God but I'm just a normal human. He told me it that takes a man or woman to understand they have made a mistake and try to fix it. He put his hand or my shoulder and told me I see a man who stands before me.

I told Aristotle thank you for your kind words. He asked me if I had told Alexander about it yet and I said no. Aristotle said, well, let's not tell him. He already has too much on his plate. So we agreed to not tell Alexander the truth. After I told Aristotle the truth, he would always ask me about the garden. I told him no words can describe it and no words can be used to tell you how much I miss it.

He told me to write it down. The words seem to come out better when people write and not say them so I wrote this poem.

My Eden

The skies so blue
The color blue is always true
Here beauty never fades
My prison
I gladly stay for all my days
Happiness I can always find a way
The only perfection that is perfectly perfected
Am I worthy of this gift?
I gladly just sit here outside your gate
To never step in is still a beautiful fate
I just got to have faith
Sight through narrow eyes
Still gives me a surprise
I could spend a lifetime
With just the thought you one day would be mine
They say dreams do come true
So I'll dream till you come true
Outside the gate is my sin
I'll wait there my Eden

Aristotle clapped and said bravo, bravo that was great. I hope that I can see this Eden one day. I told I hope you will get to see it too. Aristotle asked what's God really like and I told him he is kind and funny and he's always there when you need him. He asked me about Gabriel. You're friends with the angel of death so how could you not be afraid of him. I understand that you cannot die but still he is death. I told him that no matter what he does or is, he has always been there for me. He is more than a friend to my heart.

Aristotle said that I was a fascinating man and that I should write a book about my life. I told him I have no idea where to start. He laughed and said where to start? Start from the beginning you have the best life story of every life that have lived the earth. He told me once you start it, it will not be hard. So from that day on I have decided to write. The first book was called my life as an immortal but just like life, things always change.

One day, out of the blue, we got the word that Alexander had become very ill in Babylon. We raced off to be by his side. Aristotle went in first while I paced around in a circle. Aristotle came back out like he just seen his son dying. He said Alexander wanted to see me and so I walked in slowly. Alexander being weak as ever said, sit my friend. He asked me how he looked and I told him he looks like Alexander the great.

Alexander said its funny you and Aristotle said the same thing. He grabbed the Aegis and said that I want you to have the shield. I told him that I cannot take this shield from you. Alexander said that I must because he cannot let his brother have the shield as he will burn the world down. I told him alright; I will take it and keep it safe. I told him that he is and always will be Alexander the great.

I sent Aristotle in while I stayed out with the shield on my lap. I heard horns of war sounded from the battlefields the shield fought. The shield was the size of a Spartan shield but it was as light as a feather. Aristotle came back out crying. He said Alexander is dead. Aristotle just lost his son and he cried his eyes out. Nothing hurts more than having to dig a grave for your own child.

I did the only thing I could do for my friend was to sit next to him and put my arms around his shoulder. Aristotle wasn't Alexander's blood father but he was there for him since he was born. He raised him since fifteen after his father died and was by his side till his death. Aristotle just lost a part of himself. We had Alexander body placed in the palace in Egypt. People wondered why Alexander body was placed in Egypt and not Greece. It was simple because he loved Egypt the most and it was his favorite place in the world.

Aristotle died a year later on an island in Greece. I just lost my last friend and I was very sad. Once again, I felt the curse of my sin. Alexander's brother was now the king of all. The years went by, ruler after ruler came and went and I once again put on my Ra mask to hide my face. Nothing happened for years, just the same old thing.

Until Rome becomes the power of Greece, everything changed from then on. Cleopatra became pharaoh. She had the blood of a Spartan woman. She ruled Egypt like she was born an Egyptian. She was born in Egypt like many Greeks at the time. No matter what, she was a Greek but that never stopped her. She had Egyptian crowns made. One made of white and one of red. She wore them to show her moods so when she has the red one on; you better do what she tells you to.

The white one shows that she was in a good mood and so if you needed something that was the time to ask. Julius Caesar often showed his face in Egypt. This was a time in Egypt were the crown was at unrest. Her father, Ptolemy XII, had wheeled and dealed his way to make is daughter pharaoh. At first, his nine year old son Ptolemy XIII was the pharaoh. Even then, Cleopatra still ruled the kingdom.

A nine year old pharaoh was a joke and we all knew what was going on. Then Ptolemy XII married Cleopatra and Ptolemy XIII to each other so no one would question Cleopatra. It was a smart move by a father who wanted his daughter to rule. Julius "the snake" Caesar is what I called him, helped Cleopatra to get the crown of pharaoh. He was in love with Cleopatra but he was not alone. His best friend Marc Antony was eying her as well.

The word was Marc Antony and Cleopatra never touched until Julius Caesar died. Do not believe a word they say, it was all a lie. A great man once taught me not to believe everything I read. A man can put anything in words to deceive. There is no story better to tell than one where you were the only one there to tell the truth. The person who holds the power will always control the information.

Marc Antony was born in Egypt also but he didn't want to be an Egyptian. He wanted to be Roman; he wanted to be a great king like Alexander and Leonidas. These two tales of heroes become more than legend. It was like my two friends never died. I would see Marc Antony and Cleopatra sneak around but they have always said that it was to talk in secret. We all knew that Cleopatra gets whatever she wanted. She wanted Marc Antony and she got it.

She wanted Julius Caesar for power to make a child who would be pharaoh and Caesar of Rome. She wanted Marc Antony because he controlled the army of Greece. Cleopatra was smart. She had everything planned out, from the start perhaps. It didn't matter that Julius

Caesar had a wife. Cleopatra was the one he loved. He was there every chance he got.

I think he also did this because he knew about Marc and Cleopatra. Cleopatra got her wish. Julius Caesar gave her his seed. This is the action that sealed his fate. He was already plotted against in Rome. This was the last straw in the stack. This action place the so called republic of Rome in danger. Rome was never a republic. It was always ruled by the nobles. Do not let the people who wrote the history lie to you.

We got word that Julius Caesar fell sick and died but no one believed that. Cleopatra's heart was broken if only for a second. Rome called Cleopatra in for questioning because they suspected that Julius Caesar was assassinated. They accused Cleopatra of the plot. Now Marc Antony was Caesar and he defended her and got her off the hook. History will tell you that was the first time Marc and Cleopatra truly met. With this so called meeting, Marc Antony instantly fell in love with her.

Do not believe that as I think that Cleopatra and Marc Antony had this whole thing planned from the beginning. I bet that was really Marc Antony's child she had. Marc raised Julius Caesar child like it was his own. Marc and Cleopatra got married in secret even though Marc already had a wife. This was the most entertaining time in Egyptian history. Marc and Cleopatra had three kids, one girl and two sons.

I was still an Egyptian advisor and a priest but I didn't get involved with the affairs of this family. To be involved with this family was certain death. Certain death to me was people knowing my secret. Word was sent that Marc Antony died on his way to Egypt from a battle wound. Cleopatra could not take the lost of another love so she poisoned herself and died shortly after.

Rome moved in on Egypt fast. This was the last time Egypt would have a pharaoh. Egypt was now a state of Rome. I heard through the mouths of my spies that the Romans told Marc Antony that Cleopatra had died. Upon hearing this, Marc Antony stuck his sword in his stomach but he didn't die from the wound.

Seeing that Marc Antony didn't die, they told him Cleopatra was still alive but she was hurt. So he rushed off to her and died while on his way. The Roman Empire had Cleopatra's first son, the son of Julius Caesar killed to ensure that the nobles still ruled Rome. They came and took the other three children but no one knows what happened to them.

As time always does it, it passes the Romans got word that the god of the placed his son on earth. No one believed it but the stories of his works couldn't be overlooked. None of the Romans want to go to Israel because they were too good for that place so guess who they sent? They sent me to find the truth about what's going on or it was God who really sent me.

Since I was bored, this was a good thing for my soul. I rode off happy for the first time in years, still writing many pages in my life as an immortal. I realized through my writings that my cursed life wasn't so bad. I found a love of a lifetime and found another love time after time. I have had many great friends who changed history and life as we know it.

Chapter 11: The King of All

From the tip of Israel, I have heard many stories of the man's miracles. Found people traveling the road to meet the god of Hebrew's son. The roads were packed. I never traveled alone as there was always a person there to talk too. I even found some Egyptians on the road. I have traveled with a blind man name Isaac while he traveled to find sight.

Isaac was a kind old man. He would tell me that I don't have to slow down my trip for him. I told him that we're going to the same place to see the same man. I had no problem with taking this nice man through Israel. I never forgot my Buddhist teaching. I tried always to do the right path. The right path at this time was to bring him along with me.

We finally made it to Bethlehem, the place where they said he called home. Isaac parted ways with me as he didn't want to be a burden to me any longer. Isaac said you have the voice of a young man but you have the soul of an old man. I can't see your face but I know who you are and may we meet again.

I gave Isaac a handful of jewels but he didn't want to take them. I told him I was a rich man and that I had more money than I could have ever spend.

Being on the grounds of the people we have once enslaved was all too real. The fact that I set out with Moses to free these people; this was one of the acts Aristotle said that made me great. I found a place that finally had a room to rent. Everywhere else had no rooms to spare. I knew I had found the right spot when I saw all the people here sleeping in tents.

Remembering the poem I wrote, I'll gladly just sit here outside your gate. He wasn't hard to find. I just followed the trial of the people. I found Isaac just like that walking around with a smile. I walked up to him and asked how he was doing. Isaac said, Cain, is that you? I can see you. It's a miracle. I couldn't believe my ears or eyes. Isaac can now see?

Isaac said, see, I knew you had a young face. It was for the first time that I can see since I was a young man. He cured my eyes. I can now see the son of God and who he really is. Isaac hugged me and ran off happily. Did the son of God really cure his eyes? It was hard to believe in seeing a blind man being able to see. I followed the flock of people till I found them all gathered. There was a man in the center being surrounded by twelve other men who looked like priests. That man seemed very familiar to me. I know I see him somewhere else before but I couldn't put my finger on it.

The man in the center was around thirty years of age. His head turned right at me I felt this chill in my body almost immediately. He looked at me as if he knew me. I didn't know what to do or how to even approach him. What should I say if he really is the son of God? I approached him while the others stayed in my way protecting him. They asked me what I wanted and I told them that I was looking for a man name Jesus.

They asked me what I wanted with Jesus and before I could finish, he walked up and said, it's ok, I am Jesus. This man's voice could calm a raging storm. They calmed as soon as he said it's ok. Jesus told me that he knew I would come. With a surprised look, I asked how he knew that. Jesus said, my father told me that you would come at this date and time.

Who is this father and how does he know me. Jesus smiled and said, surely Cain you know our father. When he mentioned my name out loud, all the men with him looked at me up and down. In my head, how does this man know my name and why does he look so familiar? Then, I heard a voice; it was his voice in my head, with him looking at me "the son of Adam, my father's first child, Cain the murderer of his brother Able."

All I could do was to fall to my knees and cry. Jesus walked up to me and put his hand on my head. I heard his voice in my head again saying it's ok Cain, everything will be alright. I started to feel better almost instantly. All my pain I had went away. Is this the power of his touch? God really sent his son to the world?

Jesus told me to come with him while the others asked if he's sure that it's ok. Jesus said yes, he will not be a problem. So from then on, I followed this man like a puppy. It was all still so hard to believe why God would send his son to this evil world. He began to teach me his ways or what he called the teachings of his father.

Well, Jesus wasn't the one trying to teach. It was the apostles. It was always a fun time because Jesus would always say you're wasting your time as he knows the word for he knows my father, perhaps even better than I know him. They would always look shocked from his words. Jesus also called me brother and they didn't like that too much. Whenever Jesus was not around, they would ask why he calls you brother even though I am not his real brother, brother.

I would always stay silent because I didn't feel like telling my story. They would ask that until Jesus suddenly appear behind us. We didn't even hear or see him coming. You would hear that wonderful voice saying, do my apostles not believe the words that I speak? They all said no my lord. We believe your words and will not question it.

Jesus would always say things like these words are spoken through me by the way of my father. Or these are not my words. My father in heaven has passed these words to me. This is where I began to truly meet the men Jesus called his apostles. Peter, Andrew, James, John, Philip, Thomas, Bartholomew, Matthew, James, Simon, Thaddeus

and Judas, Jesus also had another person follow him named Judas. I was told this was his half brother. Peter was second in command. Peter was the oldest apostle and the one all the others looked up too when Jesus wasn't around.

Jesus seemed to love and respect Peter the most. He would say my father was always pleased with your works. Since my father loves you so, so shall I. This did not make the others jealous but it surprisingly made them work harder. That was a first for my eyes whenever a king had too many sons, they would always fight for his love. They would encourage each other through kind words and acts.

Jesus began to rub off on more than his apostles and his brother. The people of Israel started to be kinder to each other being in the presence of the son of God will have that effect.

He could move a mountain with his mind. Even though he held the power in his hands, he never used it. He was perfect and not the perfect imperfection way but just perfect.

I never met a man who could do no wrong until I met Jesus. He was what the Buddhist strived for. He was the noble path. I asked Jesus why god sent him to earth. Jesus told me he was not sent but he chose to come here. I asked him why he chose to come here. He said he needed to understand and see why humans act the way they are. He said it is easy for someone else to judge when you have never walked a mile in their shoes.

Jesus said the only way to walk a mile in these shoes was to become human. Now I understand how hard it is to be human and how it feels not to be perfect. I asked him what he means by that. You're God's son hence you're perfect. Jesus smiled and said brother, you think I'm perfect? You're so wrong. Without the guidance of the father, I would be like everyone else. I am also tempted by this flesh and blood.

The flesh is nothing but a sensation where everything wrong seems to feel the best. Everything right seems to dull the senses. Touch is the most powerful thing father has given the humans besides the mind. The mind is the only thing that can control that power. It brings a smile to my heart everyone keeps saying that I'm perfect. Brother, I am not perfect. I am born with the same flesh and blood like every human has.

The sins of your father and mother flow through my blood just like every human that walks the earth. He taught me so much with just kind words. I didn't feel so cursed around him. Jesus would say to me just after thirty years in this flesh and blood, I couldn't imagine living for thousands of years filled with these sins. You're stronger than you know.

Remember what I have said. Nothing is more corrupted than religion. It was clear as day when Jesus went to the temple. He walked in the door and everyone became silent. It was creepy. The priests knew who he was without a word. Jesus looked right at the priest and told them to leave. They asked what he meant by that. It was the first time I saw Jesus use his strength. Jesus said you heard me. This is the house of my father and you bare false witness against thee.

The priest said we bare no false witness against God. Jesus voice became angered that it echoed through the temple with force knocking down all the false idols in the temple. Jesus said you dare lie to me in the house of my father? Then I heard a word that shocked the church. He said blasphemy. Those words had power and I meant power behind them.

Jesus told them all their false witness and sins will not be forgiven in the house of lord. The priests ran out the temple and didn't return. The one thing I learnt was that no matter how nice Jesus was, he is still God's son. The son will do whatever he can to not let his father be disrespected.

The temple was taken by Jesus and his apostles and this is where they shared their message. The first thing Jesus did was to take down all the false idols. All the gold and jewel encrusted symbols had to go. Jesus said his father doesn't need gold, money or jewels. Those are manmade treasures. He preached his words and said not to be a part of this world but just to live in it. To be a part of this world is a sin against thy father and a sin against the father is the ultimate sin.

This world is corrupted and evil hence the reason why not to be a part of this world. He was teaching us how to live in the world and not be taken in by the evils of man. He told the story about why he rides a donkey. He said kings ride in with horses to start wars. He rides a donkey because it doesn't show the strength but it shows peace instead. The church members grew larger day by day. Pretty soon, there was not enough room for all the people so he held the message outside.

It was a blessing just to hear him speak. He said you do not need a temple or a church. These are just walls; just a building and it means nothing. Your temple, your church is in your heart and that is the place where father will find you. Whenever you go, if your heart is true about the love of my father, he will find you. That is the meaning of my body is my temple for all the ones who took the words wrongly.

He talked about being born again and not coming back to life or being recreated. It was a message for the lost to help them find their way. Just like a parent who taught their child the right way but they stray off the path. The teachings are a guidance to make sure you find your way if you got lost. To be born again is to change your evil ways from the inside out.

One day, a woman came to hear Jesus' message. The men treated her as if she was evil. They told Jesus that she was a prostitute and was unworthy to hear the word. Being a prostitute in the presence of the son angered the men and so they started to throw rocks at her. Jesus seeing the acts of these men stood in front of them. They stopped throwing the rocks and asked Jesus to move so they could continue. Jesus said, let he who is without sin cast the first stone.

All the men then dropped the rocks. Jesus said, who here is without sin and started pointing at the men. You could see the shame in their eyes.

Jesus told them that the only one who can judge is the father in heaven. Jesus said do you not hear my words? I told you only the father can judge another man or women. I told you not to be a part of this world for no man is better than the next.

He turned to the woman and held out his hand and lifted her up off the ground. She said thank you my lord. He asked her what her name was and she said her name is Mary Magdalene. Jesus said, Mary, for this day onward, you are forgiven of your sins. Her eyes lit up with joy and she asked if she is truly forgiven. Jesus told her, yes, for you took the step in trying to right your wrongs. Now go and live the word. She then ran off happily. This was not the last time we would see Mary Magdalene.

From that day onward, she was at the temple every day. Listening and praying with Jesus and they built a great relationship. Jesus waited for her to show up every day. You could see it as the day open with new people. From what I saw, Jesus had fallen in love with Mary. I could be wrong but I doubt it. Peter did not like Mary and as a matter of fact, Peter didn't like any woman. Peter thought that women are the cause of all the problems in the world. He thought men tried too hard to please them and that men did all these evil acts just to have them near.

Peter had a great point no doubt but as a man, you're always clouded by your own thoughts. No matter how much evil men did these things for women, he always left out the key. Those men chose to be evil. Peter would ask Jesus why does he keep her around and Jesus would say, Peter; both men and women have the right to be saved. Jesus made Mary one of the apostles later on. Peter did not like that at all but being a man of God, he just turn to the other cheek.

Our little group has grown. There are sixteen of us now spreading and enjoying the word. Peter called Jesus Christ, which meant savior of the people. Jesus loved the name and he told Peter that God was pleased with the name that was given. He said that he will go by the name Christ. Jesus Christ the savior of all mankind and not just the people of Israel.

The works of Jesus must have traveled far, for now Romans, Japanese, Chinese and many others travel to find Jesus. It was a shock to see all these different people from different countries in our church. We welcome everyone with open arms and we never turn down any man or woman. No matter if Jesus was God's son or not, he still carried himself like he was no better than anyone. He wore the same old clothes and ate the same old bread with us.

Many people offered him fine clothes and meals fit for kings. He would not take any of it and instead, he would tell them that he is just an ordinary man like any of these and what does the son of God need with riches when he is the son of God and that he is richer than any kings. My father's love is worth more than the entire world. This is around the time he began teaching us about what he called the eternal life.

It is important to understand that these are not things that I read in that book. I was there and I got to hear the word with my own ears. I saw the man's teachings and I walked the same path he walked. The words today aren't the words that came from Jesus. That book has been changed too many times by men who used it for their own reasons. Religion was not meant to be a way to trick a man's heart. Jesus did not speak or have a religion.

Eternal life is the only way to the father and to heaven. He told us that he made the decision to open the gate for us. He said now he understands what it's like to be human. He told us he shall make a great sacrifice to open the gate. We didn't understand what he meant by that. He said only a few chosen men and women had ever stepped foot inside the gate. He told us with his sacrifice, the gate will be opened to all.

Every time I heard him saying the gate, all I could do is to think about the Garden of Eden. He told us that ever since the dawn of man, the gate has never opened. All this is about to change through everlasting life. He told us our souls never die. We may leave this world but our souls will continue to live on. Through the ways of the father, the gate will open and the soul will finally have a home. Is this the reason the Buddhist said our souls will become something else because our souls do not have a home?

I asked Jesus if that gate was the gate of the garden. Jesus said yes brother, the garden shall open. All my hopes and dreams will finally come true. Oh how long I have waited for this day. I asked Jesus why he calls me brother and Jesus said it is because I know his father not through his words but we both were friends. And since his father had called me son, he will address me as brother.

I asked Jesus why he is so kind to me when the father doesn't like me. Jesus smiled and laughed. He is just mad at all humans because they all forgot about him and did not do what he told them. All those things said about father are true to a certain extent. They said the father is a jealous God but that's not true. All he ever wanted was for the people to understand that he is the only one. They say you should always fear him but that is not true either. What are the reasons for you to fear him if you're following his ways?

People always speak on things they don't know or understand. Everybody wants to be someone else and not themselves. Life is a wonderful gift especially your own life. There is a different in walking in someone else's shoes and wanting to have their shoes. People never understand what they have till it's gone. For anyone who lived to thirty plus, time has always been on your side. A lot of teachings have come from this great man and I have held onto his every word.

The thought that I could be redeemed was too much for me to keep in. I was one happy man and it showed in my works. I didn't feel cursed anymore I saw brighter days ahead of me instead. We celebrated with wine and we all drank including Jesus. He didn't drink as much as we did but he still drank. We ran out of wine and Jesus told us to bring him a jug of water.

Everyone had cups in their hands when he sent for water everyone dropped their cups thinking the party is over. Judas gave Jesus the jug of water and he told us to grab our cups. The looks of disappointment were in everyone's faces and no one wanted to drink water.

He then touched the water and it turned red. We had no idea what had just happened. Jesus then asked Peter to pass his cup and poured it into his cup.

He took a drink and we all were watching like a child. Jesus said that is some fine wine. Matthew asked if that is wine in the jar. Jesus said yes, and it is grand too. Matthew sled his cup to Jesus and asked him to pour him some. Jesus slid the cup back to Matthew; Matthew said that is the best wine I ever had. John told Jesus to pass the jug and we began to pass the jug around the table. We all took a drink and the faces at the table looked as if this was the first wine we have ever tasted.

Judas said to Jesus all this time you have been holding out on us. He smiled and said, I have never needed to do it but you seemed to have turned into a fish. We all cheered his named while banging the cups on the table. We partied for hours on end telling jokes and stories. Peter told us about the time Jesus saved a boy from drowning in the river. Peter told us Jesus walked on the water and saved the boy.

We couldn't believe our ears but we still cheered for Jesus. We wanted to see this for ourselves so we talked Jesus into going to the river. We drank the whole way there. We don't usually drink this much but Jesus didn't mind this time. We got to the river and Jesus still being Jesus said, I shall show you the power my father has given me. He stepped onto the river and began to walk on the surface.

We couldn't believe our eyes. Peter with the cup in his hand turned and said, I told you guys and none of you believed me. We asked Jesus to do a little dance and although Jesus was not a dancer, he still did a little foot kick. We all laughed and cheered his name once again. Jesus smiled and said I might be the son of God but I cannot dance. Judas being the most free of us ran in and tried to walk on water but he fell right in and we laughed even harder. Jesus walked up to him laughing and said I will always love your spirit my dear Judas.

That was the night Jesus showed us that he was human just like any us. The moon shined ever so bright that night while the stars lit up the sky. The wind blew calmly with a nice warm breeze. It was a perfect night for the perfect man. We never asked him to walk on the water again but we did ask him to change it into wine. We had a great brotherhood with one women and life was good. Just as with everything, time flies whenever you're happy.

Jesus moved us to Jerusalem and continued to spread his teachings. We had no temple this time but just the streets, a field or anything else that we can use to preach. Jerusalem was full of Romans but they let the people worship whatever God they chose. It was a peaceful time in the day of the slaves. Jesus started to get too much attention when stories of how he healed the blind and sick reached every land that the Romans owned.

Jesus began to say to us that he will miss us all when he is gone. We all joke and say that he'll have a long time before that day comes or we would say that he's the son of God and he will be here forever. Jesus would always give us a big bright smile when he said that. Around this time, Jesus started to tell us how much he loved and cared for us. We really didn't think too much of it because of the kind of man he was.

Every time someone starts to tell you that they love you, it's always for a reason. Whether they had a change of heart or they finally realized how they feel. There is always a change coming for there is only two things in life that will always be. One is change and the other is death and we will always be able to see the both of it. I might not be able to taste one myself but I have seen it too many times to count them.

Pontius Pilate was the overseer of Jerusalem and he sent the Roman guards to spy on us. Everywhere we turned, we saw the Roman guards. We asked Jesus what we should do and he would tell us nothing but to just let them be. None of us like the guards following us around but we have learned to live with them. Jesus even made friends with some of them and all I could do was to smile as this man was just something to learn from. Some of the guards began to watch out for us.

They brought us water and food which caused the other Jewish priests to begin to hate us, spreading lies that Jesus was not God's son. In case you're wondering Jewish people and Hebrew are not the same. We took members of their church which also means that we took their money away. Jesus would tell the people to beware of false prophets while looking at them in the eyes as they passed. Matthew and John would always smile at the priests. Those two loves to start things up.

During our teachings, Judas would sneak off from time to time for hours. Peter started to question Judas's acts but Jesus would always said let him be. That did not stop the wondering minds of what Judas was up too. Philip, who I called the eye, always saw things for what is was said we should watch him. Jesus once again said let him be. Judas has some things that he needs to work out.

We left Judas to be while watching his every move. Jesus told us that he wanted all sixteen of us to gather for a dinner. We cheered knowing it would be more of Jesus turning water into the finest wine. Since I was the man with the money, I brought a little hut for us to sleep. We all shared money to buy

Jesus a nice cup. We sat the cup in the middle where Jesus was going to sit.

It was a gathering like any other gatherings. We sang, told jokes and drank. We always have Mary and Peter sitting beside Jesus because they are the ones Jesus knew the longest and the ones he loved most. It was just like any other gatherings till Jesus made a toast. We all told each other to be quiet as the man of the hour has something to say. Jesus was quiet for a minute. Peter patted him on the back while Mary rubbed his hand.

Jesus stood up and said that it has been a pleasure being with all of you over these years. He grabbed a loaf of bread and told us all to grab a piece each. We all grabbed a piece and he told us that this is my body. Eat from it and I will always be with you. He told us to pour a glass of wine and drink it. He said this is my blood. Drink this and the father will be with you. We asked him what this was all about.

He said someone at this table will betray me and we all got quiet. Philip said I know who it is and Peter then said it's Judas. Judas stood up and said how you dare say my name. Jesus told us to stop and turned to Peter and asked who you are to judge. Peter, you will be the only one who will deny me. Peter said, I will not deny you and Jesus said you will deny me three times.

Jesus said none of us can judge as that is for my father to decide. I already forgave you Peter and the one who will betray me. It is already done. My time here is coming to an end. Just like that, the good vibe was gone and we all retired to our spots on the floor. I don't think any of us slept that night as it was all too much to bear.

The next day, everyone had a sad look on their face, all except for Judas as he wasn't around. Jesus told us that he wanted to go to the garden. He went in and told us to wait as he prayed. No one knows what he said but he prayed for twenty minutes. He stood up when he saw Judas and walked over to hug him and gave him a kiss on the check. It was odd because we have never kissed him before and right after the kiss, the Roman guards came over and arrested Jesus.

We asked what the meaning of this is. The guards then said that he is arrested for falsely claiming to be king. We were ready to fight at that moment but Jesus said no and let it be. The guards turned to Judas and gave him a bag and said good work. They took Jesus off shortly after. Peter walked up to Judas and said that he knew it was him. Philip asked Judas how he could have done such a thing to the son of God. Judas turned and ran away in shame.

Peter screamed you better run Judas, you coward. That is where the kiss of death came from that act of betrayal from Judas. We all gathered and said what are we going to do? Another set of guards walked up to me and said Pontius Pilate would like to see you. Peter and Philip told me not to say a word. The guards took me to Pilate's palace; Pilate was there in his throne room waiting. He said Ra-Noor; tell me what information you managed to find after spending so much time with Jesus.

I told him that I found a man who could do no wrong as he never harmed a soul. Pilate said that is not what I meant. You know what I am asking you. Is this Jesus the son of God? I said from the things I have seen, I believe that this man is the son of God. Then I heard that word for the second time in blasphemy, the Jewish priests came walking in. That man is not the son of God. I am a priest and I talk to god all the time. He told me of no such son and that man must be hanged for his lies.

I looked at them and said how could you hang an innocent man? He said that innocent man mocks our God and deserves to die for it. How can a man who wronged no one deserve to die, you're mocking your God by being a judge of another man and trying to put him to death. Pilate told us to be quiet he will try him by court and let it be decided there. The priests smiled. I had nothing but sadness in my heart. The priest began spreading lies about Jesus and just like that, people started to turn their backs against Jesus.

Jesus was put to trial in front of me, the priests, Pilate, his wife and a man named Herod Antipas. They dressed Jesus in purple robes to mock him as the king of Jews. They put him on trial for his actions but Jesus said nothing to defend himself. The priest asked him many questions but he rarely ever said a word. On the first day of the trial, they told Jesus of the charges against him. His crime was pretending to be king.

Pilate told Jesus that this is a serious crime and what do you have to say of it? Jesus said, I have committed no crime and I'm true to what I have said. That was the first day and the court wasn't held long. The next day of the trial, the priest had people come in to tell lies about Jesus. They said Jesus said he was the king of all kings not just to the Jews. One man said Jesus beat him up when he didn't acknowledge he as king. Another man said that Jesus took all his money by telling him he would cure him but never did.

This went on for hours they asked Jesus what he makes of these crimes. Jesus said nothing and that long day was over and they put Jesus back into his cell. I snuck down there to see him and I asked him why he is not defending himself against the charges. Jesus said, brother, it's time I told you the truth. He told me that he is going to die so that the gate of the Garden of Eden will open. Hearing this news was both sadness and happiness.

The man I came to love is going to die for us but I still couldn't accept it. I told him there has to be another way with eyes full of tears. Jesus' hands still chained reached outside the bars and hugged me. He said I'm sorry you had to endure ten thousand years of life and he shed some tears. That didn't help me seeing him cry. He told me that all will be alright for now and everyone will be forgiven for all their sins.

He told me to go before they would try to kill me. I ran off like a child who feelings just got to hurt. I went to the hut and prayed to God to not let Jesus die. The other apostles were there praying too. Mary walked around telling us that it would all be ok. I started to understand why Jesus loved her. That heart of hers was beautiful. She said everything will be alright but the looks in her eyes was different. I could tell that Jesus had told her the truth.

Mary gave the guys hope that all would be alright. The next day, Pilate called the apostles in to tell our stories and he sent us in one by one. Everyone said Jesus did no wrong and that they believe he is the son of God. When it was Peter's turn, he denied everything including knowing Jesus. It was a sad day but it was just as Jesus said. Then Judas came in and just lied through his mouth. He said Jesus lied about everything and that he was no son of god.

Chapter 12: Death Without Dying

The priest smiled and said even two of his closest friends deny him and tells of his lies. Pilate looked at the priest and said I wonder how that came to be. Pilate said he will make his decision tomorrow. With Pilate making the statement about the priest, I had hoped for a better tomorrow. We all gathered in the hut. Peter was already there just crying his eyes out.

They all asked me what has happened and I told them what Judas said. Philip, I should find him and kill him. Before I could tell them what Peter said, Peter said I can't believe I had denied him. They all said what Philip said and how could you deny the son of God. Peter said he was sorry over and over again. That was the last time we would all gather. Mary hugged Peter and told him that it would be alright. The one he hated the most was the first one to open her arms.

Everyone left; all but me, Peter and Mary. It was hard to sleep that night knowing Jesus was about to die. The next day, Pilate made his decision.

I already knew the outcome but it was still hard to hear. Pilate said I find no wrong in this man but in order to ensure peace, I would have to kill this man. Hearing that shook my very soul to its core and hearing those words from Pilate made the priests cheer. Once again, the religious people in our world have killed another innocent man for money.

Pilate's wife yelled no when she heard Pilate say he was to kill him. She ran over to Jesus and dropped to her knees. She said I know who you are my lord and thank you. She said that with both a smile and tears. Pilate picked her up and took her off. She begged Pilate not to kill him but Pilate came back and said Jesus will be crucified in two days and took him off. I begged Pilate to spare him but he said no.

The priests pointed at me and said you should also put him on trial. Pilate said you priests are pushing your luck. That man you have just pointed at is a high priest of Egypt. If you put that man to death, the Egyptians will come for your heads. The priest got quiet and Pilate said, I have made my decision, court dismiss. I walked through the streets with my head down in shame. They began posting signs up saying the king of Jews will be crucified in two days. I went back to the hut as I didn't want to be outside. I found Mary inside crying and all I could do was to put my arms around her shoulders.

I too was crying but just on the inside. Seeing Mary cry did not help as she was always so strong. I went to the garden where Jesus made his last prayer the next day. I saw Judas hanging in the air from his neck with the twenty pieces of silver on the ground by the tree. I saw Philip at first and I thought he was the one who did it until he said that he had found him like this in the morning. It serves him right for betraying Jesus.

Now let me pause the story for a minute. For all the people who think that I am Judas, that makes no sense. If Jesus already forgave Judas for his betrayal, why would God punished him? As for killing himself, that's a whole other story there. And to the people saying that I always carry silver, I am a rich man. I have tons of pieces of silver and gold.

Alright, now back to the story, Pilate did not want to kill Jesus but the people wanted blood. Distracting the people from the real truth has always been the name of the game. The priest made a special spear for Jesus' crucifixion and they called it, Rhongowennan, the god killer. They said if Jesus survives the cross, he will not survive this spear.

For a tool to kill, the spear was beautiful. It had a blue handle with gold trimmings with the symbols at the edges of the pole. The blade was so sharp it could go through rocks. The tip of the spear looked like what is now an umbrella with little circles on the blades. It had four edges that came from the tip on four different sides. It was the greatest spear that was ever created for the greatest day for mankind.

The day finally came for Jesus to be crucified. There was no wind blowing. The weather was calm at about 85 degrees and it was the perfect day for a crucifixion to be carried out.

The people gathered with tomatoes in their hands. It was a tradition to toss them at the person who is going to be crucified. Jesus made his way through the people; carrying his heavy cross in his purple robe. The guards whipped him while the people tossed tomatoes.

It was a sad day for mankind. The man who cured the sick and gave hope to the people was treated like an animal. The people booed him as he walked through the crowd. Jesus showed his strength by carrying the cross all by himself. He carried it from the bottom of the hill till he reached the top. They made him put up his own cross. I watch him the whole time following him up the hill.

They offered him some wine, the wine was full of painkillers but Jesus refused the wine. I was hoping that he would take it but being the man he was, I knew it wasn't going to happen. He laid there on the cross with no fight. He stretched out his arms and when they had a nail through his wrist, he didn't even make a sound. The people cheered aloud when the first nail went it in.

The guards moved to his right arm and placed another nail through his wrist. The crowd once again cheered at the sound of the nail being entered. They made their way to his feet placed them both together and banged the nail through both of them. The crowd began to chant crucify, crucify. The guards moved to each side and lift the cross up and placed it in the dirt. The priests smiled at seeing Jesus being crucified. They made two thieves stay on each side of Jesus. One of the thieves fell to his knees and said forgive me my lord. The other thief just sat there and watched.

Jesus started to speak and the crowd got quiet. Jesus looked up to sky and said forgive them father for they know not what they do. Bless these poor souls for man will always have sin. Hearing these words, the crowd began to chant mercy. Hearing the crowd chant mercy, Pilate pointed to the priests. Out came Rhongowennan and they stuck it into his side, right under his ribs. Jesus eyes closed and he died minutes later. All I could do was to fall unto my knees. I saw angels gather around the cross bowing their heads. I saw

Gabriel appear. He hugged Jesus as he died.

At that moment I knew where I have seen him. He was the statue at the Shaolin Temple. It all made sense to me now on why his words and their words were all the same. I found the world's true religion Jesus was Yisu. He was the one who guided Buddha. Seeing the angels there was a beautiful yet sad sight. It was almost too much to bear. I have lost another good friend that I have in this world.

The sky instantly turned black and the ground began to shake under our feet. The people began to panic. I heard a familiar voice yelling out that you have angered God and now you shall suffer his wrath. It was Philip apparently. The people started to run around while the ground started swallowing all the people who wanted Jesus to die. During the time of the crucifixion, I didn't even notice the word Inri placed on top of the cross. Inri means the king of Jews and they were still mocking him even in his death.

The ground returned back to its original state as if nothing happened. All the priests had disappeared after being swallowed by the ground. That was the longest day of my long life. They did not take him down but left him there for all the people to see. The people came from miles around to pray at his feet. The people made cross signs over their hearts as they prayed.

While sitting there praying at his feet on one night, an idea came up. I opened the wound where they stuck the spear and drank Jesus' blood. The taste was like no other taste I had before. It was sweet and bitter at the same time. I could feel his blood moving down my throat into my stomach. His blood started to take over my body. I could feel his blood mixing with my blood, killing cells as it went through my body.

I fell to the ground shortly after. The sky became the ground and it felt like I was resting on the moon. I felt the light of the moon shining onto my back. I thought this was a good idea but I was so wrong. The thoughts in your head never turn out that way in real life. I thought the blood of the son of God would cure my curse. I couldn't move at all. My eyes were wide shut and my body was paralyzed. I heard God's voice calling unto my name.

I saw Gabriel standing over me for the first time with his wings. He said my friend, what have you done? You're a vampire from now on and you will lust for blood forever. That was the first time I heard of the word vampire. What is this vampire? I did not yet understand the words Gabriel said. I blacked out and woke up. It was still dark. I did not know if it was still the same day.

The world had changed. I could feel this power and lust beating through my body. My muscles became even stronger. I had a feeling of a twenty year old that lived for a hundred thousand years without aging. My senses were sharper with ever touch. It was like seeing new colors. I could see further than I ever could before. I could hear the wind as it passed me. I never knew the wind carried voices. I could hear the voices of the dead as it blew past.

I could hear people talking when no one was around. It sounded as if they were right beside me. I could hear the bugs move through the dirt. I followed a bug on my knees just to hear him move and as I got close, the bug stopped. Then I stood still for a while and it would continue moving again. I followed the bug for a couple of minutes in wonder. I stood up faster than my mind thought all I could think. Is this a dream? I tried to picture myself at the garden but it didn't work.

I guess this is not a dream after all. It was something about the moonlight. It gave me strength and I felt its power. I was so hungry that I had a hunger like I never had before. I went to my hut. I walked there in delight and enjoying the night. While I was walking to the hut, Philip and Mary were there in the hut. They asked me where I had been to and they thought something had happened to me. I told them I don't really know but I had a vision.

They asked you too? I saw Jesus again. We need to get them to take him down. Mary asked me what happened to my eyes. I asked her what she meant by that and she told me to take a look. I looked into a small mirror in the hut and I was shocked. My brown eyes became hazel. The yellow and green had this glow. The light shined off my eyes. It was like magic. Mary asked me if Jesus gave me those.

She said, Jesus called you brother for a reason so did he give you those eyes? Philip walked over and said, amazing, you have his eyes now. I told them I don't know how I got these eyes and there was no way I was going to tell them that I drank the blood of Jesus. I went to the cabinet and grab some food. I asked them if they were hungry and they said no. I pulled out two loafs of bread and some dried meat.

I sat at the table and started to consume the food like I haven't had anything for days. No matter how much I ate, I still was hungry. Nothing satisfied me and so I went to sleep hungry that night. Going to sleep hungry is no fun at all. The next day, they tried to wake me but I couldn't get up for some reasons. They said the rest of the apostles were going to Pilate so they can convince Pilate to let them burry Jesus. I told them to go on without me as I was too weak to go.

They told me to stay in to get some rest and I slept almost the whole day. I got up to eat again but still, my hunger remained. Mary came in the hut smiling. She said we did it. Pilate is going to bury him in the cave. I said that's great news and we should celebrate. She told me you don't look so well. You should get some rest while I'll go get you some medicine. I started to feel a little better after I walked outside the hut with the moonlight shining down.

I sat there under the moonlight thinking and remembering those words Gabriel said, vampire. Vampire, what is a vampire, am I vampire? Why does food not stop my hunger? Why do I feel better under the moonlight? I stayed there all night just thinking and listening to the sounds of the night. Mary came the next morning with medicine. She told me I looked pale and made me take the medicine. She told me they were going to visit Jesus' grave and that I should come by.

I told her I will if I start to feel better she said ok and to get some rest. Once again, I slept the whole day away. I heard someone come busting in the hut door and I jumped up out my sleep. It was Mary apparently. She grabbed me and told me to come. I asked her where we were going and she told me to hush and to just come. As I walked outside the hut, I saw the moonlight and took a long breath.

I started to feel better in the presence of the moonlight. Mary said I see you're doing better. She told me to hurry and we started to walk faster and faster. I was walking with ease. It felt like I wasn't really using any muscle. We came to a cave. Mary stop and said go in, I will see you tomorrow.

I asked her what's going on but she smiled running off saying you will see, you will see. I haven't seen her being this happy since Jesus was alive and come to think of it, the last time any of us was this happy was the last supper before Jesus had his speech. I felt the wind blowing from the cave and that gave me a creepy feeling. Part of me didn't want to go in but there had to be a reason Mary brought me here.

I felt something strange coming from the cave. I walked in slowly and I saw a light reflecting off the rocks. I got closer to this light I saw a familiar face, it was Jesus. He gave me a big smile and a tear immediately fell from my eye. The son of God has returned. I walked up to hug him but I went straight through him. I couldn't understand what was going on.

Jesus said, brother, it's good to see you. I asked him what's going on and Jesus said this is my soul. I no longer live in the body. I asked him what he meant by no longer living in the body and he told me this is how we look like after death; brother the gate is now open. Those words were like the first time Eve told me she loved me. I look at him and he said yes, he read my mind but I still needed to hear it.

Mother, father, my brother, my Eve, Menes, Qiao, Anta, Alexander, and Aristotle Jesus said yes they are now in the garden. Nothing else and no others words have brought me so much happiness. My curse meant nothing to me at that point. Then, Jesus gave me a sad look. Cain, the first time he ever called me by my name. I know what you did and you will now truly live on forever. You will never see the garden, I'm sorry my brother.

I told him it's ok. My family and the ones I loved are all that matters. Jesus told me that this is the reason I will always love and miss you. Your heart is beautiful even though you made mistakes. You never fully lost your heart. Over ten thousand years of living and you still have it. My thirty three years on this earth almost broke me. You're the Christ of the living never ever forget that.

Jesus looked over at his body when I didn't even see it there. He told me that there are three holy Grails in the world. I will take my body with me but you must retrieve that spear. It holds the power of my blood. Do not let it get into the wrong hands. The last is you my dear brother, for that stupid act that you have done; it had made you the third. You have mixed the power of the Grail with your eternal blood.

You're now the sins of the Holy Grail and you will forever be cursed with that action. I was hurt by those words. He told me no matter what I have done; I will always be his brother. I looked at him and said Yisu, and he smiled. He said I see you managed to figure it all out like I knew you would. You truly are special.

No wonder your actions hurt father so. He told me to always remember that you are my brother, Cain Christ. Through mind, heart and now blood, I leave you my eyes take care brother. Jesus then reached out to hug me. I felt the hug as I didn't pass through him. He did that because I needed it. I closed my eyes and said goodbye my brother.

I opened my eyes and he was gone. The Savior of the world has been touched by the little old me. I was so touched that I sat in the cave for a couple of hours. I got my resolve back and that I must get the spear. I went to the hut to get my sword and robes. Mary was inside waiting. She asked me what Jesus told me but I told her that I am not able to tell her and it is for her own safety. I walked into the changing room and came back out with my robe on together with my sword by my side and a robe over my face. She looked at me and told me to be careful and I told her I will.

I made my way to Pilate's palace. I was thinking the whole way on how I'm going to get the spear. I started running and something happened to my muscles. They turned rock solid and I began to move like the wind. I blinked and I was in front of the palace. It was like I vanished and appeared there. The full moon of the night is something I remembered it clearly. The guards jumped as I appeared. They asked me where did I come from and what I wanted.

I didn't say a word. They raised their spears but I didn't move at all. They said they were only going to ask me one more time. I could feel their adrenaline rushing and I could hear the blood flowing through their veins. Something came over to me and my teeth started to grow out of my mouth. It poured out blood. They swung the spears at me but I caught them with each hand. The spears looked like they were moving in a slow motion. I pulled one of the guards towards me and bit him on the neck.

I began to drain the blood from his body. My eyes rolled into the back of my head. The taste was that of the wine Jesus had turned from water. Every drop of blood that entered my mouth was heavenly. The smell was better than the locust flowers that filled the courtyard in Egypt. His blood flowing through my body started to make my hunger go away. I drained his blood until my hunger went away.

I felt stronger than I ever did before. I stuck the spear through his body I felt it go through to the outside into the dirt. The other guard was running away. He was about twenty feet away from me. I threw the spear at him and the force from the spear was so great that it moved him five more feet away. I ran through the palace doors like the wind. I forced the doors open and saw two men flying away. I made my way to the throne room. I was moving so fast that no one saw me coming.

There the spear was mounted above the chair. I felt the power as I got closer to it. I felt like a magnet and

I was drawn closer to the spear. It felt like it was calling unto my name. I grabbed it and I felt like I was God himself. So this is what it feels like to be the son of God? Jesus was a great man to hold all this power and showed nothing but peace. I heard footsteps approaching and I wanted to test the power of the spear.

The guards told me to drop the spear but I didn't say a word. I slam the spear onto the palace's floor and it went right through it. From the spot I slam, the spear made a crack five feet long. The guards looked down at the crack, dropped their weapons and ran off. That was probably the smartest thing they ever did in their life. I placed the spear on my back and took off.

I heard the bells go off. This was the sound of the alarm. It was too late. I was long gone. I buried the spear on the outside of the city where no one would find it. I made my way back to my hut as I saw guards running around. I laid down thinking of what Gabriel said to me. It was clear now. I understood what it meant to be a vampire and what a vampire was. It was hard knowing that I have to live on blood for the rest of my life.

It was very hard to sleep that night. I just laid there having flashbacks of the day I laid on the moon. I was happy that I managed to retrieve the spear. The power of it was nothing to be played with. Mary came busting in the hut the next day. Did you hear someone took the spear? They are searching for it through people's houses. She looked right at me and said I hope you didn't hide it here.

I told her no. I put it in a good hiding spot. She said well, because they will come and check the hut. I told her don't worry and everything will be ok. She told me people are gathering around the crucifixion site and going to the cave to pray. There are strange markings in the cave where his body was buried. There's a cross burned into the ground. The priests are now calling the place where he was crucified and the cave of holy places.

She told me the Roman priests are coming to bless the two places. This angered me because it was the same people who killed him or wanted him dead and now using him for their own benefits. I told Mary thank you for all the info but I still need rest as I had a long night. I woke up once again at night. It was starting to seem strange to me. I haven't seen the sun in days but the one thing I did know was that I loved the moonlight.

With my new found strength ever since becoming a vampire, I had to be smart. I only drained the blood of people who wouldn't be missed. I found prostitutes and beggars to be my victims. At first, I had a problem with putting my mouth on men but the blood lust erased all of that. I always stabbed my victims so it looked like a murder. One day, I found a prostitute in a dark alley looking for work. I told her I was looking for a woman to please me she was happy to take my money.

I drained her of her blood; her blood was like tasting a wine fresh out the grapes. It was bitter and nasty as I could taste the diseases in her blood. It was hard to drink her blood. I then heard footsteps so I left her there and vanished. I drained enough blood to kill her but I didn't stab her. I was careless because she saw my face but there was no way she could live after that. I continued doing my same routine and I wonder back to the alley to find another prostitute.

The air had the smell of blood, fresh blood something was going on. I creped in quietly to see what was going on and I saw the prostitute that I killed was draining this man's blood. What was going on? As I got closer, I smelled that her blood had changed. I could smell my blood in her. She noticed me and stood up. I was scared and I don't even remember the last time I was scared. I froze in my tracks. She said you, pointing in a soft voice.

What is going on, she said you did this to me. I didn't understand those words and I panicked. Without further thinking, I then rushed through her and broke her neck. I hid the bodies under some trash so no one would be able to find them. I went to my hut, sat on the table with my head on my hands. What did she mean by I did this to her? The next day, I went to the alley to check on the bodies. The man that I saw killed by the prostitute was moving around. At that point, I understood that my curse is contagious.

I chopped off the man's head and went to the prostitute and chopped off her head. I ran to the garden to pray. I looked up at the wall there was a sign posted. Come pray at the Roman Catholic Church where you will be forgiven for your sins. It had a picture of Jesus dying on the cross. It was the new symbol of the church. At that time, I totally forgot all about praying and my curse.

I was fired up. My emotions got the better of me and my blood was boiling. I went to the hut to get my robes and hood to cover my face. I went to get the spear with one thought on my mind. How dare they kill him and use him for profit. It was like they killed him just for this reason. Why did he have to die for us? We are not worthy of the garden. I made my way to the temple where we once used to spread our words.

The Romans now used the church for this Catholic religion. There were gold crosses encrusted in jewels with a figure of Jesus on it. Where they stuck the nails they had rubies there for his blood. This was a beautiful false idol and so I stuck the spear right through it. Shattered it into pieces, the spear felt my anger the two holy Grails together in rage. The power of us two together could shake the world.

I broke the doors down. I slammed the spear onto the temple floor until the temple shook the vale ripped. I began to swing the spear wildly, hitting everything I could while looking around for any false idol that I could find. I stopped when I saw a statute the size of a man. It was Jesus on the cross with the words he died for our sins. The eyes began to follow me. I saw the reflection of me with spear in head. I fell to my knees in front of the statute, remembering the words "do not let the spear fall in the wrong hands."

It had nothing to do with me destroying the temple. It was the anger in my heart. I ran out of the temple to the port and paid a man to take me home. I stayed below the deck the whole time looking at the spear. I told myself that I will never drink blood again. I finally made it back home. My servant asked me how was the trip but I stayed silent. They asked me what happened to my eyes as they thought I was blind. I told them life in Jerusalem had changed me but I'm not blind.

They seemed to be happy that I was ok and they asked me about Jesus. They asked me if I met him and I told them yes. They asked me what was he like and I told them the son of God was the greatest man to ever live. They asked me was he really the son of God and I told them yes as I walked away. I placed the spear over the top of the aegis and the sounds of battle and the power of the spear sent chills through my body. Seeing them together was like looking at the last power of God on earth.

I asked my servants to bring me blood from the livestock they kill. I told them I needed it for rituals for the son of God. I didn't want to tell them I was going to drink it. The blood of livestock was bitter and it was hard to drink. It did not fulfill my hunger although it did stop the lust. I stored blood for the later days when I break down.

One night, one of my servants snuck into my bed as she wanted me to make love to her. I could fill her blood flowing and the smell of her blood was too much for me to handle. I told her to wait in the bed as I went to drink some of my stored blood. I drank it; it was like sour milk in my mouth. I spit it out of my mouth. I could taste the death and I couldn't take it. The taste of this bad blood made me crave fresh blood.

I wanted to tell her to leave but my lust for blood was too strong. My fangs started to show and once my fangs comes out, there is nothing much that I can do. I jumped on the bed and pierced my teeth into her neck. She loved it and she asked for more. Her eyes began to roll into the back of her head. I understood her, for I had tasted death many times getting the breath taking away from you during sex had to be the greatest feeling.

She told me to stop after I started taking too much blood the taste of death was getting too strong. No one wants to die; tasting it is one thing but to die is another. Everything fights for life because life is a precious nothing wants to die. I drained every drop of blood I could until she died. I felt bad afterwards but not during the course as I was enjoying this fresh blood. Seeing her there dead made my heart ache is this my life forever ten thousand years more of this will change me.

I dragged her body through my hidden chamber and buried her there. Cutting off her head was torture and I must get away. I went back to my room and grabbed the Rhongowennan and Aegis and moved all the precious things into the chamber incase I have to come back to get them. The Shaolin monk attire, the blanket from my beloved Eve, the eye of the sun and most of my jewels and my gold coins all the dear things to my heart I moved there.

Chapter 13: Journey To The Past

I packed my book and took Rhongowennan and aegis with me. I put on my assassin robes and rode off to the sea. I found a crew going to China and coincidentally that was the only place I thought of going. I stood on deck watching the stars under the moonlight as we sailed off into the night. The fresh blood that I just drank and the moon with the two weapons of God gave me this glow.

The crew bowed to me saying my lord Ra-Noor, I know it's you under the mask for you carry his shield. I gave them jewels and told them to keep this quiet. I stayed in the bowls of the ship to keep away from the crew as I didn't want to take anymore lives. The men kept coming down there to check on me. I told them I was ok and there was no need to check on me. A trip from Egypt to China was a couple of months long.

I filled up enough blood from her to last me a while. It was the most blood I ever took from anyone. I did that not even knowing that I was going to take this trip. I was hoping the wind would blow and get us there faster but that didn't happen. Into the second month, I could hear the beating hearts of the crew. My fangs tried to get free but I fought it off.

Their beating hearts were too much for me to bear and I eventually lost control. I stormed out of the bowls of the ship with my fangs out. I told them to jump off the ship so they might have a chance to live. They looked at me like I was crazy but they didn't jump. I hoped they prayed that night because I killed them all, each and every single one of them.

I moved like the wind to each and every one of them. They didn't even see me moving. They just saw the other men bleeding with their heads cut off. They tried to run but it was no hope on this ship. I wasn't thinking at all. I even killed the captain and there was no one left to steer the boot it crashed on this strange island. I wanted to kill myself for my actions and for not being able to control the vampire side of me. I wandered until I found a cave and that became my home for the moment.

I killed every animal I saw. I was losing myself little by little. I became a wild animal as I let my vampire take control. I don't know what happened during those times but I do remember the day I came back. I found myself on a child's neck with my fangs deep inside of him. The child was dead. My God, what have I done, have I become?

That was a very painful moment in life and breaking his neck was even harder. I couldn't let this child turn into me. No one should ever be like this. I did the one thing God hated the most; I did the only thing I could think of. I stuck the spear through my stomach thinking this is the only power that could kill me. I blackout and finally I will rest in peace.

Everything went black and I was just sitting there. Gabriel popped up. He said, hello, my friend. I saw my reflection in his eyes. I was the man I was when I was at the garden in the beginning. I asked Gabriel what is the meaning of this and he said I have lost myself and he’s here to help me find my way. I told him it's too late. Just let me be but he said no, that's not what you do for a friend. I stood up and yelled at him to leave me alone. He smiled at me and said it will all be ok.

I saw a cross pop up and I saw myself as a vampire nailed to the cross. His eyes opened as he pulled himself off the cross and walked over to me. He said, Cain, who are you; I told him I'm the son of Adam. He asked me who he was; I told him you're a vampire and a curse upon the earth. He said, no, Cain. I am you. I told him you're not me you're evil. He said evil or not I'm you but I told him to go away.

He said, no, I will never go away and you cannot fight me. I started to hit him and he said, release your anger. He then hugged me and that left tears in my eyes. He told me it's ok, don't fight me. I am you. Stop fighting yourself. It is of no use and you cannot win. I told him I'm sorry and I accepted him as myself. Gabriel showed me a mirror. Cain, this is who you are. Do not fight it. Control your emotions and become one with yourself. Do not fight it.

You are Cain, the vampire king. Always remember who you are. Everything has two sides. Remember Yin and Yang, the darkness and light he faded away saying remember your heart, remember your heart. I opened my eyes and pulled the spear out of my body. The spear's power had a different light. I was calm and the power in it now was good. It had no anger left inside. The two holy Grails were no longer filled with anger and sadness.

I grabbed the spear and the shield and placed them on my back. I started to realize that I have not seen the sun in over a year. The sun start to rise on my walk and I started to feel weird. With each passing minute, I got weaker and weaker. What's going on? I took the assassin hood off to get my first sight of the sun in a year. It was beautiful for something so small. As seeing the sun again for first the time, it was really big. I stood there under the sun just sitting under its glory.

My face began to burn. I saw a vision the sun with his fang in my neck. I could feel my power draining and I started to panic. I started running; I placed my hood back onto my head only allowing my eyes to show. It stopped the burning but I was weak and so I ran until I found a giant tree and sat there, under the shade till the night came. Another curse upon me; the sun hates me. Great, I can't go out in the sun unless I'm covered.

I could picture Gabriel smiling at me. The thought of that made this new finding much easier. I bowed my head and said thank you my friend. I wondered around till I found a village. There were guards at the gate with armors that I have never seen before. The helmets had horns and a crescent moon on top. I heard the alarm went off, and someone said ninja. The next thing I knew, more guards came with Aegis in one hand and Rhongowennan in another and I was in fighting stance.

The sight of a man with shield in one hand and a two handed weapon held in perfect defense made the men cautious. They began to speak a language that I have never heard before but I understood it. My ears could break down words for me to understand. This was one of my new powers. I let them speak in order to understand the language more. He asked me what a ninja wants in this village.

I began to speak my words and it sounded just like theirs even though I have no idea what a ninja was. They told me not to lie as I was wearing the attire of a ninja. Did you come here to kill our leader? I told them no, I'm just wandering around and I found this place by accident. I saw a man coming from the crowd with no mask on. He looked like Qiao but he was different in a way where he has this long silky hair with a sword by his side.

I heard him whisper to them to put their swords down and they said my lord and put the swords back into something. The man said when you have known a ninja to use the gate. The men put away their swords and so I put my shield back onto my back and placed the Rhongowennan by my side with the tip pointing up. The man asked me what I wanted and I told him that I was just wandering around.

I took of my hood and their eyes immediately got larger. He said you're not Japanese or Chinese. I told him no, I am an Egyptian and I'm far from home.

I was wondering around and my ship had unfortunately crashed on this strange island. He said you're in Japan, Egyptian. I remember Qiao telling me stories of the beautiful island of Japan. He told me they practice Buddhism too. I bowed my head with palm to fist rolled up my sleeve and forward my arm out.

It was dark and so he walked up cautiously to me. He grabbed my arm and saw the dragon vs. the tiger tattoo. He had this shocked look on his face. He then rolled up his sleeve and showed me his dragon vs. the tiger tattoo as well. He bowed with palm to fist and he said his name is Hiroki, welcome to the village of the rising sun. Once again another village, story or person with the name sun in it or about it. Why do people love the sun so much?

As I walked through the village, all the people were standing outside. The alarm must have waked them. I could hear them whispering as I walked by. I heard it was a ninja attacking; the people starred at me as I walked pass. I heard them say who is this strange looking man? Hiroki showed me to the place that I would be staying. I then thanked him for his kindness. He bowed and said you're welcome, now get some rest.

The house floors had soft wood as floors while the inside wall was made of this green wood. The house was full of paper walls or what I thought was walls. I touched one of the paper walls and it shook. Something was behind it. I started to feel around the paper walls until I found a carving in the wooden border. I stuck my hand in it and pulled it. To my delight, the wall moved. It was really a door to my room what a clever idea.

The bed was on the floor like the good old days. I felt at home with just the sight of them bed. I slept well that night, finally with some peace in my heart. I must continue to learn to balance the power inside of. I knew it was the only way I would be ok. Just because I accepted who I was, it doesn't mean one day I might reject it.

The next day, Hiroki came knocking and said let's take a short walk and talk for a bit. I stepped back from the sunlight and he immediately notices it and asked what was wrong. I told him the reason that I wear the ninja outfit or whatever that was, was because the sun burns my skin. He then asked if he could come in and I told him that this is his house so he can do whatever he wants. He smiled and said this might be his village but for the moment, this is my house.

He walked in, grabbed the table from my room pour some tea into the pot and sat on the floor in front of the table. This was all new to me. I have never sat on the floor with a table before. I sat down and it took me a while to get comfortable. He laughed and said I see you have never done this before. I said never in my life but I can adjust to it as I have always adjusted before. Hiroki asked me where I got the tattoo if I don't mind.

I told him I don't mind as I have once stayed at the Shaolin Temple before. He said the Shaolin Temple; you stayed with the great monks? I said yes, they gave me the tattoo. Hiroki said if they gave you the tattoo that means you're a Shaolin Monk. I never had a Shaolin Monk in my presence before. I heard many great stories about them and they were the peace keepers of China. Their power is unmatched. They said once a Shaolin Monk meditated near a wall for a year, the wall grew a hole from the power of this monk.

When he told me this tale, all I could do was to smile, remembering Buddha and picturing that hole in the wall. I doubt they ever fixed it. I told him I saw the hole but I didn't know why it was there. Hiroki asked me how I was able to speak Japanese and understand it if I have never been here before. I told him Chinese and Japanese words are familiar and that is the reason why I can break down the words in my head and understand. I learned many languages in my life. He smiled saying that I speak as if I’m an old man.

I told him I'm not as young as he thinks I am. He said you're no older than forty. You look like you are in your twenties but the words you speak are from an older man. I just smiled and said that I couldn't tell him how old I was and he probably wouldn't believe me anyway. The tea was ready and so he poured the tea into our glasses.

He asked me what my name is and I told him that I'm Cain. Hiroki said it is nice to meet you Cain. Hiroki said I heard Egypt is a magical kingdom full of Gods. I told him no, Egypt is full of people who think they are Gods. Hiroki said Japan is the same while he raised his cup and we both hit our cups against each other's. We both bowed our heads. He told me if I feel like going out to see the village, I am more than welcome to do so. Hiroki said I will have tea with you every day if I'd like and I told him I would like that.

I went back into my room. Over my bed was a giant painting of the dragon vs. the tiger tattoo. I went back to sleep and had a dream of me and my vampire self fighting but it was a happy fight. I started off as the dragon. I had scales with long claws while he had stripes and it was grand. I turn into the tiger while he turned into the dragon. I could feel Gabriel watching us and I could feel his happiness. Then the dream changed and we were both outside the garden with the Rhongowennan and Aegis.

As the two spears clashed, a glow came from them; mine was white while his was black. The two souls were in perfect harmony. Aegis would not crack no matter how hard we hit it, the shield was happy too. His purpose was to fight. Aegis also had a glow of black and white. It was a draw. We bowed to each other with no words spoken. We knew what the other was thinking. I woke up a couple of hours later before the sunset.

I put on my assassin's attire. I opened the door and saw the sunlight. I was hesitant as the sun was strong but no matter what, I still loved the sun. I stepped out but I got weak as soon as the light touched me. I can't live my life with fear.

Understand every human in life has fear. It's what you do with the fear that counts. The ones that conquer that fear are the ones that will truly live. The village was an inspiration as it melted my heart with every look.

The village was up on a hill, the wind blew through the village like a dream. The people stood up with the wind and opened their arms. As I walked around the village, the people bowed to me. I found some men in meditation and

I sat down to join them. As the day passed, I could feel my strength growing as the sun moved to west. I walked to a hill, felt some inspiration, took a deep breath and closed my eyes.

I placed my arms forward with my fingers into a claw and felt the tiger inside. I began to swing my right arm out, knee forward and the dance of the tiger immediately flowed through me. Two arms thrusting forward, I rotated right; I rotated left back and forth. Thrust my arms back, kicked my right leg in the air and held it in perfect form. I had not practiced in a long time but I remembered everything. I channeled my spirit and I thrust the force out. The new found power together with the Almighty Push sent the force in a circle all around me.

The grass flowed with the force and it looked like the wave of an ocean. I turned and saw Hiroki. He was there watching. I asked him how long he has been standing there and Hiroki said that he has been there the whole time and that he couldn't turn away from me. He felt the power from me pouring out over the hill. Watching me was like a dream perfect form, perfect stances and perfect strikes. He then asked how I made the grass turn into an ocean.

I told him the monks taught me how to channel the force from the inside and force it out. That was the first time the force came out in a circle. I did not know it could come out all around me. Hiroki said the force of the wave moved me back. I smiled and told him that I was sorry and I didn't know that he was there plus I had no idea it would do that. Hiroki smiled back at me and said that it was ok. It was like the flow of heaven and I was touched by this power.

We sat there on the hill watching the sunset. I turned and saw the whole village watching the sunset. I asked him what was going on and he said for as long as he can remember, we have been doing it. My ancestors started the tradition many suns ago and we still do it till today. He bowed his head to the sunset. I then looked around and the whole village was bowing. My power had returned I took off my assassin's hood and the dragon and the tiger was whole again.

Hiroki said the sun is the life of our world. Without it, nothing will live. He said we show our respect by bowing to it every day. We have a saying in our village that the sun is the first father, the first father is there shining down giving life to all. Hiroki said God honored the first by turning him into the sun so that he can watch over his children forever. I pictured my father Adam as the sun; I could picture him inside the sun using the mightiest Almighty Push to give life to all. The thought of that made a tear fall from my eye.

Hiroki asked me if he had offended me but I told him that was a tear of joy. Hiroki said that he was glad his words had brought me joy. He asked me how I was with a sword; I gave him my grin and said I'm alright. He said good and maybe I can practice with them tomorrow. I told I would like that very much. I sat there under the stars all night but I made no wishes as I had nothing to wish for. I went in early that night knowing I would soon lust for blood.

The next day, I went out at the same time but I would not go out before the sun moved four hours to the west. Once again, the people bowed as I walked through the village. I found Hiroki at the training grounds. He said he was glad that I came. The swords they used were about two feet from end to end. It had a slight curve like a branch on a tree with a lot of leaves. I never saw a sword like that before. It was the best looking sword I ever seen.

The handle had some type of cloth around it with a circular piece of metal where the blade started. Hiroki handed me the sword and held it out with one hand. I asked him where the shield is and he said there is no shield; he said we hold it like this. Hiroki place one hand under the circular piece of metal and the other near the bottom. I grabbed the sword just like Hiroki did and it was light as a feather.

He pointed to a man he came over and bowed to me. Hiroki said he will be my opponent. I then bowed my head to him and Hiroki asked if I was ready and I said yes. My opponent placed his leg forward and bent it. He held the sword still in the center of his body with his shoulders squared. It's been a while since I have used a sword with two hands so I had to recall the steps. My opponent charged while I stood there waiting. I needed to read his actions. His first strike was perfect but I blocked it.

I swung back and he blocked it with the circular metal piece on the sword. He swung the sword again and I dodged it. I proceeded to step forward and swung my sword right after. He spun around me to my other side. I never saw footwork like this before. He stepped around me like a dancer's feet in perfect union. First foot stepped forward while the second foot stepped to the right; he held the sword sideways to block any attack that I would have tried. He spun his body like the wind on just his right foot.

He was behind but he didn't strike. He just used Kung Fu with the art of the sword. I would have never thought of that. Now I understood what I was up against and so I placed my left leg forward and swung. He blocked it while I sled my sword down at his blade, placing my strength forward. He tried to use his strength but that was a losing battle and so he retreated. That was the moment that I have been waiting for and so I swung forward while he was retreating. I hit his sword right under the circular piece of metal and forced the blade out from his hand and the fight was immediately over.

We then bowed to each other. Hiroki asked if I was ready to go again and I said yes. He pointed another opponent, jumped in and I wasted no time this time round. I hit his sword under the circular metal piece on the first swing and it was over. Hiroki jumped up and said excellent. One more round. This time Hiroki was my opponent. I tried the same thing but Hiroki held the sword down as I swung even though I hit his blade. He swung right after I lost my balance but I recovered quickly.

He placed the sword by his side and swung the sword from the side I blocked the first attack. He spun the sword around in the air; moving his hands off the sword. He grabbed it again with the hand he took off and came straight down with the sword. He forced my sword down and kicked me right in the chest. Hiroki said the sword is not the only weapon you have. Your body is also a weapon. Hiroki won this round and I bowed and told him that I will remember his teachings.

Hiroki said let's go for a walk and so we did. I saw the people planting something in the water. I asked Hiroki what were they doing and he said the people were planting crops for rice. He asked if I have ever had rice before and I looked at him and said come on, I lived with the monks and that was all we ate. He said yes, that's right, you did. I told him no matter what, I still love rice. Hiroki said well, because we are about to eat some rice. I could smell the rice from here as the people started to gather at the field area.

All the villagers were here; the woman, the children and all the men. There were two giant pots on fire and it smelled amazing. Hiroki told me the children will eat first, the women go next and the men will go last. I had no problem with that although it was different to the times where I was used to the men eating first and leaving the women with the leftovers. It was a refreshing change to see the women treated like gifts again. That practice has been lost many suns and moons ago.

The sun was starting to set we sat in the fields eating. We all bowed to the sun as it was setting. They lit some fire once it got dark and I can finally take this damn hood off. Under the fire, the women sang songs while the children ran around playing. The men with wives sat there with their wives embracing them with hugs. I pictured Eve on the hill with me with her head on my shoulder. I sat there eating the rice but no matter how good it was, it still didn't stop my hunger.

I must go on a hunt so I won't kill any villagers. Everybody went in after a while I stayed on the hill until the ghosts were clear. I vanished from the hill. I found a horned creature like a deer and I immediately pierced my fangs deep inside. The animals blood taste nothing like humans but it had to do. I got my fill of his blood till I couldn't take in more. I had enough blood inside for over a week. Hiroki came in the next day for tea and we sat there on the table. He asked me if I had heard that and I told him no. He then drew his sword.

He said it’s coming from your room. He sled the door open slowly and he said no one is here. He started to walk around the room and he stopped at Aegis. Now I understood what he heard. Hiroki said it's funny but I think it's coming from the shield. I asked him if he can hear it and Hiroki said yes. Where is it coming from? I told him I think you know. He said there is no way that it's coming from where I think it is.

I told him to touch it and so he walked over slowly, reached out his hand and touched it. His eyes closed and he could feel the spirit of this living relic. He jumped back and asked me how this is possible. I told him its name is Aegis. He asked it has a name that you did not name? I said yes, it is the shield of a God. Hiroki asked, what God? I told Hiroki that there is only one God and he made it.

Hiroki rubbed his hand over the Aegis; he said I can hear all the battles the shield has been in. Hiroki said, this is amazing then he looked at

Rhongowennan and said that is a beautiful spear. He touched it and I could see the fear in his eyes as he bowed to Rhongowennan. A tear fell from his eye. He grabbed his ribs and turned to me and thanked me. I asked him what that was for. With tear in his eye, he said, my pain is gone; the pain in my ribs are gone. It has healed me. I said what are you talking about? It healed you?

He said Rhongowennan took away his pain. I told him I had no idea it could do that. He asked me where did it come from and I told him to let's sit down and talk about it. He turned to Rhongowennan and bowed to it again. I told him to pour the tea. Hiroki's hand was shaking as he poured. I told him that is the spear that killed the son of God. Hiroki said that is what killed Jesus? I then asked how he knew his name.

Hiroki said that story of the son of God being killed in Jerusalem has been told to all. He said I never knew his name until right now and I think the spear did it. He asked me if I knew him and I said yes, he was my friend. Hiroki then asked if he was really the son of God. I gave him a dumb look and said, what do you think? Hiroki said that he believed in him after touching the spear. Hiroki asked me what he was like.

I told him he was a walking peace; he was the strongest man alive but never used his power to harm a bug. He used his powers to heal disease and to bring happiness. He was the greatest man to walk the earth. He will forever be missed and the world will never forget him. I really didn't think that was true when I said it neither did I think Leonidas, Aristotle, Menes and Alexander would be either. Hiroki asked why the son of God allowed them to kill him.

I told him he did it for us as his death opened the gates of heaven for us. Hiroki said I will pray to him every day from now on and get the villagers to do it too. I said he will like that and thank you for honoring my friend. We had tea every day; we bowed to the sun every day. I was in paradise. I loved to sit up on the hill and watch the stars; I did this every night while the villagers slept. I loved to practice my Kung Fu under the moonlight.

One day, while I was practicing under the moonlight, I heard a few footsteps. I turned around and it was a woman walking towards my way. She was beautiful with long silky hair and a narrow face with a small perky nose. She said I didn't mean to alarm you, keep going; I love to watch you train. I gave her a weird look; she said I come out here to see you on top of the hill. I never said anything. I just watched but today for some reason, I wanted to get closer. I told her it is fine. This village is your home and I'm just here to learn. She said do you mind if I sit down with you? I am not able to sleep.

I said sure. She said her name is Emi and I bowed to her and said my name is, but before I could finish, she said Cain. Emi said everyone in the village knows your name. It’s not often we get strangers in our village but an Egyptian that's never happened. I told her it was a pleasure to meet her and she said the same to me. She asked me what I was trying to learn. I looked at her and said everything. She smiled and said that's a lot to learn. I told her I got nothing but time on my hands.

I told there is one thing I want to know and she asked what it was. What is this ninja? She said ninjas are assassins that use the art of ninjutsu to kill their opponents. She said they fight in stealth, throwing metal stars from afar. They use small katanas and move like the wind. I asked her if there were any ninjas that have ever attacked the village and she said yes, they tried to kill Hiroki many times. I asked her why would they want to kill Hiroki. Emi then said that Hiroki is the reason the emperor can't take over the land.

I asked if the emperor is the king and she said yes, he wants all the land to himself. Our ancestors have lived in this village for over a thousand years and we will not give it up. I told her you should never give this place up; this is like heaven on earth. I told her I have been around many kings and most of them would always want to conquer lands. Emi told me Hiroki is the one who unites the samurai together. The emperor believes if Hiroki dies, the samurai will be divided.

Emi said what the emperor doesn't understand is that even if Hiroki is killed, he still won't get our lands. She said none of the villages want to be slaves and we will all rather die. I told her freedom is the only way to live and that life without freedom is nothing. She told me I have beautiful eyes. They glow under the moonlight and she has never seen anything like it before. I thank her for that and told her that my eyes were a gift given to me by God. Emi said everything is a gift given by god. I told her she's right as life itself is a gift.

From that moment onwards, I had a friend in Emi. Almost every night on the hill, Emi was there with me under the stars. She even knew Kung Fu. We practiced together and it was like a painting. We chased each other under the moonlight; we rolled down the hill many times under the moon laughing at the way down. I continued sneaking off to hurt animals and I finally got myself under control. I finally learned to like the blood of animals.

I trained with Hiroki but I never used my powers to fight him. I wanted to beat him with my own strength.

Hiroki without the rib problem was too much for me. I may never beat him, not even once. Fighting Hiroki made me so strong that no one could touch me or get close to me. I beat everyone else but never Hiroki. Hiroki was like a God with a sword in his hand unmatched by anyone. I always enjoyed tea time and training with him.

Emi became more than a friend. One day rolling down the hill, I stopped on top of her, her face and her hair shined under the moonlight and I proceeded to kiss her. I couldn't help myself. You see, when a man and a woman spends that much time with each other, magic always happens. She was my moonlight and I made love to her every night we never missed a night. Outside on the porch where she rest, the candles would always attract a moth.

No matter how hot is was, the moth never stopped. I thought which one of us is the moth, which one of us is the flame? Both of us just knew what to do to attract each other. She made me feel like I was young again. I have lived over a hundred lifetimes and only found three people I loved. Love is the most powerful feeling that we can share and have. I noticed that I could only love when I loved myself.

She made me forget that I was a vampire, that I will forever be cursed to walk this world. Emi and I always eat together when the villagers gathered once a week for feast time. She would always lay her head on my shoulder; such a beautiful feeling love is. I ran my mouth with her as much as I could. She loved to hear to me talk, let me stop lying and she loved that I just wanted to talk to her. She would tell me to be quiet with a smile saying that I talk too much.

So I would stay quiet and she would get in my face. I would turn and she would come to the other side till I said something. She would say she feels better now and I would push her and runaway. She would chase me saying I'm going to get you. Whenever I was quiet on my own, she would ask me what was wrong with a smile. I would tell her, woman make up your mind. She would jump on me and say come on, big mouth speak.

I was truly happy at this time. I never wanted to leave this place ever. I knew I couldn't stay forever because my life didn't allow me to stay in one place for a long time. I don't know how many moons and suns I have seen but it didn't matter, I was happy. I finally got to see the ninjas face to face. One day during our weekly gathering, they finally attacked the village. They came out of nowhere. We heard the alarm as soon as the sunsets.

The woman and the children ran to the houses where the men gathered their swords. They surrounded Hiroki and chants to protect Hiroki were heard in the air. I waited with my sword in hand for the attack but I didn't see anyone coming. I heard something cutting through the wind. Suddenly, I saw a metal star coming my way. I raised my sword and struck it down. I heard footsteps coming from the shadows and told the men to prepare themselves because they were coming.

They came running out of the darkness; dressed in black from feet to head; nothing was shown but their eyes. They already had their swords drawn and were aiming to kill. Suddenly, twenty plus men ambushed us from the darkness. If it wasn't for my hearing, I would not have heard them coming. They moved like the wind with the talent of a bug that crawls around a house with discreet. I took down the first one I saw.

I stepped in with force and swung the sword to the left. I could feel his flesh rip as my sword came down. The smell of fresh blood excited me but I controlled my lust. I smelt blood coming from behind me. As I looked, there were villagers there lying dead. The moonlight was the only way the villagers could see the ninjas. They would step in strike and jump back out to regroup. You have to have quick reflexes to survive the assault.

Every time one jumped at me from the shadows, I could see them before they struck. I sliced through the next one's blade, shattering it in half as my sword ripped his flesh. The next time, two came my way and I held my sword to the side so I could strike them both with a single blow. They never had a chance as they had no idea who they were up against. I turned after I killed the two the ninjas and managed to separate Hiroki from the group.

Hiroki, the greatest swordsman to ever live took on four at a time. He had a metal star stuck in his arm but that didn't stop him, not one bit. They surrounded him to strike, all at once. He wasted no time and so he struck the first one and grabbed him. He grabbed the ninja and spun him around, making one of the ninjas strike his own man. At this moment, at least three villagers were dead. The smell in the air was starting to get stronger.

I ran in to aid Hiroki. I came out of nowhere and struck the ninja through his back. More ninjas came after finding their target. Hiroki was starting to get tired. I knew I had to do something so I turned into a tiger. I cut through the wind with every strike and not a single one managed to lay a hand on me. The ninjas started to retreat while I ran after them. Once I got into the darkness, I dropped my sword.

It was time for a hunt. My fangs came protruding out from my mouth. I chased the ninja up the wall. As soon as he got over, I was on top of him with my fangs in his neck. You could hear his screams throughout the village as I drained his blood. The first taste of human blood in a long time gave me blood lust and made I want more. I tracked another ninja running through the woods. I moved through the trees so no one could see me.

I found my target. I could hear his heart beating faster and faster. I jumped out of the trees with my mouth wide open. I touched him with my fangs before I touched him with anything else. I don't have to tell I cut off their heads, do I? All my strength had returned no more half the man, I was whole, whole with power. I looked up at the moon and smiled, turned, and vanished. I appeared in the village and saw that they had a ninja captured.

The women were attending to Hiroki's wounds. He had a few deep cuts but he was ok. Four of the villagers died and they prayed for them, and rejoiced in their deaths. If you don't know one of the ways of the samurai, is to die in battle. To die in battle is an honorable death and that makes no mistakes that the men will still be missed. I saw Emi came running out the house. She had a sigh of relief when she saw my face.

After the fight, Hiroki began teaching me the way of the samurai, which is now known as Bushido. It was just like the Shaolin monks but a little different. The monks were about peace and they never wanted to fight unless they had too. Bushido was all about fighting and dying with honor. They still had some of the same principles which are to protect the weak and never fight unless you have too. The monks wanted nothing more but to die in piece. The samurai wanted nothing but to die in battle.

Hiroki took me to a special place just outside the village on a hill top. He told that me this was the place his ancestors were buried. It was a magical place with pink locus flowers. Hiroki told me that they were called cherry blossoms. They are special trees in Japan that means peace. The smell in the air was enchanting. I stared at the tree and had a flashback. I remembered seeing them in the garden, the tree of peace. I guess there were still some things from the garden that's still in this world.

They gave me hope that I would find more things throughout my life. He told me the trees grow throughout Japan in any weather. I asked Hiroki if I could have some seeds as I would like to plant some in my courtyard. Hiroki said, yes, my friend. I will bring you some. I thanked Hiroki for that and he said that I'm welcome as it is the least he can do for me. I continued training with Hiroki and loving Emi. Spending tea time with Hiroki while hill time was with Emi was pure joy.

I knew I could not stay here too much longer as the risk of me killing a villager was too great. I knew how to tell Hiroki goodbye but for Emi, I had no idea what to say at all. Hiroki must have known I was going to leave soon. I don't know how long I have stayed there but I know it has been years. We had tea as usual and Hiroki suddenly said I know you're leaving soon. I want to present you a gift before you leave. I told him that he didn't have to but he wasn't going to take a no for an answer. He unwrap the blanket and there was a sword with a kimono inside.

The kimono was blue and white with the Japanese rising sun on the sleeves. The sun was red along with the rays. I told him I loved it he told me to look at the sword. The sword sheath had a hand painting of a tiger. I pulled the sword out and there were words in Japanese. I could speak the language but couldn't read it. I asked him what it means and he explained to me that it meant the Egyptian tiger. I smiled and thanked him for that. Hiroki said no matter where I go, I will always be remembered in the village of the rising sun.

Hiroki asked me if I had told Emi about it and I said no. I told Hiroki that I didn't know how to tell her and he said the truth was all I need. I had to tell her tonight I think as I will be leaving soon. That night, while on the hill, I was quiet. She noticed and asked if my tongue was hurting. I smiled and said, no Emi. She then asked if I was leaving soon. I asked her how she knew. She said, I never thought you were going to stay here forever. I told her that I want to but I can't and she just brushed that aside and said enough about that and let's just enjoy the night.

We made love right there and then on the hill, under the moonlight. After we were done, I told her that I'm going to leave the night after today. If I stayed on any longer, I don't think I will ever leave. She said, ok, I understand. The next day at tea time, I told Hiroki that I was going to leave tonight. He wished me well on my trip and told me that I will always be his friend and he enjoyed all the time spent with me. Night came and it was time to say goodbye. Hiroki left a horse for me to travel with.

I sat on the hill for about an hour, knowing that I was going to miss this place. It was time to make my journey back home and so I hopped on my horse and immediately saw the villagers came out. They all bowed as I walked passed. I looked around for Emi but I didn't see her. I guess it was all too much for her and probably was for the best. They opened the gate and to my surprise, Emi was there on a horse. She asked me if I was ready to go. I then asked her where we were going.

Chapter 14: Can't Escape Your Fate

Emi said wherever life takes us with a big smile. We held hands on the horses as we talked. We rode off to the port and Emi was leading the way. The winds were on our side and we managed to get there in a month. During the ship ride, we slept during the day and went out at night. We sat there under the stars while enjoying the sea breeze. She would get cold as we slept and so I would just use my body heat to keep her warm.

When Emi saw Egypt, her eyes sparkled in delight. The first thing she said was it was really hot. I told her this is nothing as it will usually get much hotter. She said I'm so looking forward to that and I told her she will get use to it. As we rode further in, Emi asked me if the whole place is covered in sand and I told her yes. She smiled and said it's ok as long as we are together. We rode up to the palace her eyes lit up again. Emi said that is one beautiful castle. Whoever owns it must be happy. I didn't say a word while we rode up to the gate. Emi asked if we were going in I told her yes.

She said we can actually see the inside and I told her yes. You could see the happiness on her face. The guards said my lord; you have returned with a guess, I said yes. By the time we made it to the door, my servants were waiting for me. My lord, you have returned. I had feared you died. They then turned and looked at Emi. I see you brought a slave from Asia? I told them she is not my slave. She is my new wife and her name is Emi. Emi couldn't speak Egyptian and so she had no idea what was going on.

Emi ask me if there was a problem and I told her no and everything was ok. They took our horses and asked Emi to go along with them. I told them she doesn't understand but I will tell her to. I told Emi to go with them and that everything is ok and she agreed. I told her that I will see her soon and they took her off. They took her off to the washing area and put on new clothes. I didn't tell her because I wanted it to be a surprise. I went to my room to change and wash. Not long later, I heard a knock on the door.

It was my servants. They told me that my wife has returned. She came in confused with new silk robes, clean hair and a freshly oiled scent. She asked me what's going on and why were they being so nice. I told her it's because I told them that you're my wife. Emi's face lit up and she immediately put her arms around me and kissed me. She asked if I had really told them she was my wife. I said yes and she then immediately asked why I haven't I answer her question on why they were being so nice.

I told her it's because you're the wife of the house now. Wife of the house, is this your house. I said no and then paused for a while and said this is our house. Emi jumped on top of me. I can't believe this is your house, I said ours. She then said I can't believe this is our house. Emi asked who I was and so I told her that I'm the high priest of Egypt. There is no one else in Egypt that ranks above of me. She asked me if I was the emperor and I told her no but I'm close to it. I told Emi that she is now the empress of this castle.

She made love to me right there on the spot. She could not control herself as she was just too happy. I enjoyed that very much. One of the few times I laid there and did nothing. We slept the day away. The fact that she slept throughout the day had made my life easier. I managed to hide the fresh blood that I drank. When I took her into town with me, everyone would tell me how beautiful she was.

Emi would hear the people call me Ra-Noor and she asked me if that is what they called me. I told her yes and she then asked me what it meant and I told her it was the Egyptian God of the sun. Emi asked me why they called me that; I told her the Egyptian people thought I was the god Ra in human form. Emi smiled and asked if I was really him. I laughed and said no. I then went on to plant the cherry blossoms seed in my courtyard.

Emi loved the courtyard so we spent most of our nights under the locus trees. I don't know if it was the weather or the food but Emi started to get sick. She had a steady cough that never left. No matter what medicine I gave her, nothing stopped the cough. I was starting to get worried. I tried not to show it but it was hard. Emi was always happy even though she knew she was sick. I did whatever I could to make her happy and kept her mind off the pain.

On the days that was hard for her to move, I would carry her to the balcony to let her rest under the moon. She would tell me that she was sorry that she was sick. I told her to never apologize for something like that. I told her I will be thereby her side. The Egyptian people who found out she was sick would come and pray for her. She would tell me that she would do anything to stay by my side.

She started to get really sick one day. She could no longer leave the bed. I must do something before she dies and so I sat by her bedside. Emi touched my face. She said she was sorry that she could not stay much longer. I didn't want to lose her and so I told her that I can cure her disease. Her eyes lit up and she said to give it to her. I want to be with you if it is just for a little longer. I put my head down and told her that this cure comes with a cost. Emi said I don't care what the cost is as long as I can be by your side.

I took a deep breath and told her ok. I then released my fangs and told her to close her eyes as it may hurt a little but you must trust me. She looked right into my eyes and said I trust you with all my heart and closed her eyes. I sank my fangs into her neck and started to drink her blood. The sweet blood of my love filling my body was both a great feeling and sadness. The taste of her blood was pure joy but the thought of turning her into a vampire hurt my heart. She drifted away while I stayed there by her bedside for twenty four hours.

She jumped up out her sleep or should I say her death. She looked at me and asked what was going on. It took me a second to answer and I told her that she was alive again. Emi asked me how is she still alive with no signs of sickness. I then told her that I gave her my blood. Emi asked your blood? How could your blood do this? I told her my blood can cure death but it comes with a great price. Emi told me she never felt this strong before. Emi said she could hear and see better than ever.

She asked me what the price of this was. I told her that she has to drink blood to survive. She gave me this look of terror and said, you mean blood, blood? I said yes my love. I'm sorry that you're now a hunter of the night. Emi asked me who I was and so I told her that I'm the fourth human being to ever live. I'm older than ten thousand years old. She began to move back on the bed and said I don't believe you. I stood up and vanished and appeared behind her in the bed.

She jumped forward and asked me how I did that. I then appeared on the other side of her and she immediately took a step back. I showed her my fangs and bit her on the neck. She moaned in pleasure but I stopped and told her to try. She breathed deep and her fangs came from her mouth and she struck them into my neck. For some odd reasons, getting your blood drained felt good. I had to stop her because she was getting carried away.

Emi backed up with her eyes rolled into the back of her head. That was almost too beautiful. She said the taste of my blood was sweet so she couldn't stop herself. I took her outside to the courtyard and I told her to close her eyes and listen. She told me she could hear the voices of people talking far away. She told me she could see the fly on the wall. I started talking to her in Egyptian and she could immediately answer me back with I'm happy. I asked her how she felt and she was amazed and asked I can understand Egyptian now?

I told her that she can now hear all. She began to touch the trees and she told me that she can hear and feel their life force. She said so this is how you feel, hear and see. I'm glad you shared this world with me. That night, we wandered the desert seeking out the secrets of the night. We came in before the sun and laid in bed under me the whole night. I whispered softly to her that we can never die. She smiled and said that's good then. I can now be with you forever.

Now I didn't have to hide the blood from her anymore. We drank the blood like it was wine, making toasts to our new life. She would say this blood doesn't taste like yours. I told her human blood is the best but I don't want to kill anyone. When the servants came into the room, Emi would stare them down. I would touch her back to calm her down. I showed her the secret passage so she could move freely without being seen.

Emi was the first person that I have turned into a vampire willingly. Emi embraced the night. She was already a night owl so she took the new life with great joy. One day, while I was in the courtyard alone, I heard a scream coming from our room so I raced off. As I got closer, the smell of blood got stronger, this wasn't animal blood. It was human blood. I opened the door to find Emi in the corner crying with one of the servants dead on the floor. I went over to Emi and all she could say was I'm sorry. I told her it was ok. I even took many lives when I first turned into a vampire.

I told her that it will be alright. I grabbed the body and buried it in the secret passage. I told Emi no one would find out but still she couldn't let it go. She stayed in bed all night just curled up. She got up the next night and told me she was going to pay respect to the person she killed. I told her ok and I will be here if she needs me. I stayed there in bed, thinking that it must be hard on her. She stayed down there till the sun came up.

I was going to go check on her because she left the passage door open. I thought I was hearing things and I heard two pairs of footsteps one moving forward one moving back. I jumped up and ran through the passage. I saw Emi backing up and saw the servant she killed walking towards her. Emi asked me what's going on. I stayed silent thinking to myself. Did Emi turn her into a vampire? I smelled the dead servant blood and it smelled just like mine. She was a vampire.

I told Emi that she is now a vampire. Emi asked if it was her who did that. I breathed deep and said yes my love Emi and ran off. I walked up to the servant she stopped and bowed and said master. Why did she just call me master? What is going on? No time to think. Emi was losing herself and so I broke the servant's neck and ran to Emi. Before I could stop her, she struck a sword into her stomach.

She looked at me crying and asked why she can't die. I told her that I'm sorry and it will get better in time. She said she was missing the sun and that she wanted to see the sun. She got up and opened the door to the balcony and vanished in the sun. The sun had burned her body instantly. I immediately ran over but all that was left of her was the blood on the sword. I didn't cry because I was too shocked that it all happened so fast. I was just trying to figure out what had just happened.

The sun just weakens me but it will kill the others. When she died, a tear of blood ran down my face. I knew this tear was different. It ran down my face slowly and it didn't feel like water. I didn't know what to make of the tear or even what just happened. I was a mess after Emi died hearing the servants ask where my wife was made it hard. I told them her mother was sick and she went home to be at her side.

They said they will pray for her safe return. Months went by and they still asked how she was doing. Years went by they still asked when she is going to return. I just told them I don't know and everything was just too much to bear in my soul. I packed my belongings, setting off to never return. I hopped onto the nearest ship. This one was taking me to the land of Europe. I got on with no hesitation as it was time to start a new.

Chapter 15: The Passing of Blood

I kept myself in solitude. I didn't want to get close to anyone. I had a castle built in Britain. I instantly became a lord. Being a lord simply means that you're rich or someone who comes from a royal family. My skin started to get lighter from the lack of sun and my hair texture also changed.

I become the man that we all know today. My powers started to grow stronger and I could instantly teleport to any spot in my eyesight. I could see the heat from animals and people in the night. There was no such thing as total darkness to me as I could see everything.

The sun no longer weakened me. Seeing the sun the first time in centuries without a mask or hood was grand. I stayed under the sun in my new courtyard every day. My courtyard was full of cherry blossom and locus trees. The smell in the spring was marvelous. I heard stories about the castle where no one has ever seen the inside. They say the castle was haunted and that a wizard has lived there for centuries.

I would grin and shake my head. I loved to hear the stories plus it made the people stay away. Once in a while, the youngsters would come to my palace to see if it was haunted. I would put on my Ra mask and scare them away. That brought me much joy as I was alone and I managed to find ways to amuse myself. I had two pet wolves, moon and star and we hunted at night together. We cornered many animals and chased them to each other. This was about four hundred and fifty years after the death of Jesus.

One night while on a hunt, I got lost in the feeding. I heard footsteps and as I looked up, there was a blonde hair girl starring at me in terror. Usually, I would kill anyone who had seen me as a vampire but for some reasons I didn't. I let her run away as I had no reasons to kill this girl. The next day, I heard someone at my gates. The smell was familiar and moon and star got up ready to see what was going on. It was strange because they usually growl when someone was at the gate. I heard my gates opened and so I jumped up immediately. No one has ever been bold enough to open the gates.

My door began to open and I heard the words hello. I hid behind my steps. Thinking to myself, damn, I really need to lock my door sometimes. I looked out to take a peek and it was the girl from last night. How did she find me? Then, I thought, yes all the stories about the castle and seeing me last night, this would be the first place that I would look for too. Moon and star approached her slowly. She backed herself against the wall. I guess anyone seeing two larges wolves would do that as well. They began to sniff the air and to my surprise, they walked up and licked her.

Her fear turned to happiness and she began to rub them. She moved through the fur slowly like she was trying to feel every part of them. She stood up again and said hello, is anyone home? I know you're here and I mean you no harm. She started to look around the castle while staring at all the paintings; she saw Rhongowennan on the wall and reached out her arms. I then appeared right behind her. She jumped back asking where I came from.

I asked her what she was doing here and what she wanted. She told me that her name was Elizabeth and so I asked Elizabeth, what do you want? She told me nothing and said that she saw me last night and that she wanted to see me again. I asked her was she not afraid to die? She said if you wanted to kill me, you would have done it last night. Even though I knew the answer, I asked anyway, how did you find me? She said as a child, she heard a lot of stories about the wizard in the castle.

So I figured that, that was you in the forest last night. She said don't worry, I won't tell no one about what I saw. I told her to leave this castle as it is no place for a woman. Elizabeth said I'm not afraid and I told her no matter what, it is still no place for a woman. I walked back upstairs and she said she was sorry and ran out the castle. I was relived. I thought I might lose control. It was better for the both of us but still, it was nice to have another person in my house even if it was just for a little while.

I continued about my business the next day. The gate opened again with that smell of Elizabeth. Moon and Star jumped up to meet her, so much for my loyal companions. I don't know if it was the fact that they wanted someone new around or did she have something special. No matter what it was, they still betrayed me for Elizabeth. They came running up to her while she was on her knees. They licked and rub themselves all around her. I do admit I was a little jealous.

I walked down the steps and she asked me what they were doing and I told her that they were marking their territory. They seem to like you and she smiled as I said that. I asked her what she was doing here holding a basket in her hands. She said I brought you some food, you do eat food right? I told her yes and to come with me. I don't know why I let her in but I guess I was really lonely.

She smiled the whole way to the table. Moon and star followed her all the way in those little traitors. They even sat down beside her under the table. I took her to a small round table outside my kitchen. She said my house was beautiful I thanked her for that. I asked Elizabeth if she is afraid of me. She said yes, I am very afraid right now but I never let fear get the better of me. Listening to her words made the chains rattle in my heart.

She took some bread, red wine and chicken outside of the basket. She gave Moon and Star some bones and asked me what their names were. I told her the black one is Moon and the white one is Star. She asked me why I named it Moon since it was all black. I told Elizabeth ever since he was a cub, he would howl at the moon. I named the white one Star because she shines bright with Moon.

I found them after a hunter killed their parents and heard them in the den crying. I was going to kill them to ease their suffering but I couldn't do it, no matter if they were just animals or not, it was hard to kill anything so young. Since that day, I have taken care of them and they're my family now. Elizabeth said that's a sweet story. I'm glad you didn't kill them. I got up from the chair and disappeared into the kitchen to grab some glasses for the wine. I was only gone for a second and she asked me how I did that.

I asked her if she remembers I'm a wizard and told her that I have a lot of powers. She asked me how old I was and I told her that I was over ten thousand years old. Her eyes lit up with the sound of my age. She asked me if I was really that old and I said yes, she said you must really be a powerful wizard. I said something like that with a big smile. I haven't smiled at anyone in a long time. It was nice to have company and I told her that it's been years since I had anyone at my table.

Elizabeth said it was an honor to be here at your table and proceeded to raise our glasses for a toast. The only time I saw Moon and Star that quiet was when they were sleeping. I looked at them under the table to give them a dirty look. Those smart little traitors would not look at me in the eye. I guess they enjoyed the company too as we never had a guess in the house before.

We sat there at the table for hours just talking about nothing. I could tell she wanted to ask me more questions but she didn't want to over stay. She got up and left and said I’d love to do this again. I stayed silent and said we shall see. I stayed at the gate until she left my eyesight and continued staying there even after she had left my sight. The fact that she wasn't scared or had the nerves to come over interests me. The next day, she came over again. This time, Moon and Star were waiting for her at the door.

Those little traitors turned on me as soon as someone new comes into the picture. She asked if she can look around but I told her I will show her around instead. I took her to the living room first. She walked around looking at the paintings. I had a picture of Eve over the fire place. Elizabeth asked me who she was and I told her that she was my wife. Elizabeth said she was sorry and that she was beautiful. I thanked her for that. We walked through the hallway leading to the rooms. I had pictures of my old friends over there. Gabriel was first followed by Jacob then Michael, Menes, Ra, Nor-Aha, Anta, Djer, Joseph, Ramses, User, Moses, Qiao, Buddha, Ramses IV, Gorgo, Leonidas, Amyrtaeus, Alexander, Aristotle, Isaac, Jesus, Peter, Philip, John, Matthew, Mary, Hiroki and Emi.

She asked me who all these people were and I told her that these are the people who I called friends throughout my life. Elizabeth said for someone to have lived tens of thousands of years, you sure don't have a lot of friends. I told her that should tell you something the word friend actually means a lot. You can live for hundreds of years and still not find a single friend. A friend is not merely someone you know or even someone of your family. You could grow up with someone and know them until you die and still not be friends. A friend is much more powerful than the word alone.

A friend is someone who loves and cares for you even when you're wrong. They will tell you the truth no matter if it will hurt you. Even after that, you will still be friends. Elizabeth looked at me and said I never had one of them. I told her she is still young and that she will have plenty of time to find one. She smiled and gave me this weird look and said I hope so. She continued to come over every day. I began to look forward to her visits and so did moon and star.

They would leave their beds whenever it is time for her to come over to meet her at the door. I never locked my door so she would just come straight in. I finally asked her on why she would come over every day. She then told me that she was alone as her parents had passed away and that she has no one. I told her I was sorry about that. Hearing this made me understand why she wasn't afraid of me. She started to stay the night in my castle and for everyone with a dirty mind, she had her own room.

Moon and Star would sleep with her; she always kept her door open. I think she did it for them because the little traitors loved her. It was nice having someone in the castle. I would walk by her room to check on her. Seeing this lovely blonde hair woman in my castle was exciting. I kept my distance from her bedroom by putting her on the far side of the castle. One night after a hunt, I found her sleeping in my bed. I didn't know what to think of this. I starred at her and she must have felt me there because she woke up.

She told me she was sorry that she was in my bed but she had a nightmare and she thought this was the only place to be safe. I told her it's ok. Just continue sleeping as it was just a dream. She fell back to sleep. My room smelled of her, roses and oils. All the women during this time wanted to smell like flowers trying to attract men like bees. I walked downstairs to my chair and slept. I felt star hop onto the chair and she slept on my lap. She didn't move till I woke up. Finally, one of traitors remembers who raised them.

Elizabeth would come with me on my trips to town. I would buy her nice dresses. She would twirl around whenever she tried on a new dress. The beauty of youth can always bring joy. I might look young but I'm far from it. I had the wisdom of someone who lived for over ten thousand years but yet I knew nothing. Yes, even at my age, you can be taught or learn again, remembering things that were once lost. We tend to forget a lot of things that we should never forget. Knowledge is an thousand page book. I'm over ten thousand years old and only on page one hundred. This is a book that I will never finish even if I continue to live forever.

Elizabeth made me remember that life is no good alone. There is a reason we're born helpless in the world. She made me remember laughter, the escape from sadness. What is the point of living if you're not going to be happy? She made me remember overcoming fear. We have nothing to fear but fear itself. She made me remember that I need to go with the flow. You can't always think your way through things as sometimes, you just have to go with the flow.

Whenever she had nightmares, which seemed to be every so often, she would crawl into my bed and try to curl up with me. I would let her stay by herself at first; I would go to the couch to sleep. After a while, that got old and I would just turn over. The smell, her beauty, her blood and her heart beat was hard to resist. I stood over her one night with my fangs out but I stopped myself. That was the first time that I have actually stopped myself once my fangs was drawn.

She would ease herself over towards me in my bed. I would move but she would keep moving closer to me.. It was pointless so I would just turn and her butt would be on my back. I wanted to jump her bones as her butt was round and as soft as a pillow. I stayed on my course. I didn't touch her at all. I might have put my arms around her if she was cold but that was all. Elizabeth would try to join us on hunts. Although I have told her to stay in the castle, that didn't stop this carefree women at all.

I could always smell her even though she did try to keep her distance. I would just shake my head and think to myself that this woman never listens. I would tell her I know she was there but all she would do was smile and said she knows. I told her that it was dangerous in the woods at night but she never listens. The ignorance of youths never fails. They would always need to touch the fire to see if it's hot.

No one ever sees harm until they are harmed. The animals that we hunt might be scared but they would still fight for their life. A bird cornered by a snake will fight till its last breath. A male deer that we hunted ran straight for Elizabeth, stuck his antlers in her chest raised her up and tossed her like a tree branch. Moon and Star ran to her side and I immediately felt the rage entering my body. I let out a roar with fangs drawn and ran up to the dear and broke his neck.

I never let go of the dear. I squeezed his neck so hard my thumb was touching my fingers. I ran up to Elizabeth. She was there on the ground bleeding. I picked her up and raced off to the castle. I placed her on the table and got some thread and a needle. I started to close up her wounds but she was losing so much blood. Her heart started to beat slower and she was dying. I felt Gabriel and said out loud that I'm not going to let you take her.

I bite her on the neck as I wasn't going to let her die. The taste of human blood was always the best, that sweet taste; the best of wines. I had to stop myself as I was starting to take too much blood. I sat there thinking to myself if I had just made another mistake. I thought about grabbing a sword and slicing her head off but I didn't. Moon and Star stayed under the table the whole time. We didn't move one inch.

24 hours had passed. She jumped back up and took a deep breath. I was relieved but I showed nothing. I was also mad but she did not listen. Elizabeth asked me what was going on and all I could remember was her being hit by a deer. Before I could speak, she looked at her body and saw no wounds. She looked at me and said that you healed me with your wizard's powers. It was time to tell her the truth; I told her I wasn't exactly truthful with her. She asked me what I meant by that and I told her that I am no wizard.

She asked me if I was no wizard then what I was. I am a vampire, I am the king of the night; the night belongs to me. In order to save your life, I turned you into a vampire. I told her I can show better than I can tell you. I grabbed her hand and told her to follow my steps. We moved like the wind. I ran at a slower pace for her to keep up but we still couldn't be seen by the human eye.

She smiled the whole way through; she said she couldn't believe she was moving so fast. I told her this was just the beginning and there is more to come. I took her into the woods and told her to close her eyes and listen. She smiled and said I can hear everything, I can hear the bugs crawling. I can hear the wind blowing. I never knew the wind carried voices. I told her to open her eyes to see the night for the first time.

She said I can see further than I can imagine. I told her she is now stronger than ever. I told her to go over and shake the tree. She grabbed the base of the tree and started to shake it. She smiled as she shook the tree. I had to stop her eventually as she was getting carried away. I grabbed her hand and said, I can see that you are having fun but please do not hurt the tree. The trees give life to our earth and we need them to survive. She understood as she could feel the life force from the tree.

I told her that it's time to hunt and this is the really fun part. I tracked a deer and told her to follow my steps. She ran side by side and stopped as we got near the deer. I continued until I had my fangs deep in his neck. She stood over the top of the deer and I could feel her blood lust. She asked me what that lovely smell is; I told her it was blood. She said I can control myself but I want to taste it. I told her not to fight the feeling but to embrace it instead.

Her fangs came out of her mouth and she sank them deep inside the deer and began to drink. Her eyes rolled to the back of her head and she was happy. She stopped for a second to tell me how good it was. Moon and star came running up and ripped the flesh from the body. The four of us were having our feel of this deer; one happy family. I had to stop Elizabeth from drinking. I told her once something has been dead for a while, the blood will begin to turn bad.

Still, in her blood stained dress, she twirled under the moonlight. I cheered as she danced. She grabbed my hand and pulled me towards her and asked me to dance with her. It's been a while since the last time I danced but I remember everything very clearly. We danced in the wind. Whichever way it blew was the way we went. We danced all the way to the castle and it's strange that the wind blew that way.

I'm sorry I had to ruin the mood; I told her it's more and I need to tell you. She said what it is. I told her that along this power comes a cursed. I told her that she can never see the sun again. She gave me this confused look and said but you can go out in the sun. I said I can because I have been this way for centuries and I still don't fully understand it. I told her that she will continue to lust for blood forever. You can live forever as long as no one cuts your head off or break your neck.

And lastly, the most important thing to remember is to not feed on humans as they will turn into vampires. Elizabeth said don't worry, I could never kill anyone. I told her it's easy to say but much harder to restrain yourself from doing it. Human blood calls us and it's the hardest thing to resist. You will hear and feel the blood flow; the heart beat is beautiful music to our ears. Always remember the things I tell you and make sure you stay hidden.

Oh yes, one more thing. Blood makes us stronger so make sure you feed regularly. We can still eat regular food but it's just not the same. Elizabeth embraced the fact that she is a vampire as she loved every moment of it. She stayed in the woods; just enjoying the night. The sights, the sounds, feeling the flow of life she was just like a child with a new toy. She loved to pop in and out of rooms. I would be talking to her and she would just leave.

I would stop talking and she would pop back in asking why I stopped talking. She said you know I can hear you so keep talking. I would still stop whenever she left because I knew how much she loved to do it. She would say you're doing it on purpose. I smiled and say I would never do such a thing. She loves to go on hunts with us.

Moon and Star loved having her there on the hunts. Star would run by her side and moon at mines. She never seemed to get enough of the hunt. Creeping through the woods, hiding in shadows using our sense of smell to track our prey was a delight in her heart. Through her embrace of being a vampire, we became closer. I don't know what to call our relationship. It was different as I wasn't in love with her but I loved her.

Remember when time goes by and you spend time with someone, the relationship grows stronger and things will start to happen. When things start to happen, feelings will grow. We had a bond like no other. She was the first vampire that I had spent this much time with. Having someone of your own kind around you brings a sense of belonging. It was first time ever since I became a vampire that I didn't feel alone.

That was one set back and she started to fall in love with me. She would come in my bed naked, hoping that I would make love to her. I never did and it in rage, she would storm out of my room saying why won't you touch me. I would find her in a tree crying. She always knew when I was there always asking me what I wanted. I would tell her that I'm sorry as it has nothing to do with you.

Elizabeth would ask if I'm not pretty enough for you. I would say, Elizabeth, you're beautiful never forget that. I just can't give my heart to another woman. She would say I understand but I could tell she really didn't. We started to grow further apart and she would hunt on her own. I would go in my armor chamber to write when she was away. I would usually leave the chamber before she got back but one day I got lost in my writing and I looked up and saw her in the doorway.

Elizabeth asked me what this room is; I never knew you had all of these here. I told her this is my armor room where all the weapons I had over my long life is stored here. She started to walk around the room, looking at all the weapons and armor. She asked me if I hear that sound, it sounds like a battle. Where is it coming from? She began to walk over to the Aegis as it sounds like it is coming from there.

I told her that shield's name is aegis. She then turned around and asked you named the shield. I said, no, I didn't name the shield and she said the shield has its own name. She turned and touched it and jumped back immediately. It is alive. She asked me where did I get the shield from and I told her that a friend of mine, Alexander the great, gave it to me. Elizabeth asked if it was the Alexander the great, the one from all the legends. I told her yes, that is the shield from the god himself. She said she could hear all the battles the shield has fought.

She started to walk around the room and more and stopped at Rhongowennan. She said this is the most beautiful weapon I have ever seen. She reached out and touched it; she closed her eyes and stood still. She turned around and looked at me with tears in her eyes. I asked her what's wrong she asked what that is. I asked her why, what did you see or hear. Elizabeth said the spear showed her parents to her and they said they love her.

I told her that is the spear that killed Jesus. She then asked, Jesus as in our lord? I told her yes. She fell to her knees in front of Rhongowennan and whispered thank you. Elizabeth turned to me and said do you mind if I come here to see I spear every so often. I promise I won't get in your way but I just want to be near it. I told her yes. After that day, she seemed to be obsessed with

Rhongowennan. Whenever I couldn't find her, I knew where she would be.

I told her she was sending too much time with the spear and that she was getting obsessed with it. She would tell me to leave her alone. I told her the spear is showing things you already know, you know your parents loved you do not need to keep seeing it. She turned around with a cold look in her and said it's the only thing that shows love around here. I stood there silent for a moment. I wasn't going to say anything but sometimes things needed to be said.

I told I know you're upset so I will let that go but if I didn't show you love, would you still be here? Elizabeth said these exact words "then maybe I shouldn't be here anymore." after that she wanted nothing to do with me anymore. I had a castle built for her over a hundred miles away from mines. I gave her enough money to last her a lifetime and she became the countess of castle Morgan.

I told her to be careful and remember the rules that I told you and you will be safe. I told her I wish things could have been different but she didn't care for any of my words. For a while, I kept my eyes on her to make sure she was doing what she was supposed to do. She stayed on her course so I stopped watching her, thinking in my head that it was all for the best. One night on a hunt, I felt my blood that was not in my veins.

I rushed to the castle immediately. I smelt Elizabeth as she was in my house. I rushed to the armor chamber and there she was, right next to Rhongowennan. I asked her what she was doing here and she said she needed to see it again. I told her that she doesn’t live here anymore and she needs to let the obsession go and move on with her life. She said you're right with a sad look in her eyes and vanished immediately.

I thought nothing of this little encounter but I kept a watchful eye on Rhongowennan. On the night of the full moon, I felt Elizabeth’s presence in my castle. I hopped up and then I smelt fire. I raced to the scene of the fire and the picture of Eve was burning right before my eyes. My blood began to boil and then suddenly, I felt the presence of two other people in my house. I raced off to my armory to find Elizabeth standing there with two men.

I stood there in shock. She broke one of the rules by creating two other vampires. I was already enraged from the painting being burned. One of the men reached out for Rhongowennan. I appeared right in front of him. In his eyes, I saw fear and rightfully, I grabbed his head and ripped it off clean from his body. The other man tried to attack me with my back turned but I reached out my hand without turning around and grabbed his neck.

He screamed no but it was too late. I broke every bone in his neck. Elizabeth tried to runaway but I met her at the doorway and she jumped back in fear. Before she could speak, I grabbed her neck and raised her off the ground. How dare you come into my home and burn the picture of my wife? I wanted to kill her right then and there but I couldn't do it. A tear fell from Elizabeth's eyes. I released her from my hands and told her to leave my sight.

I told her to take her bodies with her. She then grabbed them and vanished. I must now keep a watchful eye on the spear at all times. The years went by she never gave up trying to get the spear but she never came herself I would leave the dead bodies at her castle's door. I grew tired of this fighting and I must find a way to get rid of it. I was going to bury it but it might fall into the wrong hands.

I have heard stories of this new legendary king who wielded a sword from the gods. They said he never used the sword unless he had too. The many deeds of this man travelled throughout the land. I decided to pay him a visit myself to learn more about this man. I traveled to his kingdom with Rhongowennan and the aegis on my back. Elizabeth couldn't be trusted with aegis either.

I made it to his kingdom and asked the first person I saw where the king was. He pointed and said that man right there. The king was among his people, playing with the children and shaking the hands of men. He hugged all the women. I never saw a king who ever cared about the common folks. I kept a watchful eye on him as I needed to see if he was really worthy of Rhongowennan.

I brought a house in his kingdom to observe this man's actions. At least once a week, this man would check on his people. He made sure everyone in his kingdom had food and no one was hungry. He didn't wear jewels or gold but just one ring with a lion engraving. I needed to observe him in closed quarters as it's easy to deceive in plain sight. I then took up a job inside the palace. I was careful not to be noticed by him.

Once a man knows you, he can change himself around you. Another measure of a man is how he treated women. Women have always been treated as objects to men. He treated his wife as an equal entity; he treated his knights like brothers. He listened to every one of them. Everything they said to him seemed to carry weight. He always asked his council how the people were doing. He was truly a remarkable man, at least in the things I see.

The knights always went in this room where no one else could go. That was the room I needed to get in. I knew he wasn't going to just let me in and I couldn't do it in the daylight. One night, one of the knights went in to clean. That was my chance and so I ran in right behind him. I looked around but there was no place for me to hide. It was a large room with a round table. I ran back out thinking how the hell I was going to get in this and not be seen.

He used to take late night rides alone and so I decided to follow him. He used to go to the lake almost every night just talking to himself. I thought the king was losing his mind. I still followed him every time he did. This time, he was on his knees talking to himself. I was like man, he is losing his mind. No way I can give this man the Rhongowennan. I turned around to walk away but I then begin to hear some footsteps.

Did he get up that fast? I felt no one else's presence but I still turned around anyway. Everything seemed to move in slow motion and time stood still. I could see the light from the moon standing still and the stars stood in mid twinkling. I saw a woman walking on the water and the hairs on my body rose immediately. I was getting goose bumps. She looked right at me with her small eyelids. It was only for a couple of seconds but it felt like a lifetime.

I stood there in the shadows. I could see her mouth moving but I could understand no words. What is going on? Why can't I understand her words? The king got up and left. I then walked over to the lake. She stood there watching my every move. I was afraid but I didn't know what to do. I stood there at the edge of the lake and she started to walk towards me. Each step made no ripple or movement to the water.

Seeing her reminded me of my dear friend, Jesus. I stood there in silence and she said Cain, what is it that you want? I was shocked. I asked her how did she know my name. She laughed and said who in heaven doesn't know who you are? In heaven, what do you mean? She said you understood every word that I spoke. I said out loud, not really and asking how can this be. She looked at me and said, of all people, you should understand.

I asked her if she was from heaven and she said yes, my name is Viviane. I said to her I thought that all angels were men. She said who did you hear that from and I told her I heard it from all the priests. She said exactly. You heard the words from someone who has never been to heaven. You of all people understand that you cannot always believe what you hear and read.

She asked me why I was following the king. I then told her that I needed to see if he was a good man. Viviane said a good man, there has only been a few in this world like him. She told me I needed to see it for myself. She began to walk away but I told her wait. She stopped and said Cain, I'm not here for you; you already have your own guides and disappeared into the lake right after. I stood there at the lake waiting for her to comeback.

I heard her voice saying the knights are gathering, go see for yourself. I then raced off to the castle. I don't know why I kept saying raced though. That is what I used to do now. I just vanish and appear. I'm sorry but it just sounds good to say raced. I appeared inside the castle.

What am I going to do so that I'm not seen by the people? It came to me just like that. They left the door open for a minute and I went inside. They sat down and the king called for an emergency meeting.

He said the kingdom is about to be attacked and we need to secure the people into the inner walls. He said we must protect the people. I stood there teleporting in a circle moving faster than the wind. Every now and then I would produce wind that would knock something down. They would just pick in back up like nothing had happened. Saying I hate these drafty castles the king said that is no draft and that is a ghost. The knights started laughing. Yes that's right. I remember now that all castles are haunted.

They sat there making a strategy to defend the kingdom. I moved in that circle for about an hour. They dismissed the meeting saying one for all. I knew at that moment that he was more than worthy to have Rhongowennan. Now, how do I get this to him? Simple, just place in it his chamber. I wrote a note "this is a gift for the king. I know you will find a use for it." I kept a watchful eye on the king to make sure that everything was ok plus it was easy as the kingdom was only 30 miles away and I can blink to that.

I came back home to find the familiar scent of Elizabeth. Hmm, was she here while I was gone? I walked to my armory and Elizabeth was sitting there. She asked where did I put it. I told her far away where you will never find. She smiled and said good and those words shocked me. I'm glad you did that. I was tired of thinking about it all the time. She stood up and said I would like you to come over for dinner. I told her ok and I will see you on the morrow.

I know what you're thinking. It's a trap, don't go but that was the furthest thing from my mind. Plus, I understood and she understood that she had no chance in killing me. I approached her castle with anger. I wanted to kill every vampire in there but her and even that could be held on a tight rope. I didn't want to cause more problems. I just wanted to make some sort of peace.

If I was the king then that means she was the queen of the vampires. She had completely changed the person that I knew. She was no longer the sweet innocent girl or the fun loving person that I had love for. She grew up fast and she even thought of herself as a queen. I sat down at a long table with tons of chairs but just us two sat there. She was at one end while I was at the other.

We stayed quiet for a while until the servant came with the wine. She asked me how have I been. I said good and you? She said I'm great. Time has taught me so much. I must look out for my own kind; I know you don't approve of what I do. I think we can live as vampires if we so choose too. I remained silent and she continued on saying we will only kill the bad ones.

I told her it will only be a matter of time before someone breaks it. Do you hear yourself? You are playing god judging and who are you to say what's right on wrong? Elizabeth looked right at me and said if you murder innocent people, that is wrong and so I will take their lives. I see there was no point talking to her as it was useless. She said I know you don't approve of me turning people into vampires but they wanted the life. They embraced everything that comes with being a vampire. Who am I to stop that?

She had on the attire of a queen and even wore a crown. She sat and ate like she was a noble. Everything about her shows of a queen even the powder on her face. I told her I didn't want us to fight as we were once very close friends. I know we will never get back to that but I would like us to be friendly. We both agreed and raised our glasses from these words. She said no matter how good the blood taste, I will never stop loving wine.

I said me too as wine will always have a place in my heart. We sat there for a while talking. I told her that it was time for me to go. She said she understood and told me that we need to do this again. I said yes, we will without moving my lips. In her head, she said I must be hearing things. I looked right at her and said no, you're not in her head. She hopped up and said how are you doing this. In her head, I said I am more powerful than you will ever understand.

I appeared right in front of her and she couldn't follow my movement at all. Her eyes got big. I hit my glass on her glass, kissed her hand and vanished. Whenever she had a party, she would invite me. She loved the people who kissed her ass. I think she threw the parties just for that reason and to get gifts. I never understood why rich people always get gifts. They already have everything and so why would they need more. She always paid me the most attention. None of nobles or the vampires like it but there wasn't anything they could do this was my world.

About twenty years past since I gave the king Rhongowennan I had spies in the kingdom to give me information on the king. I made the right choice that he was truly the king of kings. One night, I heard a horse riding up and I could feel the fear of the rider. I met him at the door and it was one of my spies. He told me the spear has been stolen and the king is in a fight with the man who stole it right now.

I told him thank you and gave him two rubies and wanted for him to ride off. As soon as he got out of my eyesight, I vanished as I must get there fast. By the time I got there, it was too late. I heard the king had suffered a fatal wound. He was taken off to his room and so I made my way to his room through his window. I hid behind the curtains. He was there lying in bed. He told everyone to leave and to let him die in peace.

I stood there silent, just listening. He remained silent for a while and no words were spoken. Then, I heard him saying I'm not ready to die. Then I spoke from the curtain, are you sure you don't want to die? He said who's there? Are you an angel? I said no, and came out from the curtains by his bedside. I told him I shall take away the death if you're ready.

Glossary

Aaru: Egyptian Heaven

Able: my brother the third human ever born

Able (lion): a cape lion that I named after my brother

Abraham: the man who gave me the spear at the village of the sun

Adam: my father, the first human to ever live

Advisor: the title that stuck with me throughout my life Egypt

Aegis: a shield given to me by Alexander the Great, it was said that it crash on Mount Olympus

Africa: the land of first life, the home of the garden

Afterlife: the life after you die

AH: after human

Akh: Egyptian word of spirit

Alexander the Great: the king of Macedon, one of my closet friends

Almighty: another name for God

Almighty push: the power that God gave us forced out of the body

Amen: an evil priest who tried to kill me

Ammit: the soul devourer in the underworld

Amyrtaeus: the one who took back Egyptian from the Persians and became pharaoh

Andrew: one of the apostles of Jesus

Angel: God's warriors

Anoxandridas II: king of Sparta and Leonidas father

Anta: queen of Egypt wife of Pharaoh Menes

Anubis: Egyptian god of the dead

Anubis: an evil priest who robbed the poor

Apep: Egyptian god of chaos

Aristotle: a Greek philosopher, Alexander the Great father figure and a dear friend of mines

Athens: the Greek capital home of a strong army

Atum: the father of gods, the god of creation

Babylon: a city state of pure evil

Bare False Witness: to lie

Bartholomew: one of the apostles of Jesus

Bastet: Egyptian goddess of warfare

Bethlehem: the birth place of Jesus

Bible: A religious book written by man

Blasphemy: insulting God or something sacred

Bless: to bestow good of any kind upon

Blessing: invoking of God's favor upon

Britain: a place I called home after I left Egypt

Buddha: the founder of Buddhism and a dear friend

Buddhism: a religion practice by Buddhists

Buddhist: a follower of Buddhism

Bushido: the way of the samurai

Cain: the first murderer my original name

Cain Eden: my name with Eden as a last

Cambyses: a king of Persia

Cherry blossom: a tree of pink and white flowers from Japan

China: the home of the Chinese

Chinese: people from china

Christ: a name given to Jesus by Peter which means savoir

Cleopatra: the first and last woman pharaoh of Egypt

Crucified: death on a cross

Darius: the third king of Persia

Disciples: the followers of Jesus Christ

Djer: the third pharaoh ever in Egypt my grandson

Dodo bird: a tasty flightless bird

Dracula: the name that everyone calls me now

Duat, Akert: realm of the dead

Egypt: the place I called home for thousands of years

Egyptian rebels: the ones who fought the Persians

Egyptians: people from Egypt

Elizabeth: the queen of the vampires

Emi: the third love of my life from Japan

Emperor: the king of Japan or China

Enlighten path: the search for peace of mind, body and soul

Eve: my mother the second human to ever live

Eve Sea: my wife and my first love

Eye of the sun: a necklace given to me by Pharaoh Menes

False idol: a false image of God or something sacred

Forsaken: forgotten by God

Gabriel: the angel of death and my best friend

Gan Eden: Hebrew name for the Garden of Eden

Garden of Eden: Heaven on earth now heaven in the sky

God: the creator of all

Golden Haired Spartan Helmet: helmet given to me by King Leonidas

Greece: home of the Greeks

Hathor: Egyptian goddess of motherhood

Heaven: paradise for man after death

Heaven's doors: the door to heaven

Heaven's thunder: the voice of a lion

Hebrews: the people chosen by God

Hercules: Zeus half human son

Herod Antipas: One of the men who sentence Jesus to death

Hiroki: a Japanese samurai and a dear friend, the greatest swordsman to ever live

Holy Grail: of the pure blood of Jesus

Horus: the Egyptian god of protection for the pharaohs

Immortal: someone who can never die

Inner peace: having true peace inside

Inri: the king of Jews

Isaac: the blinded man who I met on my way to find Jesus

Israel: home of the Israelites

Jacob: the elder of the Village of the Sun

James: one of the apostles of Jesus Christ

James: one of the apostles of Jesus Christ

Jerusalem: the place of Jesus death

Jesus: God's human son

Jewish priests: ones who pretended to be Hebrews, the ones who got Jesus killed

Jochebed: the mother of Moses

John: one of the apostles of Jesus

Jordan: a land of slaves

Joseph: a Hebrew slave I spoke to every night

Judas: one of the apostles of Jesus, the one who betrayed Jesus

Judas: the half brother of Jesus, one of the apostles

Julius Caesar: king of the Roman Empire

Kadjet Narmer Menes: the first pharaoh of Egypt

King of beasts: a lion

King of the village of the sun: a name the people called me

King's thrust: striking straight down with unmatched force

Kingdom: a state or government with a king or queen

Kiss of death: the kiss Judas used to mark Jesus

Kimono: a robe from Japan

Kung fu: the art of the fist and foot

Lamb blood: a marker used to keep out Gabriel

Last Supper: the last dinner of Jesus and his apostles

Law of the priest: a law that no man of God can be questioned

Leo: one of the lions I named

Leo Sun: my name at the Village of the Sun

Leo the King of the Desert: what the Egyptian people called me when I first got there

Leonidas: the Spartan king, king of the Legendary 300

Libya: a land of slaves

Lotus tree: a tree of lotus flowers

Ma'at: the Egyptian goddess of truth

Ma'at: queen of Egypt, wife of Nor-Aha

Ma'at feather: the feather used to weigh you heart on judgment day

Mark Antony: a Roman general

Martial arts: way of the fist and foot

Mary Magdalene: a former prostitute, one of the apostles of Jesus, the one who Jesus loved

Matthew: one of the apostles of Jesus Christ

Mazaces: the Persian king handed over Egypt to the Greeks

Meditation: the act of finding inner peace

Mediterranean Sea: the sea of life, the in between Africa and Europe

Michael Sea: the elder of the Village of the Sea, the father of my wife

Middle way: the path that leads to Liberation

Miriam: the sister of Moses

Monks: men who are members of a monastic order

Moon: my black male wolf

Moses Ramses: Moses' name when he was in the palace

Mount Olympus: the highest mountain in Greece, the place where Aegis crashed

Mount Sinai: the place where Moses talked to God

My Eden: a poem I wrote to express know I felt about the first thing I loved

Nepal: region located in South Asia

Neter-khertet: the divine underworld

Ninja: an assassin that uses martial arts to kill

Ninjutsu: technique practiced by ninjas

Noor: Egyptian word for light

Nor-Aha: the second pharaoh of Egypt

Nut: Egyptian goddess of the sky

Origin of evil: what I am called when my name is brought up

Osiris: Egyptian god of the afterlife

Perfect defense: the formation uses by the Spartans

Persian Empire: one of the largest empires to ever exist

Peter: one of the apostles of Jesus Christ, the one who coined the name Christ

Pharaoh: the ruler of all of Egypt

Pharaoh Djoser: the pharaoh who brought upon the living death

Pharaoh Khufu: the pharaoh who brought upon the plague of death

Pharaoh Nynutjer: the pharaoh who won Egypt when it was divided

Pharaoh Ramses II: pharaoh son of Seti I, the brother of Moses

Pharaoh Semerkhet: the greedy pharaoh who taxed the people once a week

Pharaoh Senedj: pharaoh son of Nynutjer

Pharaoh Seti I; the pharaoh who killed the first born sons of the Hebrews, Ramses II father

Pharaoh Sneferu: the pharaoh would built the free true pyramid

Pharaohs Raneb: the pharaoh who divided Egypt so his sons would not fight

Philip: one of the apostles of Jesus Christ

Pontius Pilate: the one who had Jesus crucified

Pride: a family of lions

Priest: a man who pretends he talks to gods

Ptolemy XII: the father of Cleopatra, king of Egypt

Ptolemy XIII: son of Ptolemy XII, prince of Egypt

Pyramids: a tomb for Egyptian royalty

Qiao: a Shaolin Monk, a dear friend of mine

Queen Gorgo: queen of Sparta, the wife of Leonidas

Queen Tuya: queen of Egypt, Seti I wife, the no birth mother of Moses

Ra: the most important god of the Egyptians, the god of the sun

Ra mask: a mask I put on to hide my face

Ra-Leon: the name I was called in bed when I made love

Ra-Noor: the name the people called me after I became advisor

Rahahankh: the sun gives life to this land from heaven, Egypt's original name

Ramses IV: the Egyptian king who fought the Persian Empire

Red sea: the sea that Moses parted with his staff, the sea Moses turned to blood

Reed fields: Egyptian heaven fields

Religion: a set of beliefs with a god involved

Resurrected: to come back to life

Rhongowennan: the spear used to kill Jesus, one of the Holy Grails

Ripe in the Veil: the day I used Rhongowennan to destroy the church

Roar: the sound that comes from a lion's mouth when enraged

Samurai: a Japanese warrior of peace

Sekhmet: the Egyptian goddess of healing or war

Seshat: the Egyptian goddess of writing

Shaolin temple: the home of the Shaolin Monks

Simon: one of the apostles of Jesus

Sins of the Holy Grail: when I became mad after I turned into a vampire

Spartans: people of Sparta

Staff of Moses: the staff used to part the Red Sea

Star: my female black wolf

Tattoo: to mark the skin with ink

Taxes: money collected by the people for a government or kingdom

Tefnut: the Egyptian Goddess of air

Ten Commandments: rules of God delivered by Moses

Thaddeus: one of the apostles of Jesus Christ

The Apostles: the people who followed Jesus Christ when he was alive

The Four Immeasurables: the practice of developing qualities of equanimity, love, compassion and joy

The Lake of Fire: Egyptian hell

The Noble Eightfold Path: the practice to end suffering

The Plagues of Egypt: the plagues of God used to free the Hebrews

The Three Marks of Existence: to see things as they are

The Weighing of the Heart: judgment in the underworld

Thomas: one of the apostles of Jesus Christ

Tiger vs. dragon: offense and defense

True pyramid: the large grand pyramid

Trunks: an elephant

Underworld: place where Egyptians go when they die

Usermatre Serpenre Ramses II: Ramses II full name

Vampire: an immortal person who feeds off of blood to survive

Village of the Rising Sun: a village in Japan where I stayed for years

Village of the Sea: home of my wife

Village of the Sun: the village of the first people I even found

Viviane: an angel on earth

Wishman: the name my wife used to call me

Wizard: a person with magical powers

Xerxes: king of the Persian Empire

Yin and yang: darkness and light, two sides of a whole

Yisu: Chinese name for Jesus

Zeus: the most power Greek God

www.ingramcontent.com/pod-product-compliance
Lightning Source LLC
LaVergne TN
LVHW050916080826
845145LV00001B/101

9780615913377